In the Mood...
For Murder

D E McCluskey

&

Tony Bolland

D E McCluskey & Tony Bolland

In the Mood… For Murder

ISBN 9781549619847

A Dammaged Productions Production

www.dammaged.com

For Ann McCluskey... My mum, and my greatest fan
(even though she won't read any of my horror stuff)

For Bill Bolland...

1.

'HOLD IT THERE gents!' A huge hand appeared from out of the night and stopped the first of the five young men from entering the door of the ballroom. The youth stopped, mainly because the potential power in the appendage that had halted him looked to be greater than the power that he had in his entire body.

As he stopped, the youth looked at the hand's owner.

He was mountain of a man, dressed in a black three-piece suit, complete with a white shirt and thin black tie. His neck wouldn't have looked out of place as the trunk of an old oak tree; and his face was covered in a dark beard that had its fair share of grey flecks hiding within it.

'I hope we're not going to have any trouble tonight,' the giant continued in a heavy accent that verged on a full baritone.

The young lad turned back towards his four companions, and raised his eyebrows before smiling, a less than sincere smile, towards the towering doorman.

'Us?' he asked, feigning hurt at the implication. 'Not from us, sir. We're only here to partake in the famed festivities and the convivial atmosphere that your fair city has to offer. We're on a rare night off from protecting His Majesty's seas from invasions and pirates.'

The doorman narrowed his eyes; he'd understood less than every other word of what the youth had just said. This was not only because he was dim and had trouble understanding longer words, but also because the lad's accent was strange. These boys were not from anywhere in Liverpool that he knew about.

'So, where're you boys from then?' he asked, eyeing the uniforms they were wearing.

'From the HMS Belfast, sir. She's in port for a few nights. We're sampling the Liverpudlian night life and hospitality,' one of the others, a taller boy who was standing behind the first sailor, piped up.

'Oh yeah? Well, I'll just let you know, we'll be keeping an eye on you in there, so no funny business… you got that?'

The first lad nodded, smiling a sly smile to his mates behind him. 'No funny business? We've got that, right boys?'

All four sailors nodded their agreement; each smiling a similar grin - the kind that dripped with mischief.

'Well, OK then,' the bouncer replied, taking his huge hand off the fist sailor's chest. 'But only because you're servicemen, and you probably saw some action in the war. You can go in.' He pointed at each of them, individually; the point had an implied threat attached to it. 'But heed my words gents, no messing about. OK?'

All five of the lads snapped to attention and saluted the big man.

'Ron,' the doorman shouted through the closed door behind him. 'I'm letting these five lads in because they've been on His Majesty's service. Although to look at them, they don't look too far out of short trousers.' He began to laugh at his own little joke and the 'huk-huk' sound confirmed that he was as dim as he looked.

Much to the annoyance of the other punters who were still waiting in line, the five sailors were ushered through the doors and into the grand foyer of the theatre.

Inside, there were two staircases; one lead left and the other right. In the centre was a small booth; inside the booth sat a woman. She looked old, yet, in a certain light, she also looked ancient. She didn't like to smile; it was her job to demand the entrance money from the partygoers, stamp their hands with ink they would be trying to get off for a week, before ushering them in with a wave of her hand. She didn't believe in being nice to them. Patricia had been with The Rialto for years and was considered part of the furniture.

'These five are gratis, Pat.' Ron said as he led the sailors passed the booth, towards the left-hand staircase.

'How come?' she asked with a scowl, a deeper one than she used on the regular punters.

'Seamus said so.'

She turned her scowl on the boys and all five of them shied away from her. Her face was nasty when she was happy, but when she scowled it had been said that she was vile enough to scare a ghost. 'Just because they're wearing sailor's uniforms, doesn't necessarily mean they're sailors.' She rolled her eyes and sighed. 'Oh, go on then... let them through. I'll let Red deal with Seamus later.'

Michael, the doorman on the inside, led the sailors up the left-hand staircase. They followed him like ducklings following their mother, all on their very best behaviour.

He stopped before he got to the door at the top, the one that led into the main ballroom. The sailors stopped behind him, almost banging into each other in their eagerness to get inside. He put a hand on the handle of the door and turned towards his wards. His face was stern and serious, and the boys knew that, although this doorman was also dim, he was a whole lot brighter than the one outside who had let them in. 'Now listen to me, and listen good,' the deep rumble of his thick Irish brogue working to full effect on each of them. They all fell silent and looked at him as if he was about to say something spectacular. 'We won't be dealing with any trouble here tonight, will we lads?' He paused expecting an answer. When none was forthcoming, he continued. 'This place is a respectable gaff and we don't want any scallywags coming in and ruining it. We don't sell gin, we don't sell beer, and we don't take kindly to drugs either. So, play nice and play safe, eh boys?'

The five sailors nodded.

'Good, then all that's left is to wish you boys a great night. In you go but remember...' he gifted them all a threatening glance, '...behave!'

He pushed the door, and the heat, the noise, and the smell from the room beyond, hit them all full in the face.

2.

THE BALLROOM WAS filled with sweating, young bodies. The phrase 'swinging from the rafters' was apt for how this room looked. Even though there was a strict 'no alcohol' policy during the evening's entertainment, the distinct smell of fermented grapes, hops and distilled juniper berries hung heavy in the air. Some younger members of the crowd, and to be fair many of the older members too, were writhing and gyrating themselves into a frenzy on the dance floor. Some of them obviously aided in their recklessness by the fermented grapes and juniper berries; others, the more reserved dancers among them, just enjoying the music and the ambiance of the night.

There was a sign on the wall that was currently being ignored by everyone in the room. It read; *NO JITTERBUGGING*

The room was large, the tables had been pushed back to make a larger area available for the banned style of dancing that was happening everywhere. The curved walls of the ballroom depicted a life-like mural of a beautiful Venetian scene. This was to facilitate a feeling as if the partygoers, inside, were looking out from the balcony of a fancy hotel overlooking the romantic canals of Venice. Gondolas floated past with pretty girls sat in them being courted by handsome young men. The gondoliers, wizened to the young couples, eyed them with levity and envy at the joys of their youth.

The five sailors surveyed the scene before them with wide, boyish grins. 'OK boys, I think we've hit the jackpot here tonight.' The first youth said as he spread his arms and slapped two of his colleagues on the back. Laughing, they all entered the hot ballroom.

~~~~

It was Friday night and Liverpool was, quite literally, swinging.

The live band were into the second of their three sets, set back, away from the main dancing area, separated by a small stage that elevated them from the revellers below. A curtain behind them offered a classy backdrop. It concealed a small backstage area where the musicians could sit in between sets, and smoke and drink, out of the view of the main crowd. There were seven of them in total; a cut-down version of the usual swing bands that were currently blowing up storms, up and down the country. However, they were blowing up their own storm tonight at The Rialto.

Even though the night outside was cold and wet, it was of no concern to anyone inside. It was Friday, the last weekend in February. It was payday!

An early onset of spring was in the air and, most importantly, the war was over, and had been won!

The party was in full swing.

Nobody noticed the five latecomers as they made their way into the ballroom. Everyone was far too busy dancing and enjoying the effects that of the gin, wine, or any other alcoholic beverage they could consume before making it into the club, was having on their night out.

The men in the ballroom were dressed smartly. Most of them wearing shirts and ties, with matching jackets, waistcoats, and straight trousers. The fashion of the day was to slicked back their hair with copious amounts of grease. More than a few of them had made up for the lack of hair product by using fat, right out of the chip pan, and sprayed with their father's best Sunday cologne to mask the stink.

The women's fashion was colourful calf-length dresses that buttoned up to their necks. Each one of them was having a ball being swung around the dance floor in time with the beat, by their boyfriends, or boys vying to be their boyfriends. With each swing, a certain amount of leg would be displayed, to the obvious enjoyment of the men on the fringes of the dance floor. Their enjoyment coming from the flash of American tan and the tantalising stocking tops, further up the thighs, with each swing. Real nylons were still very hard to come by so soon after the war, so the girls who weren't lucky enough to have them, had to make do with carefully painted gravy browning and a thin line of eyeliner drawn up their calves.

No one really cared what they looked like, all they cared about was having as good a time as they could.

The sailors were in their element.

3.

'FIVE GINS PLEASE,' Clive, the sailor who had done all the talking outside, ordered at the bar. The lady behind looked at him as if he was from another planet.

'What?' Linda, the barmaid asked, thinking she'd misheard him.

'I said five gins, please!' The last word had been emphasised.

She shook her head and smiled. 'Oh, no! I'm sorry love but we're a dry bar. We only serve tea and coffee. I can get you five teas.'

'I don't want any fucking tea. If I'd wanted tea, I'd have stayed back at my nanas. No, I want a proper drink,' he snarled at her.

The poor girl recoiled as if she'd been slapped. 'Erm, well, there's a pub just a little bit further up the road, they'll sell you gin. We don't have a li…'

'Are you telling me that all these people, all the ones dancing like lunatics, are sober?' he snarled again, pointing towards the full dance floor.

Linda followed his gesture and smiled an uncertain smile. She was feeling out of her element here. Normally she would have had a snappy, and witty, comeback for any potential troublemakers, but these young boys seemed different somehow. 'Well, I don't know if they're *all* sober, but certainly some of them are.'

Clive's face changed in an instant. His lip curled and his brow ruffled as he pushed a stack of cups that were placed on the bar. Linda jumped, just in time to get out of their way, as they fell, crashing onto the floor. The crescendo of smashed crockery alerted the other barmaid, working a little further up the long bar; she was quick to turn at the loud crash.

'What's going on?' she asked. 'Linda, are you all right?'

'Yeah… she's all right!' Clive spat in his West Country accent. 'It's this bar that isn't!' He turned towards his small crew behind him. 'No ale here tonight boys! It looks like we're going to have to make our own fun.'

He walked through the others who were standing behind him, as he headed towards the dance floor.

Linda was on her knees trying to pick up the broken crockery, with tears in her eyes.

'You leave that girl,' Brenda, the other barmaid whispered. 'I'll get it. You go and find Red, let him know what's just happened.'

Linda nodded as she wiped her eyes. She stood up, brushed off her skirt, and walked off in the direction of the offices. She only glanced back once to see where the five troublemakers had gone. She spied them on the dance floor.

All of them were now, actively, looking for trouble.

The band had slipped into a medley, merging some modern songs in together with classics, and the crowd were loving it.

As the crowd whipped themselves into another frenzy, dancing to the classics, the lead male vocalist, an older gentleman wearing a tuxedo that looked maybe a few years older than he did, suddenly stopped singing. The band continued playing, overcompensating for the sudden loss of vocals. He looked like he'd forgotten the words to the song they were playing; it also appeared as though he had forgotten where he was.

The attractive blonde, who was the lead female vocal, took over the duties a man from the side of the stage came on and escorted the older man off.

It was a sad scene.

But not for most of the punters, who hadn't even noticed, nor the sailors, who had found the funny side of the drama and thought it was hilarious. They were pointing and laughing as the older man, struggling against his escort, tried in a vain to get back onto the stage.

'Look over there.' Bored of the tragedy that was happening on the stage, Clive was pointing to the side of the dance floor where a group of young girls were standing together, enjoying the music and giggling between them. The other four nodded their agreement - these girls were fair game.

They made their way over and stopped in front of their prey, blatantly staring at them. The girls noticed and began to giggle even more than before.

'So, girls, do you like this kind of music?' Clive asked, attempting to break the ice. The others were standing behind him, looking over his shoulder, egging him on.

The girls turned away from Clive and began to laugh.

He smiled, as he did he was glad for the low-level lighting, so no-one could see the blood rush to his face. 'What's so funny?' he asked, feeling like he was on the outside of a joke. He could feel his friends behind him, looking, and probably laughing at him. He turned and was disappointed to find out they were. He turned back towards the girls, his smile was now replaced with a mean scowl. 'Look, do you want to dance or what?' he snapped, not even caring which one might take up his offer.

'What? With you in that stupid uniform?'

'And with that accent?'

'Are you joking?'

All five of girls turned away from him then, giggling at his stunted advances.

He could hear his friends behind him, they were now openly laughing at him too. He prided himself on not suffering fools, lightly, and he was also known to have quite a short fuse. Right now, he could feel a match, hovering over his blue touch paper, ready to light it. He didn't mind being the mouthy one, playing jokes on his friends, but he didn't take kindly to being the butt of anyone else's joke; *especially not from a dopey group like this lot,* he thought. He felt as the fuse of his own personal firework began to fizzle away, as he reached out and grabbed one of the girls by the arm. It was the same girl who had rebuffed him first.

'What the fuck's wrong with my uniform?' he demanded; his eyes and his nostrils were flaring.

The girl smiled a humourless smile as she tried to back away from him, but the vice like grip on her arm made it difficult. 'There's nothing wrong with your uniform… It's the prick inside it that's the problem,' she replied, twisting her arm to free it from his grip.

The other girls were laughing aloud at their friend's comeback. This embarrassment, coupled with his shipmates laughing behind him, was too much, and a pink mist descended over his brain. Without warning, he pulled the girl away from the rest of her group and spun her around to face him. Her scoffing face fell in an instant, as she looked his psychosis in the eye.

'What do you think you're doing?' It was her turn to demand. 'I'm dancing with my friends here. Is that OK with you?'

The other girls had stopped laughing now and were staring at the other four sailors who were all looking, menacingly, back at them. One by one the girls began to back off towards the dance floor, in the hope that someone, anyone, might come to their aid from the five sailors, and soon.

'What's going on here lads?' A voice from behind them spoke up. All the girls, including the one still in Clive's grip, turned to look towards where it had come from. Their faces changed from scared to relieved in a flash.

'I'll tell you once to fuck off,' Clive warned, without even looking around at the source. 'This doesn't have anything to do with you!'

'It's got everything to do with me when you've got hold of my sister like that,' the voice continued.

A heavy hand landed on his shoulder and dragged him around, away from the relieved looking young lady. As he was pulled, the sailor, this not being his first fight in a club, balled his hand into a fist and swung it at his aggressor. The punch landed square on the newcomer's nose. He felt the satisfying crack of the bone underneath his fist, and blood began to flow down his face. The newcomer let go of his grip on Clive as his hands automatically went to his nose. Dark blood was spurting between his fingers and down the front of his waistcoat, ruining the white shirt underneath.

The bleeding man stumbled backwards and knocked into a man who was escorting a young lady towards the dance floor. As he fell in turn, he knocked into the girl and she tripped on the lip of the wooden floor, falling over onto her front, her arms splayed out before her.

'Watch it will you, mate?' The newcomer snapped as he swung himself around, ready to start an argument. He stopped short as a strange look spread across his face as he saw blood already pouring from his adversary's nose. Then, at the very last second in his peripheral vision, he saw two sailors coming at him, one from either side.

The original group of girls had scarpered, all except for one who had stopped to help the poor girl, splayed out on the dance floor, to get up. She looked dazed, as if she didn't quite know what had hit her. Several people around them on the dance floor had also stopped dancing and were gawping, with rapture and growing delight, at the drama that was unfolding before them.

The two sailors were on the man in an instant, one of them had wrestled him to the floor while the other was raining punches down on his face.

The man with the bleeding nose regained his faculties and lunged at Clive. He grabbed the sailor in a chokehold and attempted to force him down, onto the floor. The blood that was dripping from his nose rubbed off, over his crisp, white, tunic, ruining the fabric.

One of the other sailors was stood on the edge of the dance floor, waiting for whatever was about to come at him. It came in the shape of two local lads, excited rage on their faces, gin on their breath, swinging wildly.

The fifth sailor, the smallest of the group, had ducked out of the way of the fighting and was sidling up to a group of young girls who were stood, watching the events, from the side of the dance floor. They were obviously enjoying what they were seeing.

'Do you know what?' he asked, and all three girls looked at him at the same time, all of them sporting smiles, one of them sporting a smile that was brighter than all the rest as her eyes roamed over his tunic. 'I can't take them lads anywhere,' he laughed as he shook his head. 'Have you got any idea who they are?'

The girl with the biggest smile pointed towards one of the men who was currently wrestling another sailor on the floor. His hair had lost its greasy hold and was flopping about his bloodied face as the two of them rolled around the dance floor.

'That's my fella there,' she said, rolling her eyes. 'He's always doing this.'

The sailor grinned as he put his arm around her and gestured towards the dry bar. 'Should we go and stand over there, just to get out of the way like?'

Her eyes lit up at the offer from the handsome, uniformed man, and they sloped off, his arm still hanging around her neck.

As her friends watched them saunter off the other way, they shook their head, tutting. 'I can't believe she's doing that…again,' one of them muttered, her face looking like she had just sucked on the sourest lemon in Liverpool. In reality, she was jealous that she wasn't the one walking off with the exotic sailor.

They all were.

A shout rang out from somewhere within the melee and the short sailor turned around, just in time, as a chair came sailing across the room, heading right towards him. He ducked, the missile narrowly missing him and the girl, as it sailed on, smashing into the bar next to him. Cups and saucers went crashing onto the floor before it ended its short-lived flight into the long mirror that adorning the wall behind it.

The sailor held his hat at a jaunty angle as he regarded the devastation the chair had caused. He grinned and helped his young lady friend up from the floor where he had pushed her. 'I think me and you need to go outside, don't you? It's safer out there!'

Her shocked face that was looking at the devastated bar before them, turned towards him, and a small, sly smile crept salaciously over her face, as she allowed herself to be helped up. The top button of her dress had popped open revealing a little more cleavage than she had originally intended.

The sailor looked at it and winked at her.

She looked down at herself, to see what he was looking at. Her smile widened as she looked back up at him. 'Maybe we should. I'll go and get my coat.'

The band, fronted solely by the attractive female singer, were halfway through one of the crowd's favourites, *String of Pearls*, when they had to stop. The fight had spread across the dance floor and fists were flying far too close to the musicians for their comfort. The tall trombone player looked over the melee and saw a small figure enter into the ballroom. The moment he saw him he knew that their set was over, for now. He leaned over towards the drummer, a smaller man who was also watching the progress of the fight with some interest.

'George, maybe we should wrap this up. This one looks bad.' As he spoke he pointed out the small man he'd seen arrive.

George looked over his drum kit and nodded winking his acknowledgement. 'I see what you mean.' As he stopped playing, the rest of the band noticed the downswing in the music, and they all followed his cue. One by one, they looked at him and he inclined his head towards the curtain at the back of the stage. This one gesture was enough for the rest of the band to understand what was happening and begin to gather their equipment off the stage.

'Red.' George spoke the single word as both a warning and an instruction.

Within less than a minute, the band were packed away and back behind the large red curtain. George and Brian were peering out towards the proceedings on the dance floor.

There were more than thirty men fighting now. There was blood, hair and fists flying everywhere.

Moving from behind the brawl was a wall of black.

Several large men, all wearing black suits, waistcoats and black ties, were wading through the trouble grabbing at anyone who was fighting, regardless of whether they were protecting themselves or were aggressors. The unsuspecting brawlers were tossed aside as if they were ragdolls.

Brian winced a few times as he watched a few of the men throw punches towards the big men. Every time it happened he tutted and shook his head slowly. He didn't really want to know what happened to them after that, but he was helpless to turn away.

The four sailors that had started the brawl were faring quite well for themselves; the fifth was faring very well too - he had exited the building with an excited looking local girl and was currently in a dark alleyway behind the theatre, engaging in a pre-marital, passionate embrace with the first man's girlfriend. This dark alleyway, just off Parliament Street, had seen its fair share of passionate embraces.

The wall of bouncers pushed through the melee until inevitably they came to the four sailors. Their white uniforms were torn, dirty, and covered in blood, but each of them had grins on their bloody and bruised faces.

One by one they were plucked from their individual fights and hauled away by the big men in black. The men they were fighting with scarpered as they saw which way the wind was blowing.

The four sailors were dragged out of the dance hall and out into the foyer.

'Get off me, right now. I'll kill you. I swear to God I will,' Clive spat through his bloodied lips; pink spittle flying as he mouthed the words. His left eye was bruised and rising nicely, it would be completely closed over by this time tomorrow night, if a steak wasn't applied to it, and soon.

'Oh, you will, eh?' A thin, reedy voice came from behind the large men, as the door to the foyer swung shut. It was a quiet, reserved voice, with just a tinge of a London accent. 'And just how are you boys going to go about killing us then?'

The foyer was silent, in comparison to the riot that was occurring not a few feet away from them, behind the heavy doors. The man with the quiet voice stepped out from behind the four big men holding the sailors. His appearance complemented his quiet voice as he differed, substantially, from the other bouncers. He was a small man, thin with very short, very thin ginger hair on the top of his head. His face was clean-shaven, pale, and sculptured. He looked delicate, but there was as air of malevolence about him, especially if you looked into his eyes.

'The way I see it gentlemen, is that you have no leverage here, whatsoever. I think you're going to be in trouble tomorrow when you turn up for duty full of cuts and bruises. But then, if you continue this path, making baseless, idle threats, then maybe, just maybe, you won't turn up for duty tomorrow, or ever again.'

The four sailors fell silent as they recognised the threat. Real fear shone through their bruised and swollen features, as the enormity of their current situation dawned on them. Even though this man was a lot smaller, and slighter, than they were, they had come across his kind before.

Dangerous men!

He stood before them, fingering a key that was hanging around his neck on a golden chain. He did this almost absently, but Clive could tell that there was an absolute reverence to the charm.

He raised his eyebrows and addressed the nautical patrons one more time. 'Now, the way I see it, you've come into my club, you've had your fun, but now I think it's time that you all left.' He turned taking in all four sailors in one look. 'Before you can't leave, OK?'

The big men all let go of their wards, and all four sailors attempted to fix the tunics of their uniforms.

The thin man pointed back out of the door to the office, out towards the main exits. 'Now, if I were you, I'd find the other little toe-rag you came here with, I'd leave through them doors down there, get back on your little boat… and never set foot in Liverpool again.'

The sailors looked back towards the large men stood behind them. They were bloodied too, but none of the blood seemed to be their own, it all belonged to other people.

'It's not a boat, sir,' one of the sailors piped up.

Red turned to look at him, his head was cocked slightly, and his eyes were devoid of emotion.

'It's a ship, sir…' the sailor continued.

Red's eyebrows raised and the sailor stopped talking.

Clive turned back to look at the gangster before him; there was a defiant scowl on his face, but he knew that they had been bested here tonight, and they didn't have any more fight left in them. 'It's shit in here anyway, no ale,' he snorted before he, and his colleagues, turned to make their way towards the exit.

Red scoffed as he watched the sailors skulk out of his office, making their way towards the door.

When they were gone, he addressed the men in the office. 'Within ten minutes, anyone still bleeding in my club will be out too. I won't have this level of disruption. Not at The Rialto, this is a respectable gaff.'

With that, he waved his hands at them, dismissing them from his office. As they were filtering out, he looked up. 'Oh, Ron,' he addressed the last bouncer left. 'A word please!'

Ron, the bouncer who had initially allowed the sailors into the club, swallowed hard. 'no worries, Red,' he replied, before closing the door, sealing him in the office with the smaller man.

The rest of the bouncers made their way back into the main hall ready to perform their duties to the best of their abilities. Anyone with blood on their faces were about to get a little bit more.

A young man burst into the foyer. His flopping black hair was matted with the blood that had been pouring from his nose; he was busy looking for his girlfriend.

~~~~

Ten minutes later and the band were back on stage. They were minus the older lead male vocalist, but they began to swing the night away again, it was as if nothing had happened.

~~~~

Outside, the four bloodied sailors were making their way around towards the back of the club, searching for their missing friend. Clive heard a low moan coming from one of the back alleyways and peered down. Alfie, the smallest of them was halfway down the alley, his trousers were hanging down his legs, and before him, facing the brick wall, was the girl he had left the club with.

He offered a thumbs up to his friends.

With a roar, all four of them charged up the alleyway and grabbed him, wrenching him away from his conquest and dragging him off, out of the alleyway; leaving the surprised girl attempting to save her modesty from her, now exposed, compromising position.

4.

'HOW CRAZY WAS that fight last night? I mean, Jesus, we've seen our share, but that one! The punters were slipping on the blood for the rest of the night.' Brian Malone was a tall man, thinning on top with round glasses and a gentle looking face. He was essentially the brass and wind section of the Downswing Seven, the resident band of The Rialto. He was currently struggling down a narrow corridor that was dimly lit. A few bare bulbs hung here and there from the ceiling, casting their dim, yellow glow that only succeeded in adding differing levels of mystery to every small obstacle in the way. At present, to Brian, that felt like every obstacle in the entire world.

He thought the large boxes that he was attempting to carry must have had minds of their own; and their only mission in this life was to bounce off every bit of wall possible along the corridor. Twice he stumbled and more than once he took the Lord's name in vain, as he felt the grip on his burden slip due to his hands growing sore and sweaty.

The tunnel that led to the backstage area of the theatre, where the auditions were being held today, was notorious for being unforgiving to the many musicians who had had the unfortunate *privilege* of negotiating their way through it. Many a cut and scrape to guitar hands or saxophone fingers had ensured any number of nervous performances.

Some of the more 'diva-like' performers paid lackeys to carry their equipment in for them.

George and Brian were not quite at that level of privilege, yet!

George Hogg was lagging Brian; he was struggling, even though he was carrying substantially fewer boxes than the taller man. They looked lighter, but to be fair to him, he would struggle more than most of his colleagues down this tunnel anyway. This was due to his limp. George had always hated the word *cripple,* but he had long ago resigned himself to the fact that that was, exactly, what he was.

When he was a child, he had caught a severe case of polio, which had stunted the growth in one of his legs and distorted his foot. This caused him to develop what was known as a *clubfoot* and he had to wear a metal leg brace to allow him to walk with a semblance of normality, ever since.

To this day, he was embarrassed by it every day of his life, and even though it shamed him, and he saw it as a disability, he had never once allowed it to shadow an opportunity to further himself. He had always struggled through, overcoming any adversity, and had become something that he always dreamed of becoming when he was a child. George was a fantastic drummer. His father, also a drummer, had helped him along with his dream by rigging up a bass drum pedal that he could use with his leg brace. After that, there had been no turning back.

He also never missed an opportunity to use this disability to his advantage too. It had managed to be overlooked during the draft for the war. He was deemed not fit enough to serve his country, so he had spent the entirety of the war at home, servicing the local communities as a blackout warden. He also serviced them by running a rather lucrative black market, selling the people of Liverpool extra rations - eggs, sugar and anything else that he could get his grubby hands on, which was usually quite a bit.

He was using the disability even now, guilting Brian into carrying the lion's share of his equipment up and down stairs or along narrow, treacherous corridors for gigs.

'Can you hurry up? I'm getting frigging welts in my hands from carrying your rubbish,' Brian snapped as he stopped a little in front of George. He looked back at him, offering a scolding expression as the thought he was being used crossed his mind.

'I'm going as fast as I can. I don't know if you've ever noticed that I'm a cripple! Have you?' he shouted back, the annoyance in his voice was obvious even though it was mostly said in jest.

'Only every day of my miserable life that I've been unlucky enough to spend with you. And, yes, I am aware that you're a cripple, and that being a cripple prevented you from seeing active duty.' Brian shouted back to him with more than a hint of sarcasm in his voice. 'And from carrying these bloody boxes,' he continued.

'So, who've we got today then?' George shouted back along the corridor. He was catching his breath as he'd stopped to rest his leg.

Brian turned to see him sitting on his drum stool with his braced leg stretched out before him, absently rubbing it up and down by the knee. The sweat that beaded on his forehead reflected the dim yellow light emitted by the single, stark light bulb hanging above him.

'Oh, just another wannabe. Some cat with a great hairstyle and a mediocre voice to match. Same old, same old,' Brian replied. He took advantage of the rest and stopped too, laying some of his burden down on the floor. He stretched his red, welted fingers backwards and forwards; the cramp made them feel more like talons as he worked the tendons slowly.

'Well...' George began. 'I noticed that I was, once again, overlooked for the role.'

'George, we've been through this...'

'No, we haven't, Brian. You know as well as I do that I'm the perfect fit for the lead male vocalist. You've heard me sing.'

Brian had heard George sing; the guy had the best set of pipes on him that Brian had ever heard. His timing and pitch perfect voice did make him the ideal candidate to take over Tex's role, but his appearance, and his ego, let him down.

George was short, he stood about five feet seven at full stretch, but he was very seldom at full stretch due to his clubfoot. He would normally be seen bending low, or even crouching as he walked, giving him a kind of Hunchback of Notre-Dame like appearance. This, coupled with his thinning hair, were not deemed attractive enough when it came to selecting a lead male vocalist.

Brian was lighting a cigarette when he heard a clatter, then a crash followed by the sound of something metallic rolling along the floor. Brian snapped his head around towards his colleague, just in time to see him rolling about on the floor. The contents of the boxes; cymbals, and metal stands, were scattered all around him. George was on his back in the middle of it all, with his eyes closed, fuming!

'I'm OK, I'm OK…' he hissed, '…but I don't know if I can say the same about the kit!'

Brian got up and offered out a hand, which George reluctantly took. He could see the embarrassment on the drummer's face but did his best to ignore it, knowing that he wouldn't take too kindly if he had to acknowledge it. The pair of them began to busy themselves, collecting the scattered drum paraphernalia from around the floor, before storing it all back in the correct boxes.

Brian couldn't say that he really liked George; he could be unnecessarily cruel to some of the other band members, and to some of the punters who frequently wanted to come backstage to congratulate them on a great show. It wasn't all the time though; George could also be extremely charming when the mood took him. But he only ever seemed to have any time for others if he was something in it for him.

There was something about the drummer he'd always been wary of. It could have been his cold smile; or the fact that sometimes he would catch George looking at him as if he was thinking of different ways of killing, cooking, and serving him up, but mostly Brian just didn't trust the man.

From the very first moment that they had met in Rushworth's Music House, there had been something a little off about him. It was almost as if he was hiding something. Brian had been attracted to this side of him at first; he liked the moody nature and the doubtlessness of his attitude. He refused to be taken for a fool, and he refused to suffer fools. Because of his clubfoot and his limp, he had often been underestimated, usually at the peril of the person doing the underestimating.

The day they met, he was attempting to return a set of drum brushes that had fallen apart on him and the man behind the counter was having none of it. Brian had watched, with a strange satisfaction, as George had talked the salesman around to not only refund him, but to give him a new set of brushes in the deal too. Brian liked the dark, almost sinister, side to him. It appealed to him as he too had his own dark and sinister secrets, that meant he couldn't be too choosy about who his friends were.

In George, he felt he had found a kind of kindred spirit. Given the fact that he had an idea George knew about his secrets, and wasn't too bothered by them, he supposed, for now, he could live with his more unpleasant idiosyncrasies.

'I told you I was a frigging cripple.' There was a lack of humour in George's face as he dusted the lighter dirt, that had clung to him from the well-trodden floor, from his dark trousers.

'Yeah, well, forgive me for not remembering,' Brian replied as he mooched around the dimly lit area for the wing screws off the top of the cymbal stands. 'I mean, there must be thousands of cats with dodgy legs who play drums like you, hanging around Liverpool, don't you think?'

George smiled another humourless smile and winked at him. 'Yeah, well, tell it to the big-time recording companies eh, and don't forget to tell them that I can sing too.'

Breathing a heavy sigh, Brian continued his search for the wing nuts, before eventually locating them hiding in the shadows of box that had been discarded against the wall. They continued their short journey to the concert hall, mostly in silence.

Where the corridor ended, there was a small black door that they both struggled to get through with the boxes. Once through, they were in a dark backstage area, where the artists would gather, before entering onto the large, elevated stage before them.

As they walked through the door, the room opened like a vista before them.

To the uninitiated, the stage could be an intimidating place; it could steal your nerve, your identity, even your breath, but these two veterans took it all in their stride. They had been playing this stage night after night for the last two years and had gotten rather used to it.

Brian only just made it onto the stage, before he had to dump his cargo in a pile as it felt like it was slipping from his grip again. They were the first to arrive, which was normal, as all the others knew that if they turned up at the same time as George they would end up helping him to carry his kit down the corridor, and no one really wanted to do that.

Brian turned to look at his colleague, his face was bright red and he was panting with the effort of the Herculean task they had just endured. 'Don't you believe in second trips?' he asked. 'Haven't you ever heard of a lazy man's load?' Brian bent over with his hands on his hips, attempting to relieve himself of the stitch that had developed in his side.

'Have you ever heard of a clubfoot up your arse?' George laughed. 'Or maybe you'd like that eh?' He winked at him.

Brian laughed a strained little laugh, pulling an exasperated face as he began to unpack his own instrument; the trombone. As he sat down with his polishing cloth in his hand, he shot the smaller man a second look; this was not lost on George who smiled wryly to himself before turning his attention towards his dismantled kit.

Brian watched as George untied the straps on the individual drum cases, watching as he cast a pathetic figure, struggling to remove the drums inside; a simple task that many others would take for granted. George's disability wasn't as bad as it could be, but Brian was a sentimental fool and he couldn't help the feelings that flowed from him. He knew that if George had an inkling of the sympathy he felt, he would be in big trouble –George never took kindly to charity - but he couldn't help himself, it was the way he was wired. *I can't help that just as much as I can't help...* He never finished his last thought; it was too awful a thought for him to even contemplate.

Unlike his own disability, the one he could hide from most people, he knew that George had to live with the fact that everyone he met would judge him by his clubfoot. It was his defining feature; the only feature anyone would remember.

That was until they heard him play the drums.

When he was behind the kit, the man transformed from a cripple with a bad attitude, into a musical god. His rhythm and timing were perfection itself, and if he was ever called upon to do a drum solo piece, he would rattle the skins like no one Brian had ever seen before.

Unfortunately, for him, drummers were usually pushed to the back of the stage, upstaged by the singers, the horns, and even the bass players. George was always doomed to be in the back.

Off stage, he'd always tried his best to hide the metal calliper and the extended shoe that came with it, which he could do to a good degree, but there was no disguising his limp.

'What are you staring at?' George asked. The spite in his voice was obvious.

This attack snapped Brian out of his thoughts, and he shook his head, turning his attentions back to the cleaning of his instrument. 'Nothing, I was just wondering when you were going to go and get the rest of your kit, that's all.' Brian's face was reddening as he turned away from George's fierce gaze.

He began to busy himself, setting up his trombone and music stand, as he listened to the irregular thump of George limping backstage to retrieve the rest of the kit that they'd left in the corridor.

5.

THE ANGER INSIDE George was building. He was always angry when the band held auditions for new members. The rapid demise of Tex, the lead male vocalist, had meant that they had to expedite the recruitment for a new front man, and it didn't sit right with him at all.

All six remaining members of the band were present for the upcoming audition. George on drums, Brian on brass and woodwind, Eddie was the guitarist and sometimes band leader for bigger numbers. Faye was the sexy female lead. That left the last two members; Tam, no one knew his second name, and no one was really interested in finding it out. He played double bass, smoked, drank, and kept himself to himself. Finally, there was Joe 'Big Joe' Franklin on piano. Joe had never once had anything to say in the running of the band; to him it was somewhere he could go to drink, play music, get paid, and spend it all on finding woman to fall in love with.

George was a founding member of the band and had come up with the name; The Downswing Seven. But over these last two years he felt like he'd been pushed further and further back, out of the way. The band had been formed around Tex Ryder. He'd been the natural choice as the lead male vocalist from the beginning. Back in the day, he'd been a fantastic crooner with a career touring around Europe and America, before the war came and killed the industry.

Over the years he'd become far too old and too frail to make it through the long sets. This coupled with the fact that sometimes he forgot the words to the songs and, more disturbingly, he would sometimes be found sitting and staring into space for lengthy periods of time, didn't go in his favour. Once he began doing it in the middle of the sets then everyone knew that his days were numbered. At first the audience thought it was funny, as if it was a new comedy part of the show, then after a few uncomfortable minutes, when he began to mumble incoherently into the microphone, the joke soon wore off. More often than not, Faye would lead him off stage and the band would carry on into an instrumental, or a medley, until she could make it back on stage alone.

Since then, the temporarily re-named Downswing *Six* had been through several singers. None had wanted to stay too long for one reason or another, always citing *musical differences* as their excuse for quitting, but some members of the band had held other suspicions.

Tex had been allowed to dip in and out of the band to make him feel like he was still part of something – even thought there was little he could bring anymore – and last night had been the final straw. When one of the doormen had stepped in and escorted him off stage, the whole band, including Joe and Tam, had agreed that they needed to get someone in on a permanent basis, otherwise they would have to split up.

The main reason George hated auditions was because he himself had a fantastic singing voice. His baritone and crooning were second-to-none, and due to his perfect timing, his rhythm was excellent. Although no one had told him to his face, he knew exactly why he had never been allowed to front the band. It was all down to the fact that he had a clubfoot, and he wasn't what you would call a classically good-looking bloke.

He didn't 'look the part'.

The band had decided that to get larger crowds at the gigs, they needed someone who the ladies could fall deeply in love with, and who the men would want to be like, both in persona and in looks. They said that they were attempting to present an image, prying people away from the everyday dirge of rations and post-war depression, and giving them an escape.

It was exactly what they had with Tex in the early days. He'd been a fantastic singer and a very good-looking man, broad at the shoulders, and he could speak with an authentic American drawl. This was all put on; he had spent six months in America before the war, trying his best to make it with the big bands over there, but had come home with his tail between his legs and an American accent. Everyone knew it was false, but it fit and pandered to the escapism that everyone in the clubs dreamed of.

Everything about the music scene these days was image; very little depended on substance, talent, or skills. This was the reason George Hogg had been overlooked time and time again, it was also the reason he was so testy today. Once again, he had been unanimously ignored for the front man's position, a role that he knew would fit him, and one that he could wear so well.

So, all this going on, coupled with the fact that none of his horses had come in yesterday so he now owed a huge chunk of his wages from the next gig to Red, meant that he wasn't having the best of days.

'Right, let's get set up eh, the guy will be here in less than an hour.' Eddie spoke to the rest of the band after he had spent the twenty minutes meticulously going through the set for the audition.

George sighed and shook his head in despair, he didn't care what time the new guy would be here. With the air of a child who had been scolded and forced to tidy his bedroom on the threat of no supper, he sulkily set up his kit.

6.

WITHIN THE HOUR, all the members of Downswing Six had set up their instruments, tuned up, and were back on the stage; most of them carrying cups or glasses, and all of them smoking.

Tex Ryder had made it to the audition too. Everyone was always glad to see him but none more so than George. He had always had a soft spot for Tex, as he had always been a good friend to him. He had served with George's father in the latter years of World War One. Both of them had survived, and on their return to Liverpool, they had embarked on a living, playing in bands all over the country. George's mother had never liked him, mostly she blamed the eternal bachelor for her husband's wayward attitudes, George thought it was more likely his mother's nagging that had kept him away. On his brighter days, he would regale George with fantastic tales of adventures that the two of them got up to on tour. These tales had always fascinated George; due to the rigorously religious upbringing enforced upon him by his mother, and his father being away most of his childhood, he had never really gotten to know him.

After the disastrous events of last night when the band had let him come back on stage for a few numbers and ultimately having to be led off, Tex had been more than a little confused, he was living in the past, not really connecting with things going on around him.

'I got to tell you, George, I hate these audition things,' Tex confided as the rest of the band set up and tuned in around them. 'It always brings home to me the fact that my singing career's almost over.' There was more than a sprinkling of melancholy in his voice, and it made George sad. Very few things could elicit emotion in George, but the agonisingly slow demise of Tex was one of them.

He put his arm around the older man and gave him a hug. 'Tex, you know you'll always be the best lead singer that the Downswing Seven ever had. All this…' he waved his arm around, indicating the rest of the band, '…it's just a new generation.' George then indicated off stage, towards the rows and rows of empty tables in the theatre. 'All them people out there Tex, they'll all remember coming to The Rialto and watching the Downswing Seven, fronted by Tex Ryder.'

The older man was looking out at the seats, his eyes were rheumy and red, and they looked heavy with tears. He was nodding as if he was considering some distant memory. A ghost of a smile broke on his once handsome face.

'You're just passing on the baton, Tex, that's all, passing on the baton,' George whispered into the old man's ear. It made him sad to see such a once great man reduced to the rubble that he now was. *It'll come to us all sooner or later,* he thought, as he made his way back to his kit. He sat down, heavily, on his stool, fixed the bass drum pedal to his clubfoot and let loose a serious roll on his finely tuned skins.

He watched with a tinge of sadness when Tex jumped a little at the noise and then began to shuffle off stage.

'Who invited the fossil?' Eddie Martino asked once Tex was safely out of earshot.

George couldn't stand Eddie; he was the band leader and played a little bit of guitar. *'All he does is wave a stick about and sometimes play a few guitar chords, rather badly if you ask me,'* George could be heard grumbling about him, usually when they were divvying up the payment at the end of the night, and mostly when he was handing over the lion's share of his divvy to Red. 'He doesn't bring anything to the table, he just smiles at the audience, pretends to conduct us and comes in as and when he feels like it. I can tell you for a fact that I've never, not even once, took any notice of what that duffer's doing up there.' George would complain, loudly, to whoever would listen, but then, as he usually complained about everything, he normally ended up complaining to himself.

'Look at him, all dressed up and ready for the audition,' Eddie continued, laughing like a schoolyard bully as he pointed to where Tex had sat himself back down. 'He's even wearing his old band leader's suit. I can't believe he's turned up wearing that moth-eaten old thing.'

'What's wrong with that?' George shouted towards him, his anger was simmering like a boiling pot, he knew that sooner or later he was going to blow his lid and when he did, he wouldn't care who was in the blast zone. 'He just wants to make an impression that's all. Do you have a problem with it?'

'He's making an impression all right, one that says we're living back in the twenties. If we ever manage to get out of The Rialto gig and actually take this band touring, that fella has to be our first casualty.' Eddie scoffed as he watched Tex sitting in the wings, looking like he didn't even know where he was.

George had had enough. He stood up from behind his drum kit; his face was flushed dark red. Brian was the only one who noticed this and, seeing which way the wind was about to blow, he had to think fast to diffuse the situation.

'You're thinking of taking this rag tag band touring?' Brian laughed.

Eddie spun around to him; his face still filled with mirth from laughing at Tex. 'Yeah, why not? You got to have dreams, don't you?' Eddie defended his stance.

'Dreams are for the kids! You're closer to fifty than you are to forty, maybe you need to get yourself a woman, have a couple of kids and think about settling down before you start dreaming of international stardom.'

As the rest of the band began to laugh, this time at Eddie, Brian spared a quick glance over to George whose face had now turned back to the correct shade of pink, as he sat back behind his drums. He let out a sigh then turned back towards his own job at hand, polishing his trombone.

At that precise moment, as if on purpose to diffuse the situation that was building, Faye Farrell floated back into the room. Faye was thirty-five years old. When she was up on stage, she could pass for twenty-five, up close, on a bad day, she looked in her forties. She was petite and very pretty. The rest of the boys in the band knew that it was her immaculately prepared make-up that was covering the cracks, but none of them minded; the audiences loved her. Her short, blonde, bobbed hair cut into a sexy 1920's retro style and fantastic figure made her the envy of most of The Rialto female clientele, and the desire of most of the males.

The fact that she was plagued with very low self-esteem coupled, paradoxically, with a huge ego, made her a very complex and very vulnerable woman.

'Hi Georgie...' she flirted as she wafted past.

Eddie stopped talking instantly as she entered the room. His eyes followed her like a puppy dog's, following every move his new master made. Everyone in the room watched as she drifted past into the wings to stop and give a Tex a big kiss.

'There you go, fella,' Brian said nudging George as she went past. 'Faye would be perfect for you.'

'Oh, thanks mate, yeah, hook me up with a fortysomething has-been why don't you!'

'She's not forty; I'd say that she was mid-thirties at most, and she still looks good for it.' Brian countered.

George shook his head and began to tighten the nut on the top of his cymbal stand. 'Believe me, she's forty, if not physically then mentally. Nope, she's not for me that one.'

'Well, even so, forty's not so old these days, it's not like she's been working down a coal mine, now is it?'

George looked up at her, as if he was contemplating something. 'You know what Brian, you're right! She wouldn't be so bad, I mean, she's got a few bob, hasn't she?'

Brian laughed as he walked away. 'Man, you are one sick cat.'

'Maybe I am but you know what? You're an eligible bachelor too. Why don't you make a move on her? You've got as much a chance at that as I do.'

Brian's beaming smile became a little more uncomfortable as he sat back down at his stool. He gave George one more cursory look before finishing off his instrument.

Got you there, old pal, George thought as he swapped his sticks for the catgut brushes favoured by the swing bands.

'Hey Faye, where have you been baby?' Eddie Martino shouted to her as she breezed back onto the stage.

'I've been in your dreams, honey,' she replied, not missing a beat.

Everyone could see that she was toying with Eddie, half flirting and half condescending. Everyone that was, except for Eddie himself. He still thought that he was genuinely in with a chance of bagging the girl who was at least ten years younger than him.

'You know it, sugar,' he replied, his smile beaming from ear to ear and looking around at everyone in the club just to make sure that they all heard this exchange.

'Hey, George, can I have a word?' she asked, shouting over to where he and Brian were talking about her.

'Just as long as it's not going to cost me any money,' he retorted.

'You wish you could afford this, honey,' she laughed as she slipped off her coat. Underneath she was wearing a tight outfit, one of the ones that was continuously getting the band outrageous reviews. The women all wanted them, and the men all wanted to take them off. They were considered both sexy and controversial in whatever circles you happened to be in. There was cleavage on show. Though Faye was quite petite she made the most of what God, and her mother, had given her. The whole thing didn't leave much to even the most vivid imagination.

George liked it; he liked it very much, but not anywhere near as much as Eddie did. He made a show of checking all his pockets, as if he was looking for his wallet. 'I got some loose change around here somewhere,' he laughed. 'Sure, sister, what do you want?'

She nodded towards backstage. 'In private if you would, mister.'

'Sure.'

As George got up off his drum stool, and limped off towards the backstage, Brian punched him in the arm.

'Go on laddie,' he whispered, winked and then smiled at him.

As they both walked off stage, George was gleefully aware of the stare that Eddie was currently boring into his back. *If looks could kill,* he thought to himself with a wry smile.

7.

AS THEY ENTERED the small office backstage, George closed the door behind him, giving a quick look to make sure that no one had followed them, before closing the curtains over the windows ensuring them all the privacy they needed. He had a good idea what this conversation was going to be about. He turned back into the room and beamed a smile at Faye who was sat on the corner of the desk on the other side of the room, lighting a cigarette.

She was looking at him for a few seconds before she began to talk. Her mask of flirtatiousness dropped and the real Faye, the flawed individual, was now clawing through the cracks of her façade to reveal herself to the world or, more particularly, to George.

He took one look at her and his smile widened. There was not even a hint of levity in it; he looked like a cat toying with a mouse it had caught moments before he got bored; and killed it.

Her eyes began to redden as tears welled up within them. Her heavily made-up skin looked pale and cracked, as if it had been administered hastily, with a shaking hand, instead of the carefully crafted work of art she usually portrayed. Only someone who was looking closely would notice it at all. This, of course, was George's job.

Silently he stood, observing as the nervous wringing of her hands began to escalate and the rapid twitch of her eyes flicked from him to the door and then back to him several times.

'Hey, what's the matter doll?' he asked eventually, the sympathy pouring out of him was insincere and mocking. He knew exactly what was wrong with her and that, right now, he was the only person in Faye's world who could help her.

'I need some of that stuff you can get, baby, and I need it now.' She wiped at her nose and sniffed. 'This flu is getting really bad. I don't think I'll be able to sing without it.' The tears that had been threatening, broke the dam of her eyelids and flowed freely down her cheek, leaving a single tramline through her makeup. She was flustering, trying to get her words out, but her breath seemed in short supply. She was worlds apart from the Faye everyone outside this room knew. This was the Faye that only George saw, and the one he really appreciated.

He put his hands on her shoulders to steady her shaking. He needed her to stop crying and bring the 'fake' Faye back, just until tonight, when she was in his house doing exactly what he wanted her to do. 'Sure, sure I can get you some, but I'm not going to be able to get it until tonight.' He looked at her as her face changed. He sighed and nodded, as if her had sympathy for the desperate woman before him. 'The guys I'm going to have to get this lot off are not going to be happy with the short notice though.' He exhaled slowly through his nose, enjoying every second of the power and control he had over her. 'I can see them putting the price up for this hit. Are you going to be OK with that?'

As she wiped the tears from her face, a large clump of powder that had been laid thick on her cheeks, came on her hand. *She's going to have to fix that before going back out there,* he thought. Her shaking hands reached up to the lapels of his collar and she smiled a smile that she might have considered sexy, but George found repulsive and for too desperate for his liking.

41

'I don't mind, George,' she whispered, trying her best to sound seductive. 'I'll pay. I just need it to get myself through the next gig, that's all.' She pulled him a little closer, almost close enough to kiss. George could smell her breath; it was the sour stink of a desperate woman and it made him wince. 'I'll do that thing you like. You know, even that thing with my mouth...'

'Oh, I know you'll do it,' he said pushing her and her stench away, the sickly warmth radiating from her was making *him* feel nauseous.

'Because if you don't you won't get what you need, will you?' An ugly smile broke on his face. 'And you'll need to clean your teeth too, your breath is rank.'

She recoiled as if he'd slapped her. She let go of his collars and stepped back, away from him. Her face had the look of a spoilt child who was being told 'NO' for the first time. Angry, hurt and defiant. George knew the defiance was just another façade.

'What if I go to the source myself?' she asked as if thinking this would shock him into some kind of action.

George smiled again. He looked down his shirt and straightened his collars, taking an age to look up at her again. When he did, there was a smug grin on his face; he loved this feeling. 'Feel free, darling. You go and do that, you go and see if they'll sell to a woman, and a strung-out woman at that. I'm pretty sure they won't, no matter what 'favours' you offer them. After that, I won't sell to you either. What will you do then? You'll have to go to the street, and God only knows what you'll get there or who you'll have to use your little mouth trick on to get it.'

'You're a bastard, George Hogg.'

He stepped up close to her despite the rancid smell of her breath and leaned in so that they were almost nose-to-nose. His smile was dangerous, and nasty. 'You're right, Faye, and you'll do well to remember that. Now, be at my place tonight. Shall we say about seven?

We'll both get what we need, and the next gig will go without a hitch. We'll both do it with a spring in our steps. Are you OK with that?'

With more tears welling in her eyes, she turned away from him and stormed off towards the small office door.

'I wouldn't go out there looking like that. You look the colour of boiled shite,' he snarled. 'Get yourself together girl, we don't want your adoring fans thinking that you have a problem now, do we?'

There was a full-length mirror in the corner, for artists to get a last-minute appearance check before going on stage. She opened her handbag and began to fix her hair and powder her face, making herself look, at least, semi-presentable again. She shot one last glare back at George, who smiled back at her before shooing her away, out of the room, like an unwanted dog.

Once she was happy with her appearance, she left the room without another word.

Back on stage, nobody would have guessed that she had almost been on her knees begging in the back room. She was all smiles and flirts, stirring Eddie up into a near frenzy. Just a few moments later, George limped back and sat behind his drum kit. Brian idled over, a contented little smirk on his face. 'What was all that about?' he asked conspiratorially

George winked at him and smiled back. 'That woman can't keep her hands off me. Seriously, I think she has an addiction.'

8.

'EVERYONE, THIS IS Carl Bennett, he's going to be auditioning for the lead male vocal today,' Eddie announced; the smile on his face widened as his eyes searched to meet George's. Out of them all, he knew that George would be the big problem today, and he wanted to keep him as sweet as he could, for as long as he could.

The newcomer was stood next to Eddie looking at the rest of the band. He looked nervous and a little troubled at the introduction as he leaned in close to Eddie and whispered something into his ear.

Eddie looked at him and his brow furrowed. He then raised his eyebrows and turned back to the band. 'I'm sorry everyone, it's Carl Cole, not Bennett.'

This made the newcomer smile a little, as he bounced back on his heels.

'Oh brilliant.' George said to Brian, just loud enough for everyone on the stage, including Carl and Eddie, to hear. 'Just what we need, a prima donna with a frigging stage name.'

Brian frowned and leaned closer towards George. He hadn't taken his eyes off the newcomer yet. 'Give him a chance eh? He might be good.'

George looked at his friend and shook his head, slowly. Brian was still looking at Carl, his eyes were wide and there was a dreamy smile on his face. George could almost hear the romantic music that must have been playing in his head.

Carl walked to the front of the stage. He was tall, six feet at least, maybe even a little more, he had broad shoulders, his thick head of jet-black hair was waxed back to perfection. His complexion was healthy brown with a rugged, thick, one-day shadow stubble on his chiselled chin.

'What the hell does he think he looks like with his hair all up like that, and what's with that tan?' George whispered.

Brian turned to him, there was a deep scowl on his face. 'George, would you just shut up? You said you wanted to tour with this band didn't you? Well, your wish might have just walked through that door. The women are going to go crazy over him.'

Not just the women, George thought, raising his eyebrows. 'Fancy him do ya?'

'Just eff off and play your bleeding drums, will you?' Brian cussed as he moved away from George, giving him a look as if he was a dead cat he'd just found in his kitchen.

Smiling to himself, George leaned away, noting Brian's reaction to his almost playful question.

'Carl's pretty new to the band circuit.' Eddie continued. 'He's just left the army where he saw some action. He used to sing in the swing band that they had there. He's recently back from America and is looking to settle into the gig circuit here in Liverpool, so he does have quite a bit of experience.'

'I bet he has experience in other areas too,' George whispered towards Brian, nudging him with his elbow. 'Swing band in the army? Just a load of old queens singing together to get out of the fighting if you ask me.'

Brian looked angry as he turned around. 'Oh right, just like using your *slight* disability to get you out of any active service eh?' he spat.

George knew that he was trying to cut him, but he had a much thicker hide than that. He narrowed his eyes before answering. 'You know that I'm going to be at least ten times better than this joker here, don't you? The only difference is, I don't have a full head of hair and a tan, do I?' he asked; there was a dangerous spark in his eyes, like a shark sensing blood in the waters.

'Aw bloody hell, would you look at her,' Brian pointed towards the newcomer, doing his best to change the subject.

Turning back to look at Carl, George was having trouble seeing him, as Faye was currently draped all over him, like a rash. She was running her fingers through his hair and cooing as her hands travelled over his broad shoulders. Carl seemed to be loving the attention.

Brian laughed as he turned back. 'Jealous are we, Georgie?'

George snapped his head around towards him, his face was nasty, his top lip was curled. 'No, Brian. I'm not!' he snarled. He leaned in and lowered his voice, adding to the level of threat, 'And don't ever talk to me like that again.' He leaned in, raising his eyebrows at him; his face was close, and serious. 'I'm warning you. Do you hear me?'

Brian backed away with his hands in the air, in surrender. 'All right, all right...' he shrugged. 'I'll leave you alone, you can stew in your own juices.' He walked away and headed towards the newcomer.

George tutted as he watched them all fraternising. Brian was gushing now too. He was all over Carl, whose face was reddening at the attention and the flattery coming from the newcomer.

You fucking queen, he seethed in his head. The anger was bubbling inside of him now, so much so, he could almost envision steam coming from his ears.

'OK then... right!' George shouted, bringing about an abrupt end to the over-friendly greetings. Everyone in the group stopped what they were doing and looked at him. 'Are we going to play here or are we all just going to fawn around admiring Carl's good looks?' His face was now displaying his own façade, the one that looked like his old congenial self. 'Oh, and I'm George by the way, George Hogg, the drummer!' He said the last part with an abrupt emphasis.

Carl attempted to walk over to him to shake his hand, but he had already sat back down at his drums and was readying himself to play.

'Right then, let's get about this audition. How about Benny Goodman's 'Sing Sing Sing' to get us off to a good start? Carl, are you OK with this one? If you're not, then I'm sure Tex over there can give you some pointers.'

The old man sat in the wings waved a little as he heard his name mentioned.

'No, it's good man. I know this one. Right, after three… hit it. One, two, three.'

The band kicked in with the fast tempo swing number.

It was clear to George even before the first dee-dee-dees, that this newcomer was nothing special, just another bog-standard singer. He had no flair, no feel for the music, or for the melody. He could hold the notes OK and George could see, with dismay, that the bastard looked good doing it, but as far as classics go, this guy was no Mel Tormé, *or even Tex Ryder,* he thought.

They brought the song to a crashing crescendo, George showing off a little on the drums; he tended to do that when there was a new person about. A silence fell about the room as the music stopped and everyone looked at each other. It was clear from their expressions that Carl hadn't quite cut it, and a smile spread slowly across George's face. He was just about to stand up and thank Carl for his time when Faye got there before him.

'Well, I think this guy is in…' she brayed across the stage, trying her best to contain her lustful looks towards the singer, but was not doing a very good job of it.

'He gets my vote.'

George turned towards Eddie, the older man in the suit had a stupid grin on his face as he looked about at the other members. He would have gone along with anything Faye suggested. All she needed to do was to show him her puppy-dog eyes and he was smitten.

Frigging sap! If only he knew how much of a whore she was for her special medicine, he thought to himself. *I wonder how in love he'd be with her then.*

'I loved it too,' Brian gushed, clapping a little too boisterously and mooning a smile in Carl's direction.

Why is it only me that is even registering that Brian is queer? he thought again. *That's a situation I need to keep my eye on.*

'Well, I thought it was decidedly average at best.' George put his sticks down on his snare drum and limped towards the congregated band who were stood around the newcomer, congratulating him.

There were only Tam and Big Joe who remained impassive about the singer. Neither of them particularly cared who fronted the band, as long as they got to play and drink; it could have been fronted by Beelzebub himself!

Once again, everyone stopped what they were doing and turned to look at George. Brian rolled his eyes and Faye looked at him through tilted eyes; a small, secret smile on her lips.

Carl watched the smaller man's laboured approach, his eyes were constantly drawn towards his club foot, and George could see something in his expression. *Is that sympathy? Would that be another reason for me to hate him?*

Carl dragged his eyes up from George's withered leg and smiled an uncertain smile at him. 'Well, it's certainly good to meet you.' He held out his hand for George to shake. 'That was some fantastic drumming, man.'

George nodded at him, ignoring the offered hand, and limped past him. He stopped before he got to the backstage curtain and turned around. There was a sneer on his lips. 'Your phrasing was out, your timing was awful, amateurish really, and I could hear you breathe between lines.' He looked around at the rest of the silent band and sneered some more. 'But then, I'm just a drummer and don't know nothing about all these things… So, I suppose you're in, on good looks alone. Congratulations, Carl *Bennett*.'

George limped off stage towards the exit, his head held low, and everyone knew he was in a bad mood.

They watched him go, mostly with sighs of relief.

Carl didn't know what he had done to annoy the strange man, but then he didn't really care, it seemed that he had got the gig, and now he was earning, he could begin to put his plans into action.

Faye watched George leave, knowing that she was going to be seeing a lot more of the angry little man tonight. The thought depressed her a little, but she had a need, and needs must!

9.

A FEW NIGHTS passed and the 'new and improved' Downswing Seven were a hit. Carl was proved to be popular, both with the ladies and with the other band members.

This was all to George's obvious resentment. He would do anything he could to put the new singer off his stride; subtly speeding up the rhythm, changing the musical cues ever so slightly so he'd miss an intro, anything that would make him look unprofessional on stage.

The rest of the band knew what was happening and they all did their best to counter George's obvious, sly deeds. Everyone apart from Tam. Tam sometimes played along with the jest, just for the deviousness of it.

Carl and Faye were an excellent team and their chemistry was fantastic. Everyone knew that the chemistry between Tex and Faye had been magnificent, but it had been paternal, almost as if the father was teaching the daughter the ropes. Between Carl and Faye, it was sexual; it was explosive and exciting, and it dragged the dance hall-goers into their world.

Much to the disappointment of Faye, the chemistry didn't transfer off stage. Although he was nice and affable, he always seemed distant. To her it seemed like he was searching for something, something, or someone that was never there. She had even, unsuccessfully, come onto him one night after a rather successful gig. She had been rebuffed, but in a manner that made her think there may be something between them in the future.

She was fine with that.

~~~~

Thursday night came around and they were finishing their third and final set. Thursdays were always an early finish for the band; it gave them a little time to get ready for the long run of the weekend. After completing a rather jazzed up version of *Rum & Coca Cola*, Carl and Faye finished the song, finding themselves in each other's arms, with him looking down into her starry eyes, and grins that spread right across their faces.

Once the curtain had closed, stealing them away from the adoring punters, Faye and Carl were still in the position. 'Are you gonna let me go big boy or are we gonna be stuck like this forever?' she asked, hoping beyond hope it would be the latter.

He winked and moved his face forward to kiss her. Faye closed her eyes, thoroughly open to the expected kiss, and ready for the impact he would make on her lips. Her heart dropped when he bypassed her mouth and kissed her cheek instead.

The moment had not gone unnoticed by most of the other band members. Big Joe and Tam couldn't have cared less about what was happening as they packed up their kit, with only three things on their minds; cigarettes, alcohol, and women.

Brian had also witnessed the exchange; he watched as Carl expertly missed the kiss, and whereas Faye's heart fell, his fluttered.

When he had first met Carl, he was instantly struck by his beauty. He didn't think that he had ever seen such a beautiful man before in his life, *and I've been looking,* he thought with a secret grin. There was something, he didn't know what, in his eyes. He'd seen it that day, and now, watching this embrace, or lack of embrace, he was almost- almost, sure that Carl was a kindred spirit. This thought made him polish his trombone a little faster before he realised what he was doing and slowed down again, looking around him his face turning crimson.

Eddie had witnessed it too.

His heart had sunk at Faye's willingness to give herself up to the newcomer. He had harboured feelings for her since the first day she had come in to sing for them. He knew that it was sad, not to mention pathetic to love someone from afar, as he did, and he was no stranger to the heartache watching her leave with one punter after another over the years, and not doing anything about it. Still, he harboured romantic ideals of being her protector, the rock for her to build her foundations on, but more recently, he'd seen that rock erode. She'd become closer to George over the last few months and Eddie knew that could *not* be a good thing.

George also watched the embrace. He didn't care either way how the embrace ended. He knew he had Faye exactly where he needed her. He also knew that she would be in his house tonight, begging for what he had.

She needed her fix after all.

'Right guys, I'm away. I can't be seen hanging around with you shambles. I've got people to see...' George looked directly at Faye, who was still mooning over her near embrace with Carl, she shot him a dirty look, it was all he needed. 'Some of those people I'll be seeing sooner rather than later. Goodnight all... oh, and great gig.'

No one took much notice as George limped out of the stage area.

'So, who's for drinks tonight? I know a great pub on Hope Street that'll serve until three in the morning - if you know the right people and are willing to pay, that is,' Brian announced.

Faye was dusting herself down as she looked at Brian. She had been getting the familiar itches and twitches that she associated with the need for what George could give her, but she figured that a night out, drinking rum, in a bar filled with dockers and sailors might also be just what she needed. *Besides, it might give Carl the final push he needs to get some of my delights,* she thought with a sly smile.

10.

GEORGE WAS WAITING, impatiently, in the house he shared with Tex. The older man was stood behind him with his evening jacket on and a broad smile on his face. 'Are you sure you don't want to come? It'll be a laugh you know.'

'I'm sorry Tex, but I'm in no mood for a good laugh. You go; I'm expecting some company anyway.'

Tex's eyebrows lifted, giving him a slight comical look. 'Company eh? Anyone we know?'

George managed a small smile as he regarded the old man in the coat, 'No one you know, but I certainly know her, very well!' He winked at Tex who smiled and continued to fix his hair in the mirror over the fireplace.

'Well, don't wait up for me,' he winked back at George. 'You never know, I might get lucky myself.'

He smiled as he waved Tex out of the room. He turned the radio on and tuned into a swing show being broadcast by the BBC.

His fingers were tapping along with the music, as he sipped from the large glass of whisky he'd poured himself while he waited for the evening's entertainment to arrive. The whisky was black market, but it was surprisingly good for a cheaper-end blend. He couldn't really afford the good stuff right now, but he was the ambitious kind, and truly believed that if he wanted something bad enough, it would happen.

Some of his neatly greased back hair had flopped onto his face and he pushed it back with an irritated flick. He took another sip of his whiskey and tapped along to the beat of the song as if it was a punishment to the artists playing it. He was livid about today's proceedings, despite the knowledge that he was about to take most of Faye's wages from the next gig and receive a delicious sexual favour for the privilege of it too. The money he would make for Faye's 'snow' would be just enough to pay Red back what he owed him for his recent loss on the horses.

These thoughts made him feel a little better about himself and the situation he found himself in. *Who needs this band anyway?* he thought bitterly.

As he grasped his cigarette between his fingers, he was using all his concentration to stop his hands from shaking. He knew it was just lust-induced adrenaline coursing through his body, due to the anticipation of what he would be getting Faye to do to him for just a small tasting of her current poison, but he could feel his anger building again. This time it was due to the annoyance at Faye for having the audacity to be over half an hour late. He'd already decided that he was not going to give her what she needed tonight, but she *was* going to give him what he wanted.

It was nearly half past ten when, finally, there was a knock at his front door. Rising from his chair, he twitched the curtain, looking out of the window wanting to make sure it was her; but he couldn't see anyone in the darkness.

This made him even madder than usual.

'That bitch, making me wait. She'll get hers, you'll see,' he spat as he limped towards the front door. He held the brace on his bad leg as he did, knowing that it made him go that little bit faster. He didn't want her to wait any longer for her punishment than she had already. He paused before opening the door, flicking at his hair one more time in irritation. He looked at himself in the mirror in the hallway and smiled a cold grin before straightening his shirt, tucking it into his trousers.

He gripped at the latch on the door and opened it in a hurry. 'Well, Missy, it's just about time you made an appear...' he began. The words stuck in his throat as the visitor at the door was not who he expected it to be. In fact, it was the last person he expected, or wanted, to see.

'Hello, George.' The person stood on the step greeted him in a thin, reedy cockney accent.

George stopped dead in his rantings. The colour drained from his face as he stepped back a little, subconsciously putting room between him and his visitor.

'Red, erm, come on in, will you?' he stuttered, offering his arm out to the smaller man, inviting him inside.

'I don't mind if I do,' the visitor replied in a pleasant voice.

Red stepped inside the small house and brushed past him. He poked his head out of the door, looking up and down the street. There was a posh Ford Anglia parked a little way up. He could count three, large silhouettes inside. The headlights were on and the engine was idling.

George closed the door, gently clicking the latch, and went back inside. He made his way into the living room and found his guest already sat on the couch, making himself comfortable.

'Red, this is an unexpected... erm, surprise. How are things? Can I get you anything? Coffee? Whisky?'

Red was a short man with thin ginger hair, cut so short that he really looked bald. His features were weasel-like and he had small, black, beady eyes. His frame was slight but menacing. Everyone knew that his size and appearance didn't mean a thing, he was all muscle and wiry sinew. George had personally seen him take down opponents almost twice his size.

He was also well known for his abruptness when it came to business.

He was sitting on the couch, leaning forward with his leather-gloved hands joined before him. He was looking at George.

Too intently for George's liking.

The key that he was always so proud of was dangling from his neck from the gold chain; it was currently George's focal point.

'How about my money, George? Can you get me that?'

'I, erm….' George stuttered.

Red stood up and straightened out his long black overcoat. 'I thought not.'

'Hang on now, Red, that money isn't due until next week. I've got the gigs at your place this week, you'll get your cash on time. You know I'm good for it.' George was almost pleading now; he was confused at why tonight was not going as smoothly as he had envisioned it.

Red looked at him as if he were a piece of dirt on his new shoe, a sneer stretched across his face. George fancied that he could feel the malice in the man's eyes radiating like a warm wind in his face. 'I reserve the right to amend my arrangements as and when I need to. You best get it to me by then, George, or see that clubfoot of yours?' Red's voice never rose above a threatening whisper. 'That'll be the least of your worries. I want the fiver that you owe me for the bets and the other fiver for the snow I gave you to sell. I want it tomorrow, and no excuses.'

Red stood from the couch and stepped forward, crunching George's bad foot underneath his own, fine Italian, leather shoes. He didn't exert too much pressure, just enough for George to wince at the threat.

'Ten pounds? Where am I going to get that kind of money from?' he asked through his wince.

Red shrugged. 'I don't really care where you get it from! Ten pounds, on my desk tomorrow night, or I come back to…' he indicated the room around him, '…this charming little shithole. Believe me, that is *not* something you want to happen.' He exerted more pressure on the foot and George could feel his knees almost buckling under the pain.

He brought his face up close to George's. He could smell Red's expensive cologne and the mint on his breath, but he could also smell the wild, ferocious animal that was lurking somewhere, not too far, beneath his calm veneer. It was like a coiled spring, eager to pounce, longing for it even. He was fingering the thin chain that hung around his neck over the collar of his shirt. He was rubbing it as if it meant something to him, as if it soothed him. He buffed it like an elderly widow clasps at her rosary beads in church on a Sunday.

'Do you see this, George?' he asked holding the chain towards him.

George nodded, his eyes flicking between the offered jewellery and his guest's crazy looking eyes.

'This is my power, right here.' He held the small metal key that was dangling off the chain between his forefinger and thumb. He pushed it into George's forehead. 'This is my key to everything. It's because of this key that I have the power to come into your…' he looked all around him at the room that George lived in, his face pulled another disgusted grimace, '…home, and demand my money. It's down to this key that I have the power to drive around in that flash car out there,' he said, indicating outside George's window. 'And, did you see them three men inside the car?'

George looked in the direction that Red was indicating. He couldn't see any car or men due to the chintz netting and the curtains, but he knew they were there; he knew the two men in the back and the one sat in the front.

He looked back at Red and nodded.

'Well, this little key gives me the power to command them to do anything I want them to do. You understand me, George?' To add emphasis to the question, he exerted a little more pressure onto George's foot.

George was still nodding. He didn't really understand where this conversation was going but the pain in his foot told him that it was serious and that it might do him good to listen and listen well.

'I can command them to come in here and do you over; I can command them to do your lovely place here over too.' Red brought his face even closer, his black eyes boring holes into George's face. 'Does Old Tex still live upstairs?'

George nodded, slowly. Sweat was dripping down his brow into his wild, and petrified eyes, causing them to sting.

It was obvious that Red was enjoying himself; that he was the zone, doing what he lived for. A smile crept onto his thin lips. 'Well, if I wanted, I could command them to go upstairs and do the old duffer over too. Come to think of it, I might be doing him a favour, the old fart. Are you grasping the context here, Georgie?'

George hated being called Georgie even more than people staring at his metal leg brace.

'Whatever I command them to do, they will do. Is this understood?'

George swallowed; he could feel acid in his stomach churning due to the menace of the situation. After everything that he'd been through in life, he always swore to himself that he'd never ever get into a situation like this again, not after the bullies at school, not after the ridicule he had endured at the hands of mean girls, never again.

But, alas, here he was.

'Understood!' he seethed through gritted teeth.

'Excellent! Then our business here is complete.'

Red removed his foot from George's and the relief was instantaneous. He fell back onto the chair behind him looking up at his aggressor, who was looming over him as if he were a slave master ready to administer another lashing to a petulant slave.

'Right then, I'll see you tomorrow, Georgie, with my money. Understand that I hate making these…social calls, but I've got a feeling about you George, and let me tell you, it isn't a glowingly warm, nice feeling either.'

He leaned in and slapped George on the cheeks, twice, with his leather-gloved hands. The slaps were hard enough to leave marks. With another smile on his face, he headed towards the front door.

George didn't get up to follow him; he sat and watched the thin man leave, absently running his hand towards his calliper and rubbing it, in an attempt to soothe his aching foot.

11.

THE NIGHT WAS a success, the four members of the Downswing Seven were having a fantastic time in the Ye Cracke pub, off Hope Street, in the centre of Liverpool.

It was a pub that tolerated a diverse crowd of revellers inside.

From the moment they had entered, Eddie's hackles had been up. It seemed to him that most of the men inside were far too friendly. There was a lot of leaning into each other and far too many hugs going about for his liking.

Brian and Carl, on the other hand, seemed to be enjoying themselves immensely, and Faye was acting like the Belle of the Ball.

Everyone took to her instantly.

Eddie had taken umbrage to this, as he had seen this night as his chance to let her know exactly how he felt about her. As it was, he couldn't even get near her.

Once the patrons inside the pub found out who they were - the core of The Downswing Seven from The Rialto - the drinks began to flow, and Eddie forgot about his misgivings regarding the bar, and the people enjoying themselves within it. He began to embrace the friendly atmosphere and the convivial nature that was beginning to blossom between the new member and the rest of the band. *Out of the domineering view of George,* he thought with a drunken, twisted smile.

A couple of men had lifted Faye onto the bar and although she was complaining and protesting, when they asked her to give them a song, it didn't take her long to break into her best Vera Lynn and perform impromptu renditions of *We'll Meet Again* and *A Nightingale Sang in Berkley Square*.

Even though he was rather drunk now, Eddie could see the way she was looking towards Carl, but he also noticed the way that Carl was oblivious to the looks.

He was happy with that.

~~~~

A few hours of heavy drinking later, Eddie had gone home, and Brian had also disappeared around the same time as one of the men behind the bar. Faye and Carl were sat at a corner table still drinking.

Both were aware of the late hour; neither of them cared.

Faye was drunk. She had reached the point where she knew that her mouth could get her into trouble, but she didn't mind the kind of trouble she could get herself into with this man. To her irritation, he didn't seem nearly half as drunk as her. *That could be a good thing,* she thought, *no brewers droop to contend with!* With a salacious smile, she reached out her hand towards him and touched his fingers.

He stiffened at her touch and turned his head away from the window where he was gazing, to look at her. He then smiled and accepted her hand.

'What are you thinking about, Mr Enigma?' she asked, cocking her head to one side. All the itches and the nervous twitches that she had been having earlier had been absorbed by the alcohol; she was under no illusion that they would be back tomorrow, but she wanted to at least enjoy tonight before she had to even think about dealing with George.

Carl looked at her and smiled, then he shook his head, slowly but sadly. 'Nothing much,' he replied eventually.

'Don't give me that. I've only known you for a short while, but I can already tell that there's something up with you.'

He breathed in a deep, resigned sigh before picking up his pint of stout and taking a long swig from it.

She moved her hand away from his and sat up straight in her chair. 'Is it another woman? Do you have a wife or something?'

He shook his head. 'No, it's nothing like that...' he paused, thinking. 'But then, I suppose it *is* something like that too. There's... someone!'

Faye closed her eyes and sat back in her chair, reaching out for her half-finished drink. She had wanted Carl to take her home tonight so much. There, she would willingly do all the things that she was forced to do with George. Right now, all those dreams had been shattered. Carl had a girlfriend, or a wife.

'It's OK you know, I'm not going to jump on you and eat you alive,' she lied, offering him a slanted grin.

He laughed a small wistful laugh before looking at her. 'Come on, it's late. Let me get you home, we've got another gig tomorrow.'

Faye nodded. She knew, deep down, that nothing was going to happen between them, not tonight anyway. Her life suddenly began to drift back, far from the potential bright lights she'd envisioned with Carl, back towards the dull greys of George and life at The Rialto.

When they got to her house, it was nearly light, and the early March chill was in the air. 'Are you sure you don't want to come in? You could sleep on the couch you know?'

'No, there's somewhere I need to be, someone I need to check up on.'

Faye, now almost sober and totally devastated by the rebuff, took the rebuff on the chin. *That' the kind of girl I am. I take the hits and kept on rolling,* she thought.

'OK, are you going to be in tomorrow?'

He winked at her, nodded, and gave her a kiss on her cheek before walking away.

12.

GEORGE WAS WAITING outside The Rialto for Faye to turn up to the sound check. As he saw her making her way along the street, he slipped himself deeper into the recess of the stage door, so if she happened to glance over, she wouldn't be able to see him until it was too late. He waited patiently for her to get closer before reaching out and grabbing her by the arm.

She jumped at the attack but relaxed when she saw who it was.

'Where the hell were you last night?' he hissed.

She looked at him as if he were something unsavoury that she'd just stepped in, then flashed him a smug smile. 'I went for a drink with Carl and Brian. Is that illegal?'

'Yes, it's fucking illegal when you were supposed to come to my house for your fix.' His eyes glared as he seethed. Faye took a step back, away from the madman gripping her arm.

'Yeah, well,' she said, wrestling her arm from George's vice-like grip. 'It turns out I didn't need it. We had such a laugh, all four of us.' She fluttered her eyelashes and offered him a saucy smile. 'If you're jealous then maybe you should've been there.'

His lips pulled back in a sneer as he studied her face. The thick make-up was still there, and her eyes looked almost as bad as Tex's did when he was having a bad day. He knew that she still needed the stuff, but the gin, he could still smell on her from last night, must have taken the edge off her need.

He shook his head as he pushed her away from him. To him she was a means to an end, something for him to use and abuse, whenever he needed it. Right now, he needed her, and it angered him that she had the audacity to defy him. 'Get away from me you whore,' he spat.

The force of the push made her stumble into the main foyer of the ballroom where the rest of the band were stood, talking and smoking. Everyone turned as she fell inside. A small nervous laugh escaped her as she looked at them all. 'Well, I think someone might have overdone it on the gin a little last night!' She lied.

Both Eddie and Carl rushed over to help her up, laughing as they did.

George followed her in about a minute later, ignoring the kerfuffle as his colleagues dusted Faye off. He bustled past them into the main ballroom and hobbled over to the main stage. His limp was a little more pronounced than usual, mainly due to his unexpected visitor the night before, and he struggled with the couple of stairs before sitting at his drum kit and beginning to play.

All the others turned to watch him, or rather to marvel at him. He really was an excellent drummer.

'His rhythm is perfect, isn't it?' Carl mumbled, shaking his head as he watched George rip into a full-blown swing number on his own.

Brian rolled his eyes. 'Yeah, he is. Don't ever tell him that. He isn't as nice a person as he is a drummer.'

'I kind of get that. What's his issue with me?' Carl asked, still watching him beat furiously on the kit.

'Well, you see, first of all, George has an issue with life itself. He thinks he's been dealt a bum card. He's got all the talent on the drums and, honest to God, you want to hear the guy sing.'

Carl raised his eyebrows and looked at Brian. 'He sings too?'

'Like you wouldn't believe. He just can't see past his disability. He tells himself that it's his leg and his height that stops the band from promoting him to lead singer; no offence here, Carl, but he really is that good. But it's not that. It's his ego that stops us from giving him the gig. Ever since Tex took bad, George has had his eye on the top spot but both me and Eddie know that it just can't happen. It'd kill him and destroy the band too.'

Brian walked off then, towards the stage where he picked up his trombone and began to put the beginnings of a brass section to the rhythm that George was playing. Soon, all the others joined in and there was nice, loose, swing vibe in the room. The mood shifted and an impromptu performance of *I've Heard That Song Before* by Harry James and Helen Forrest began. George took the lead vocal and was backed expertly by Faye.

Carl was gobsmacked.

George's voice was perfect for the loose swing song; his bass complementing the nasal, female parts that Ms Forrest had recorded to wonderful effect. He was pitch perfect and could even swap to alto within a heartbeat. Carl couldn't believe his ability to keep time on the drums and sing at the same time. The song finished and another kicked straight in. Once again, Carl was blown away by the ease of the transition from one song to the next.

The performance eventually played itself out and Carl couldn't help but clap. Brian beamed when he watched Carl's reaction; his face flushing a deep crimson. 'That one was *Swingin' in the Sunshine*,' Brian explained. 'It's one of the more popular hits with all the punters. It's one of the ones that I think you'd do really…'

Carl wasn't listening to Brian; he was clapping and shaking his head as he walked over to where George was now tightening the skins on one of his toms. 'George, I've got to say, that was fantastic, your voice… Christ, it's excellent. Why aren't you singing lead?'

There was a collective intake of breath from the rest of the band members. Even Tam and Joe were looking at the newcomer with frowns on their faces.

Brian rolled his eyes, pulling a scared frown. Eddie raised his eyebrows and turned towards Faye, fawning over her so they were kept away from the fallout that was, now, inevitable.

George stopped what he was doing and looked up at Carl. He put his tuning key down on the skin of the drum and exhaled a slow, deep sigh before standing up. This exaggerated movement got the attention of all the others and they tried to look the other way, busying themselves with anything else, knowing exactly what was coming next.

The smaller man limped over to where Carl was stood on the edge of the stage, never once taking his eyes from the newcomer.

Carl stopped clapping as he watched him approach. His eyes were darting from George to the rest of the band and back to George again.

Eventually, he made it over and stood silently before the taller man.

After a short, uncomfortable pause, he spoke, breaking the awkward, looming, silence. 'You see this, Carl?' he asked.

Carl's eyes looked away again, he was silently pleading to the rest of the band for help, any kind of help, before eventually realising that none was forthcoming, so they returned to George. He smiled an awkward smile and shrugged. 'See what?'

'The limp, Carl,' he said with an emphasis on his name. 'Can you see the fucking limp?'

Carl didn't want to, but he looked anyway, at George's metal clad leg. His mouth dried instantly. Any saliva he'd had prior to this confrontation, was gone; he didn't know where. His eyes told the room that he wanted to be somewhere else; anywhere other than right here, right now.

'Yeah, I've seen you limp, so what of it?'

Carl could feel his eyeballs sinking into his head as George stared at him. He felt like a balloon with a small hole in it. He had only wanted to be nice to him and now he felt like the biggest creep in the entire world.

'Well, Carl, apparently, the punters don't want to see this. So therefore, we have... *you*.'

He looked around the room, at the other band members, still hoping for some assistance that was, apparently, not about to happen any time soon. He needed help to get out of this situation, but try as he might to grasp their attention, all he could see was the backs of their heads. Everyone was busy doing anything else other than getting involved.

'Well, I... erm...' he stuttered, the only response he could think of.

'Yes, well... you...' George mocked. 'Maybe you should think about things before you open that handsome mouth of yours eh? Maybe do us all a favour, and do it before you start to sing, eh?'

Carl felt like the balloon he envisioned earlier, was now totally deflated. He didn't feel physically threatened by this man, he knew that, if it came to it, he would be able to fight him, but the ethics of hitting a cripple were the same as hitting a man who wore glasses, maybe even worse. He also didn't want to lose this gig. He had other, more important reasons for needing the money.

'Well...OK then.' Eddie interjected, thankfully for Carl. 'Shall we get another song under our belts eh? Maybe get Carl here on the microphone; that is what he's here to do after all. Don't forget we've got an important gig tonight.' He was trying his best to elevate the situation and cheer everyone up.

'Yeah, at The Rialto. Just like every other Wednesday, Thursday, Friday, Saturday, and Sunday evening,' George said averting his glare from Carl and hobbling his way back to the drum kit.

Carl sighed; the relief was physical as he watched the smaller man limp away.

'Are you OK?' Brian asked, handing a microphone and stand to him. 'I told you not to engage. It just brings out his, erm, more destructive side.'

Carl accepted the props, nodding as he did. 'Yeah, so I see,' he replied, not taking his eyes off the drummer.

13.

THAT NIGHT, THE Rialto was swinging, and after the events of earlier in the day, the band were eager to get going. They'd announced the changing of the name back to the Downswing Seven and announced their latest addition. Lead male vocalist, Carl Cole.

Carl was excited, he was also nervous. He got like this every time there was a live performance. When he'd performed in the army it was usually to a bunch of the lads who he knew. It was different singing to an audience that comprised of just men, but these days, it was a mixed crowd, and not one of them in uniform.

There was a good crowd and a huge buzz about the ballroom tonight, everyone was in a great mood, ready for some good music and a lot of dancing.

His eyes spanned the grand ballroom, taking in the fantastic mural depicting scenes of gondolas cruising up and down the canals of Venice; giving the large hall the effect of space and tranquil beauty, and taking the punters away from the gloomy streets of Toxteth and the smoky city of Liverpool.

The room was full, and every table was filled with revellers. Everyone was dressed in their best, and ready to enjoy their Sunday night before the drudgery of the working week, just mere hours away, dragged them back down again.

He'd found that he loved singing in front of so many people at the same time. The knowledge that there was a talented, professional, and experienced band behind him alleviated most of his nerves.

He peeped his head out of the large red curtain covering the stage. He wanted to see what the audience looked like. He wanted to smell the smell of one of the famed Sunday nights in Liverpool.

He wasn't disappointed.

His eyes scanned the faces of the audience. He was looking for the one person in the ballroom who, he guessed, would be the only one looking like she was not enjoying herself. It didn't take long to locate the pretty, young wallflower.

His sister.

She was tall, slim, and very attractive. Her blonde hair was cut short in accordance with the new fashions that had made their way over the Atlantic from America and given the girls something new to consider. The dress she was wearing was a kind of silk material that clung to her hips. It accentuated her every curve with a very respectable, but at the same time risqué, split up one, smooth, silk-stockinged leg.

All the men in the room, regardless of whether they were alone or not, had their eyes drawn to her. More than a few of the women were looking too, but not for the same reasons.

Carl hated the attention she got, but it was something he, begrudgingly, had gotten rather used to, as it happened everywhere they went. It always had, even when she was a child.

She was stood against the far wall, oblivious to the amorous and lecherous looks she was receiving from all quarters. She was ravishing and innocent but there was something else about her. Somehow, she looked lost, alone in a sea of people. Her big, scared eyes were searching the room as she clung, desperately, to the wall.

Carl released a long, relieved sigh, before ducking back behind the curtain where the rest of the band were assembled, set up, and ready to go on stage in ten minutes.

'I'll be back in a moment,' he said to no one in particular, as he passed the other six performers, on his way to the stage door.

'What? Where are you going, Carl?' Eddie asked, watching his hurried exit.

As Carl left the stage, heading for the main ballroom, he knocked into George who was carrying a large glass of water onto the stage to place by his kit. 'Jesus, watch it, will you?' he snapped as water spilled spilling down his shirt. He put the glass down at a nearby table and watched as Carl disappeared through the door.

An idea came to him. As it did, a large, sly smile crept over his face. 'Well, there he goes,' he said, suddenly in a lot better a mood than he had been in all day. 'The main event, ladies and gentlemen, has just left the building...'

Chuckling to himself, he made his way towards the backstage, where he deposited his glass of water. He gave Faye a wicked pinch on her behind as she passed, on her way towards the curtain. It was a playful pinch but one that he knew would leave a bruise. She jumped, cursing him as she moved on.

Brian was watching as he did it; Faye noticed that he had seen it and tried to laugh it off, but it was difficult to hide how much it had hurt.

'Oh, you, George,' she shouted. 'Just you concentrate on your boom-boom and not mine eh?'

This derived a small titter from the rest of the band, all except Brian. His look skipped between her and George, who was now busy making some final adjustments on his kit and smiling to himself. Brian was becoming concerned about George's behaviour; he'd been bad before when they had held auditions, and on the new singer's debut gigs, but today had been ridiculous. He made a mental note to have a word with him after the gig.

Eddie, in a fit of panic, followed Carl out of the door and watched his progress across the room.

'Phew, panic over everyone, it's just a broad. He's talking to her over by the cigarette machine,' he announced on his return backstage.

Faye ran to the curtain and looked out with some urgency. It took her a moment to find him in the crowd, and when she did, she saw he was talking to a tall, attractive woman. Her heart fell into the pit of her stomach and she closed her eyes. The loss of something exciting, something that could have been special, even if it was only in her head, crashed around her. It hit her hard. Not wanting any of the band to know the true level of disappointment she was feeling, she pulled back from the curtain, harrumphed comically, and then returned to her position. 'It's always the good ones that are taken!' she quipped with a smile plastered on her face, even though inside it felt like her heart was breaking.

George was a connoisseur of reading people and their emotions; he'd had to be to make a success of his more nefarious dealings. He'd made it his business over the years to be the perfect reader of Faye, and right now he could read the sadness in her smile.

It made him feel even better than he already did.

He winked at her and pulled a smug face before leaning in to whisper something. 'So, now you see. You'd have been much better coming to mine last night than building all your hopes on a handsome no-mark like him.' He reached inside his jacket and produced a small brown medicine bottle. He shook it so the thick, sweet contents swilled against the sides. 'I bet you're starting to itch right about now, huh?' he asked.

As if on cue, she began to feel the oncoming twitch as imaginary insects ran amok, up and down her body, underneath her clothes and in her hair.

'I'll see you in the gents during the break. Normal rules apply, yeah?'

Her eyes shifted to see if anyone else was looking and was relieved that they weren't. She offered a faint nod, averting her eyes towards the floor. The deep shame and disappointment in herself coursing through her, just like the twitch.

George put the bottle back into his inside pocket, raising his eyebrows and nodding as he did. 'Yeah, I thought as much. Bring the cash.' He leaned in even closer. 'All of it,' he concluded.

Faye's eyes turned upwards; her look was sheepish and filled with hurt. She nodded her own small acknowledgement as she edged away from him. Running her fingers through her hair and straightening her, tight fitting, gown, she lifted her head high.

George grinned again as he watched her put up the façade, he knew that her spirits, and her will, were at an all-time low.

Eventually, Carl returned to *almost* everyone's relief. 'I'm so sorry about that everyone, but my sister's back from America. She got back the other day and I promised her a night on the town. She could do with cheering up a bit, well, quite a bit, actually. It's a long story…' he was panting, a little out of breath. 'So, are we going to get this show on the road or what?' His eyes met George's at the back of the stage.

He narrowed his eyes and stared back. *He's hiding something,* he thought, making a mental note to make every effort he could to speak to Carl's sister as soon as he got the chance.

Everyone agreed that going ahead with tonight's gig was generally a promising idea. Everyone except George. Outwardly, he agreed and even feigned approval at Carl's eagerness, but inside he was still fuming.

Fuming and scheming.

14.

THE SHOW WAS going down a storm and Carl was doing a sterling job. What he lacked in technical ability, he made up for in enthusiasm and charisma. He really was a great front man.

The crowd loved him.

George hated him.

Brian and Faye had both fallen deeply in love with him.

Eddie didn't trust him.

Tam, the double bass player, didn't really care one way or the other and Big Joe, the pianist, was too drunk to even notice that it wasn't Tex singing.

It seemed that the new-and-improved Downswing Seven were a hit. Backstage after the first set, the mood was jubilant. Most of the band were in high spirits and too busy slapping Carl on the back for a job well done to notice George slinking off towards the bathroom. The only exception was Eddie, his curiosity was piqued when he noticed Faye slink off a couple of minutes later.

Through narrowed eyes he watched her go. He'd noticed that she hadn't been herself at all today. She'd turned up to the rehearsal full of the joys of spring but after an hour or so she had begun to slope downhill. *It's my bet that that bastard George has something to do with it*, he thought as he watched her disappear into the back.

With a sly look, to see if anyone was watching, she slipped into the same toilets that Eddie had seen George enter. With a cup of tea in his hand, Eddie was strictly against alcohol while he was playing, he sauntered over towards Brian who was polishing his trombone again. 'You seen George?' he asked the taller man.

Brian's lips curled as he shook his head slightly. He was far too busy admiring Carl and hanging on his every word regarding the first half performance to worry about where George was.

'Tam,' Eddie shifted his attention. 'Did you see George?'

Tam had never really been part of the team; he was more of a hired hand and kept himself to himself. He pouted and shook his head before giving all his attention back to his smoke.

Eddie thought about asking Big Joe if he'd seen George, but he knew that he'd be half gone on cheap gin by now to worry about where a drummer might have gone on his break. He didn't like the feeling he was getting about this situation; it was a feeling like something was about to happen, something bad. He took it upon himself to investigate George and Faye's disappearances. 'I'm just off to the loo guys, be back in a mo,' he announced. Nobody took any notice of him.

With a determined stride, he made his way to the artist's toilets backstage. He needed to know what was going on between Faye and George. Not only did he consider the dynamic bad for the band, he thought any dynamic where George was concerned was bad for the band - but if he was in with any chance with the woman he adored from afar, he was damned if he was going to allow a crooked cripple to spoil things for him.

He opened the door into the gents' toilets as if he were handling an unexploded bomb. His hands were sweating and greasy, as he gripped the door handle and pulled it slowly towards him. He didn't want to alert anyone inside that he was coming in. Disappointment and relief washed over him in equal measures as he saw the room was empty. The toilet at the end, however, was closed. He looked back outside where the group was gathered; no one was even looking his way, so he went inside. He crept up to the cubical, feeling more like a pervert than any kind of super-sleuth. *Sherlock Holmes I'm not...* he thought fighting a small smile and the extra rhythm of his rapidly thumping heart.

When he got to the stall, he reached out and rattled the door, hoping to surprise whoever was inside. 'Hey, is there anyone in here?' he asked, raising his voice a little. There was no answer. 'Hey!' He pushed on the cubical door and it opened, revealing an empty stall.

'Shit,' he spat in disappointment.

He made his way out of the toilets at the exact same moment Faye exited from the ladies' opposite. She was smiling and looked a lot more like her normal, happy self, a million miles away from how she had looked prior to, and during, the gig. She was rubbing her nose and sniffing, and there was something about her eyes, something that he just couldn't put his finger on, but mostly she looked good, and that was good enough for him.

'Eddie!' she shouted, a little over enthusiastically, as she planted a great big kiss on his forehead. She laughed and grabbed his arm in a link. 'We best be getting back. Second show starts in ten minutes.' She guided him away from the toilets. 'So, what did you think of Carl eh? Not bad? I think he's getting better and better!'

'Not bad,' he lied, he had really liked him, but he didn't want Faye to know that; he could see which way the wind was blowing with the Carl situation. 'He's no Tex Ryder, that's for sure.'

Faye laughed a little. 'Yeah, but who is?' she asked as they walked off in the direction of the stage. Eddie knew the answer to that one but thought better of even mentioning his name. Faye was chatting almost constantly, not allowing Eddie to get a word in edgeways. He didn't mind, not one bit.

A couple of minutes later, the door to the ladies' toilet opened ever so slightly and George popped his head out. He made sure that there was no one hanging around backstage to witness him exiting from the wrong door. Happy that there wasn't, he quickly left the room. The contented smile on his face had more to do with the wad of pound notes in his inside pocket than the fact that the fly was undone on his trousers.

Smiling like he was the cat who had gotten the cream, he made his way back to his drum kit, ready for the next set.

15.

AFTER ALL THE bravado and circumstance of the first set, Carl was astonishingly mediocre during the second. Faye, on the other hand, was spectacular.

She hit every note, pitch perfect, and she owned the stage as George had never seen her do before. He watched her from his vantage point at the rear, looking every bit the star that she very nearly had been, and thought that she could still be. His smile grew wider and more devious as he watched Carl stumble and mumble through his lines and miss his cues almost everywhere. *He won't last long*, he thought with a chuckle.

The chuckle wasn't long-lived though, as he was a little dismayed to see all the women in the club swooning over him when he did get his parts right. George shook his head and curled his lip in annoyance as he struggled to keep his perfect time. As Faye was introducing the next song, George's eyes fell upon the tall, attractive girl near the back of the club. The one wearing the tight dress. She was watching Carl's every move but there was something different about her. She wasn't filled with the same lustful longing towards him as the rest of the ladies that night. There was another kind of attraction. She looked a little sad; almost as if she wanted to be elsewhere. *Maybe she wants to be inside one of my little brown bottles too,* he thought, producing another devious smile as a lick of his greased-back hair fell onto his face. His eyes flicked between the girl and Carl. Had he seen something between them? Was it... a moment? He put it to the back of his mind and continued with the song.

As the performance came to a crashing crescendo, with the ever-popular instrumental *In the Mood*, the audience was in raptures. Carl was taking his bows and the crowd were applauding the new male lead, in effect sealing his position in the band. Faye was stood next to him clapping and holding his arms up to the crowd as if he were a championship boxer who had just won a hard-fought bout. As the applause died down, George limped his way over to the front of the stage, putting on his act of 'oh look at me, I'm a cripple but I'm not letting it get to me'. He had used it so many times in the past and it seldom failed to work.

Eventually the applause began to fade, and the band exited the stage for the night, beginning the ritualistic back slapping and congratulations that ensued after each performance. George excused himself. 'I really need a drink,' he announced as the band attempted to drag him into a group hug.

Faye, on her new high, was fawning over Carl, as was Brian. *He'd better watch himself,* George thought as he made his way out. *His veneer is slipping.* Eddie was congratulating Faye; his hands a little too friendly. Tam and Big Joe were in conversation on either side of an open bottle of whisky.

George wouldn't be missed.

He limped over to the bar where the tall woman was standing, alone. There was a bittersweet smile on her face as she looked over to the stage area, obviously searching for Carl, looking every inch the lost soul and poor innocent damsel surrounded by ogres. She was doing a good job of fending off the unwanted advances from the potential, and more often not so potential, suitors of the club.

As he got closer, he mused that her smile had been nothing from on stage, compared to what it was up close.

This woman was simply stunning.

In his past, a girl like this would have been far too intimidating for him to approach, but that was in the past, and he didn't live there anymore.

As he neared the bar, some of the rebuffed suitors came over to him, clapping him on the back, congratulating him on the band's performance.

'All right mate, you were brilliant up there.'

'Dead good that mate! You guys are excellent.'

George loathed the attention from the public and was not always gracious to them when they were congratulating him. Tonight however, he accepted the adulation, as he was looking to impress the young lady. 'Cheers guys, thanks, but if I could just get to the bar and get myself a drink… I'm a bit parched, you know.' He turned towards Linda, the waitress behind the bar and tipped her a wink.

'The usual?' she asked as George got her attention.

He nodded and raised his eyebrows. She then looked around her, just to check there was no one watching, before reaching down and grabbing a large bottle, half filled with amber liquid. She poured him a large whisky, topped it up with soda water, added a dash of lime juice, before handing it back to him with a knowing nod.

'Thanks Linda. You're a lifesaver! I owe you,' he said with a conspiratorial smile before turning back to face the crowd, with his drink in his hand.

The tall woman was standing next to him, still looking towards the stage. George had observed, even in the brief time he had been standing next to her, that she had many gentlemen admirers, yet she remained alone. It amazed him as he was bowled over by her beauty, even more so in close quarters.

'Can I get you a drink?' he asked, directing the question with an air of confidence.

The vision turned around at the question; she was about to decline the offer offhand, but she must have recognised him from the band and her face changed, as did her mind.

He noticed the change and grinned, inwardly. He tipped his glass towards her; in effect showing her what was inside. 'I can get you the good stuff,' he whispered conspiratorially, tipping her another wink.

A smile spread across her face, lighting up her already beautiful eyes. 'Oh, yes! OK then,' she replied timidly. 'As long as we don't get into any trouble.'

He smiled and raised his glass to her as he turned back to the bar. 'I don't get into trouble, I'm an angel in here,' he joked. 'What's your poison?'

Her face fell a little at the question. 'What?' she asked.

'Your poison? Your favourite drink,' he replied with a smile.

'Oh,' she breathed, looking more than a little relieved. 'Would it be too forward of me to have a brandy?'

George smiled again; he liked this girl. 'No, not at all. Linda, can I get one large brandy for the lady if you please.'

'George!' Linda hissed. 'You know that this is for the performers only. If Red finds out…'

He shook his head and raised his hands as if to calm the woman down. 'Relax. We'll just have to make sure that Red doesn't find out, won't we? One little drink for the lady please.'

'Listen,' the girl spoke. 'I'm OK on the drink if it's going to get you in trouble.'

He looked at her as if to reassure her. 'No, look it's fine. One large brandy, Linda, and I swear I'll make it up to you.'

Linda blushed a little, her round face lit up like a big red balloon. She rolled her eyes and breathed a long sigh before relenting, as she usually did for him.

There was something about George!

'OK. But only the one. I quite like this job you know.'

'And so you should, because you're so good at it,' he replied, leaning over and giving her cheek a small playful tweak. She blushed again before reaching back under the bar.

The tall woman accepted the drink and sidled up to him, a grin was beginning to form on her lips. 'So, your name's George then?' she asked, her whole demeanour changing from being timid, to being confident and sultry in a matter of seconds. 'I'm Marnie, Marnie Bennett.' She held out her hand for George to take, which he did very charmingly, before handing over her drink.

'This is for you then, Marnie,' he said offering up his glass for them to clink, which she did, gracefully.

'Thank you, George.'

'So, I heard it through the grapevine that you're Carl, our new boy's, sister. Was this rumour correct?'

She laughed. It was a small, skittish sound. 'Well, news really does travel fast, doesn't it? Even if it's not that exciting.'

George shook his head and smiled a lopsided grin. 'A new, beautiful girl like you, is certainly exciting news.'

She dropped her head a little sheepishly and then looked up at him with big, mocking eyes. 'George, are you flattering me?'

He laughed but ignored the question. He had one of his own. 'So, you're married I take it?'

She looked at him over her drink, her eyes had turned a little misty and she blushed slightly. George raised his eyebrows and looked at her hand. She was wearing a wedding ring, but married women only came to this bar for two reasons; to enjoy a night of dancing with their husband or to enjoy a night of dancing with someone who was *not* their husband. She was becoming something of an enigma to him.

'I don't really want to talk about it,' she replied, taking a sip of her brandy.

'Oh, I'm sorry, I just assumed from you wearing a ring, that's all.'

On the mention of the ring, she looked at it on her finger and smiled; it was a small sad smile.

George put his hands up in surrender. 'Look, I'm sorry. I've overstepped the line. I'll leave you alone.' He lifted his drink up to his mouth and swigged it all back in one.

'No! No, please don't. You're the only one who's spoken to me tonight as if I'm an actual human being; all the others have just been trying it on.'

George shrugged and then laughed a little. 'How do you know I'm not trying it on?'

It was her turn to laugh now; it was a light noise, quite musical. 'Oh, I'm sure you are, but you've gone about it a whole different way. All the others just, I don't know, kind of swooped on me.'

He turned towards her, leant his elbow on the bar and grinned. 'That's because you're like an exotic creature, like an Amazonian bird. You're far too exotic for The Rialto. Do you live abroad?'

She laughed and nodded. 'I used to, only for a brief time. But I had to come back.'

'Well, that's their loss and our gain. That's what I say.'

She smiled another sad smile and nodded her head, before taking another sip from her brandy.

'Can I get you another?' he asked, noticing her glass was nearly empty.

'I really shouldn't.'

'Oh, come on, one more isn't going to kill you! It's Sunday night. Everyone drinks on a Sunday!'

'Sundays, or any other day of the week! It doesn't mean much to us lowly seamstresses.'

'You're a seamstress? How convenient.' George looked genuinely interested and impressed. He knew how to turn on the charm when he had to, mostly to compensate for his leg. 'So, tell me, how much would you charge to knock me up a new suit?' With a cheeky smile on his face, he stepped away from the bar and turned around, giving her an easy view of his measurements.

Marnie laughed again; she was pushing a strand of her blond her back behind her ear as she accepted his offer of a second drink.

Less than an hour later, after at least another three drinks each, they left The Rialto together, both smiling and laughing.

~~~~

Eddie was over the other side of the room talking to a table filled with couples. Red liked the band to work the room after a performance, once the dancers had sat back down, as he wanted the punters to stay an extra hour or so and buy more tea. He also wanted the 'special' customers to purchase some of the hard liquor that he had in reserve, along with his 'special stuff'.

Eddie was the first to notice George and Marnie leave. Frowning, he watched the unlikely couple head towards the exit.

Carl was also watching his sister. A look of dismay, maybe even pain, had taken over his features, but he'd been cornered in a conversation with two very beautiful young women, so, even though he wanted to go to her, to stop her from leaving with that loathsome man, he'd been compelled to let it go. He'd have words with her in the morning, just to make sure she was OK.

Brian watched Carl, watching Marnie. *I wish he'd look at me like that,* he thought, before blushing a deep crimson. Shaking his head to get the thought out of his brain, he continued his chat with the new, charming barman.

Faye was stood in the doorway of the dressing room. She had changed out of her concert clothes and into something a little more formal for the rest of the night. She knew that Red especially liked the girls to work the crowd after the shows but tonight she wasn't feeling up to the job of flirting outrageously with gangsters. She was leaning on the jamb of the door as she watched George and Marnie leave together. She was feeling a mixture of jealousy, relief, and a small spark of panic at seeing them walk off together. She was relieved that she wouldn't have to perform for him again tonight; jealous as she watched the younger, more attractive girl steal off into the night with a mysterious man, and panicky as the annoying, not to mention irritating, itch had returned all over her body. It seemed the effects of her last fix were beginning to wear off.

Tam, the double bass player, didn't even notice them go; in fact, he very rarely noticed anyone post-show. He was always far too busy burying his nose into his secret bottle of whisky to care for any of them.

16.

'EXCUSE ME! WHERE do you think you're off to, sonny Jim?'

At the sound of the reedy Cockney accent, all the blood in George's veins froze. He turned around to the direction of the loathsome voice and winced. In the excitement of meeting and getting to know Marnie, his meeting with the owner of The Rialto had gone completely out of his head.

'Red, I was actually just coming to see you. I was, erm, just getting this lady here a little fresh air.'

Red rolled his eyes and beckoned him into his small office. It wasn't a request. 'Sure, you were. Get in here, now, and don't make me wait any longer.'

The thin man re-entered the office.

'Can you wait here a moment?' George asked Marnie. 'I've just got a little bit of business with Red over here. I shouldn't be any longer than two minutes. Promise!' He wrapped her coat around her shoulders, to protect her from the chilly Liverpool night, and lumbered off in the direction of the offices.

'Don't be too long,' she replied with a reproachful smile.

'I won't,' he winked at her, *I hope*. He flashed her a smile before entering the office just behind the cloakroom.

He knew the smile would make him look more confident than he felt, but he knew that he needed to get into character if he was going to deal with Red.

'Shut the door!' Red demanded as George walked into the smoke-filled office. 'And sit down.' He pointed at a small chair opposite his desk and George obediently took it. Red sat down too and looked at him; his eyes were dark, like pools of obsidian; this man chilled George to the bone.

Still silent, he picked up the thick cigar that was languishing in the ashtray on the desk before him, popped it into his mouth and puffed on it, before looking at the end of it, a little dismayed that it had gone out. He picked up a heavy looking lighter from the corner of the desk and lit the end, puffing away as he did. The thick, grey smoke from the now glowing brown wrap made George uncomfortable.

Red never offered him a smoke.

'Don't we have a trivial matter of ten quid?' he asked sarcastically, keeping up his reputation of not beating around the bush. Everything was business with Red.

George looked at him stoically. One of the traits that George had picked up over his years was his fantastic poker face. He showed no fear to the man opposite him, even though inside his stomach was churning. He knew that if he showed Red fear now then this deal, and any possible deals in the future, would be over before they even began.

'I don't have it,' he said, keeping up his stony face. His voice didn't waver, not even a bit.

'Ron!' Red raised his voice, only slightly, and the door that George had just closed, opened to reveal a gorilla of a man. He stood by the door as if awaiting instructions. 'Go and tell that beautiful young lady out there that she'll be going home alone tonight.' The big man nodded and turned to re-open the door. 'Oh, and tell her that she might do well to invest in a black dress very soon.'

The big lout smiled behind George as he gripped the door handle. 'Yes, boss,' he mumbled dutifully.

'But I do have half of it,' George said calmly, as he reached into his inside pocket in his jacket. He produced a small bundle of notes and spread it over the desk towards Red.

Ron looked back at his boss, unsure if he should still speak to the woman. Red shook his head and dismissed him from the room. The big man shrugged, then left.

'Half?' Red looked at George, his stare was dangerous. It was cold and filled with malevolence. The hint of a wicked smile broke on his lips as he sat back, regarding the crumpled notes on his desk. 'Do I look stupid to you?' His voice never raised above a half whisper.

George stared back at him. There was a small twitch in his eye that was the only real giveaway that he was scared out of his wits. He knew that now he had started this game; he would have to finish it. 'Half now, then the other half in five days. But there's a rub.'

Red sat back in his chair and puffed away on his cigar, slowly, never once taking his small, black eyes from George.

'To get it all, I'm going to need more snow.'

There was another pregnant pause as Red pondered George's request. He leaned forward, elbows on the table, and, if it was possible, his stare doubled, penetrating George's head as if attempting to read what thoughts were etched onto his brain. He began to laugh; it was a quiet, dangerous chuckle. He shook his head and caught George's eyes with his own. 'George Hogg,' he laughed. 'I knew there was a reason I liked you. Let me get this straight. You want me to give you more produce, allowing you to get in more debt with me, and to only pay me back half of what you owe me up front?'

'I know how it sounds but I've got a bigger customer base right now, and it's expanding. Look, it's only for a few days. I'm paying you most of my wages here as it is. It's bread and water for me all month.'

'That's not my issue, is it?' Red replied with a smirk.

'No, not at all, but give me five days and I'll pay you the other ten pounds, the rest of what I owe you for the extra stuff, plus a further five for your... inconvenience. You don't really have anything to lose here.'

All the faux humour disappeared from his face in a flash and Red eyed George suspiciously, as he considered the offer. 'I'm not a man to allow people to run ragged around me, George.' He paused, more for dramatic effect than anything else; he wanted George to sweat a little.

'You're a weasel. I can tell that you're a weasel, but you've been good for it in the past.' He sat back in his chair again, puffing at his diminishing cigar, appearing to contemplate George's offer. 'I'll tell you what. I'll give you another ten-quid's worth now and I'll expect the whole twenty-five back, let's say by Thursday. I'll come and collect it personally Thursday night. If you don't have it then I'll...' he shrugged a little, again for effect, '...also personally, slit your throat from ear to ear! Do you hear me, Georgie boy?'

Red had begun to absently finger the little key around his neck. George knew that he meant business. He swallowed, hard, and felt a click in his throat as he did. 'I hear you! Personally, on Thursday night!' His voice remained calm, but there were trickles of perspiration dripping from his brow.

'Right, get out of my office you fucking weasel and start making me my money,' Red ordered as his hand left the key and he opened a large book that sat on his desk before him, pretending he had other business to attend to.

George stood and offered his hand out towards the thin man. Red ignored it, burying his head into the book he was reading. After a moment, or two, George wiped the sweat-slicked hand on the leg of his trousers. 'Right, I'll be off then. See you on Thursday,' he said turning to leave.

As the door closed, signalling George's departure, Red got up and twitched the small curtain over the window, he watched as George limped over to where Marnie was waiting, looking a little worried. He watched him as he put his arm around her, and she began to giggle. 'How does a cripple like him get a girl like that?' he wondered aloud, before returning to his desk. 'Ron!' he shouted. The big man lumbered back into the office.

'Yes sir?'

'I need you to go and get me some more snow. I need ten quid's worth here, first thing in the morning.'

The big man nodded and turned heading for the door again. 'Yeah, boss, not a problem,' he mumbled before leaving the office; leaving Red sat at his desk with a pensive look on his face.

17.

'SO, THIS IS where I live,' Marnie announced proudly as they stood in the street, outside a large house. It was situated in Bootle, a quiet suburb of Liverpool, with a great view of the park opposite.

George knew the area well. His ARP warden days had seen him traverse around Derby Park many a night.

He gazed up at the tall house. It was modestly decorated but it was nice, it beat the dingy little place that he lived in with Tex, by a country mile. 'This is really nice. Do you own it?' he asked, as all kinds of ideas flashed through his mind.

She scoffed at the question. 'No. I wish! I only rent a room. It's the whole of the loft though. I have my own space up there, two rooms; one bedroom and one living room. There is an indoor toilet as well!' she said, making a statement.

'Get you, how very fancy,' he mocked in a posh voice, making her laugh again. 'No more cold bums for you in the middle of winter!'

Marnie laughed and nudged him, then her face changed as she looked at him. 'Do you want to come in for a cup of tea?'

He could tell that she was nervous.

Although slightly taken aback by the offer, he thought about it for a little while before smiling and shaking his head. 'I don't think I should. I've only just met you tonight; besides you're our new singer's sister. I don't want you going and getting yourself a reputation on my account, now do I?'

She looked at him a little shocked, but playfully so.

'Mr Hogg, I do hope you don't think I'm inviting you into some kind of den of iniquity.' She had her hand on her heart as she said this, making George laugh. 'I'll have you know that my intentions are completely innocent.' She raised her eyebrows and smiled. The smirk had more than just a hint of the Devil in it. It was the kind of smile that George liked.

'Well, when you put it like that! I can't really refuse, can I?'

'No, you can't.' She took hold of his hand and almost dragged him up the short path to the large, black front door.

Once inside, standing in the front parlour, the ornate beauty of it struck George all at once; the decor and the ornaments were exquisite. True to his nature, pound signs began to flash in his greedy eyes.

There were porcelain figurines placed strategically around and the room was crowned by a large, glass cabinet at one end. Inside the cabinet there were several small golden trinkets, including a magnificent pocket watch on a thick golden chain.

George was lost in a world of avarice as his eyes darted from trinket to trinket, mentally tallying the potential profit of everything in the room.

'Now, I don't want to appear insensitive...' Marnie began, ripping him out of his profit fuelled daydream of gold and splendour, '... but there's loads of stairs up to my room, do you think you'll be OK with them or should we stay down here?' She asked this, obviously concerned.

'Madame, when I was a child I suffered muscle atrophy as a complication of polio, this resulted in retardation of bone growth in my tibia,' he replied in a mock foreign accent. 'I'm not injured; I'm actually physically fit.' Inwardly he cursed himself for telling her this as he had used his leg to dodge the draft into the war, and for other things on numerous occasions. He didn't want it to become a 'thing' between them.

She shrugged and continued up the stairs. 'Do you even know what all that means?' she asked looking back over her shoulder at him.

He shook his head. 'Nope. I just use all that mumbo jumbo to get myself into ladies' bedrooms.'

As he watched her shapely form mount the stairs, she giggled.

A noise from behind him caught his attention. It was only a squeak, but George's keen hearing picked it up. It sounded like a door opening, just a crack, before closing again. He smiled to himself. *Her landlady doesn't like her, or at least doesn't trust her. Very interesting,* he thought.

18.

MARNIE'S ROOM WAS lovely, and George liked what he saw. The furnishings that she had put together in the meagre space were very stylish and he had an idea that they had cost her a pretty packet. He picked up a porcelain dancer and looked underneath it. The stamp was French, and he had an idea it was expensive.

When Marnie came back into the room with two large and steaming cups, he put the ornament down and helped with the cups.

'I'm sorry, the kitchen is all the way down on the ground floor; it's the only place with a kettle. You did say no sugar, didn't you?'

'No!' he replied. 'I asked for two lumps.'

Marnie's face fell as she resigned herself to go all the way back down three flights of stairs to get him the sugar lumps.

'I'm joking,' he laughed. 'I don't take sugar. It's fine as it is.'

She shook her head and laughed as she handed the cups over to him.

He took the offerings and set them down on a small coffee table, making sure he pulled over a couple of doilies to set the cups on first. He sat down on the two-seater couch and relaxed, absently rubbing his bad leg. 'So, Marnie. Tell me something about you. A beautiful woman, all alone in this bedsit,' he indicated around him. 'Albeit a lovely bedsit. Surely a lady like you must have any number of suitors.'

She dropped her head and began to play with the hair behind her ear again; she was looking anywhere other than at George. 'Well, none of this stuff in here is really mine. I've not long moved in. I've just returned from America.'

'America!' George exclaimed almost excitedly.

'Yeah. It's a long story, I'm sure you don't want to hear all the boring details.'

George really could be charming when he wanted to. 'Of course, I do. I find you fascinating. Think of me as a sympathetic ear.'

Marnie sighed and sat on the chair opposite her guest. She leaned over and picked up her cup. 'Only if you're sure you want to hear it!'

George winked.

'Well, I met a man a few years back - Bradley - he was an American GI on assignment over here during the war.' She regarded George for a few moments as if she were trying to gauge a reaction from him, maybe even a judgement; when she didn't get one, she continued.

George noted that her eyes had turned a little misty.

'He was the most handsome, charming man I've ever met. I think I was taken along by the fact that he had a bit of money in his pocket and could get all the things that the American GI's could get. You know, like chocolate, nylons and make-up, proper make-up that is, not the cheap stuff we had to make do with. Well, we sort of hit it off from the very start. He used to take me dancing.' A wistful look had taken over her face as she looked up at him again. 'We even went to The Rialto once or twice. Although I was far too young to be allowed in, somehow Bradley always managed to do it.' She laughed, it was a bittersweet noise, before she turned her attention back to him. 'We might have even seen your band play.'

George was taking a sip of his tea, as he listened intently. His senses were tingling, and he had an inkling he was about to hear something that would be very interesting to him.

'So, I was pulled around in his whirlwind. My dad hated him. He said he was a Flash Harry and was only after one thing. I didn't know what he meant at that time, all I knew was that I was having a fantastic time and that whatever it was Bradley wanted, he could have it for all I cared. This one time I told my dad I was going to a cottage in Wales with one of my friends when really Bradley took me to the Lake District. There was an air force base there filled to the brim with Yanks. We danced all night,' the faraway smile was back on her face as she relived the night in her head. 'We were jitterbugging and everything. After that, we walked through the beautiful countryside until it was morning. Then we…' Marnie suddenly stopped, and a deep crimson crept into her face.

'Then you what?' George asked, genuinely interested.

Marnie looked at him, she was blushing harder before she began playing with her hair behind her ear again, averting her eyes from his, coyly.

'Oh…' George said, his own eyes widening as he dropped his gaze down towards his tea. 'Erm, right,' he said, a small smile growing on his face.

Marnie looked at his smile and began giggling herself.

'So, what happened next?' he asked, trying to relieve Marnie of her embarrassment.

'Well the next thing, my dad found out about us. I don't know how, but he did. He shouted and raved on about how a good Catholic girl could do such a thing. He called me all sorts of names, terrible names, before throwing me out on the street, to be with my 'heathen bastard'! I think that was how he put it.'

George's face regarded her with shock. 'That was a bit harsh, wasn't it?'

She paused before answering. 'It was, but then I was always his little girl. Now, suddenly I wasn't. How did he put it?' She thought for a moment before continuing. 'I'd been... deflowered, that was it, by a dirty Yank.'

George pulled a disagreeing face, although he was rather enjoying this tale. 'What did your mother have to say about it?'

'My mother died during childbirth. Apparently, she was told that she would never be able to carry another child after the complications with Carl, then she fell pregnant with me.' She stopped and looked back down towards the floor. 'My father doted on us. He gave us everything that he could, everything he never had. And that was how I repaid him.'

George leaned over and grabbed her hand, giving it a reassuring squeeze. She looked at him and smiled. *Carry on,* he thought, *you can't stop now!*

Almost as if she had heard his thoughts, she continued. 'So, Bradley asked me to marry him. I said yes and I became Mrs Marnie McFell. The US Air Force flew us over to Utah where his family lived. I was introduced to them as his beautiful war bride, and I was instantly disliked. None of them, not one, took me under their wing. His sisters were horrible, his mother was cold and his father...well, after he tried to get me into his bed and I refused, he never even spoke to me again.'

'Oh, my God, that sounds awful,' George said, squeezing her hand again.

Marnie looked close to tears, so he put his cup down and moved in closer to put his arm around her. As he did he felt her flinch under his touch. He didn't mind, he was expecting it, and it didn't deter him. He held her for a small while and eventually she began to relax, almost to melt into his embrace.

He grinned like the cat who'd tasted the cream.

'And then the worst thing in the world happened,' she continued, almost unexpectedly. 'My entire world came crumbling down around me. I was three thousand miles away from everything I knew and loved, surrounded by people who were openly hostile towards me, when one day, while he was out on a training mission, he was flying over the ocean and his engines cut out. Both of them!'

George held her a little tighter; he could feel the shiver run through her as he did.

'The US Air Force said that he ejected successfully from the stricken plane, but his body was never found. Oh, they looked; they looked and looked, but they think he was too far out. They tried to comfort me by telling me that his death would have been rather swift but then continued to tell me that the search must be called off, as it was unlikely that they'd ever find anything left of him by now. Imagine telling a grieving widow that! That her husband couldn't be buried in a Christian grave because it was likely he'd been eaten by fish.'

George tried hard to stifle a small laugh; he raised his hand up to cover his mouth and forced a cough, as Marnie turned towards him. There was a small, playful smile on her face that contrasted somewhat with the tears in her eyes. 'Are you OK? Am I boring you with my tales of woe?' She asked with a small laugh.

George shook his head and beat his hand on his chest. 'No... no, not at all, just a little attack of heartburn, that's all. Please carry on; I think you need to get it off your chest.'

'Well after that there was no point staying in America. I had no friends, no family, no one to turn to.'

George, sensing that there was more to this tale, allowed her to compose herself for a few moments and continue.

'There was something else too. Something important. I was pregnant! I was pregnant with a dead man's baby. There was no way I was going to let that family know about it. The strange way they rounded together, keeping their family close, I knew that they wouldn't have had an issue holding me captive, at least until the baby was born, before discarding me off into the wind to fend for myself. No, I knew then that I had to get away - from them and from America. I had to get home. I contacted our Carl. It was out of pure desperation. He arranged everything for me. He got me a free flight via the UK Air Force for ex-servicemen. Apparently, I wasn't the first war bride to need a cheap way home ,and I really don't think I'll be the last. I flew home in a cargo plane. There were thirty soldiers with me, all shouting lewd obscenities between themselves whenever they knew I could hear. That was one of the worst times. But when we landed, and Carl was there, my world seemed a little lighter.'

George smiled to himself. There had always been something about him that people tended to trust, making them think that they could tell him all sorts of things in confidence. Marnie had just fallen into the same trap. He now had everything he wanted; the leverage he needed, that he could use against her as and when he needed to.

He opened his arms towards her. The smile on his face looked genuine but it was a crocodile smile. Inside he was cold and scheming.

Marnie wiped the tears that were flowing from her eyes and fell into his open embrace. He hugged her tight and she responded in kind.

She couldn't see it, but the tender moment had been ruined by his roaming eyes. His pupils were widening as they darted around the room, drinking in all the expensive finery dotted here and there. In his mind, he was wondering where the best place would be to offload some of these, obviously expensive, trinkets. He knew a few places and a few people, and even some people who knew other people. For someone as enterprising as he was, it was never hard to offload items for a few pounds here and there. He guessed that there might be as much as a couple of hundred pounds' worth in this room alone, not counting the exquisite trinkets in the front parlour, downstairs. He salivated at the thought of the golden watch in the cabinet, and how good it would look on his waistcoat, and how much profit might be in the rest of the house.

'I had to get rid of it. I just had to. Who's going to give a chance to a single mother in this world eh? Who?'

George snapped out of his money-induced daydream when he felt the dampness of her tears on his shirt. He had nearly forgotten that she was still there and had almost completely forgotten what she had been talking about. He had been lost in his dreams of money. He searched his mind trying to remember, then it came back to him. He remembered that she had found herself pregnant and widowed in the same week. *Stay with it, George, this could be your gravy train.* He smiled as he rubbed her back. 'Come on now, I bet there's loads of people out there who'd give a lovely young woman like you a chance. I'm sure of it.' *Oh yeah, most definitely,* he thought.

19.

THE NEXT MORNING, the band were meeting backstage in The Rialto as they did most Monday mornings. They usually met to discuss how the gig went the night before and to go through any ideas of numbers that they could drop from, or add to, the set.

Everyone was there apart from George. Even Joe and Tam had turned up.

Carl was looking a little dishevelled, his normally impeccable hair was unkempt, and his eyes were distant and black as if he hadn't slept. He was fidgeting nervously and there was a frantic air about him. 'Did anyone see them leave? Are you sure they were together?' He was asking anyone who would listen.

Tam was about to pipe up and tell him that he had seen them leave together, but then his cigarette burnt out, and he felt it was more important to light another than to cater to the ravings of a mad man.

Joe didn't even know who he was talking about.

'I saw them go,' Brian piped up. Carl instantly rounded on him. 'Well, I saw them leave the ballroom and then I saw George talking to Red.' He was blushing a little at the sudden attention. As his eyes met Carl's intense stare, he looked away, rapidly.

'Red? But isn't he a…'

'Majority shareholder in The Rialto? Yes, he is, Carl,' Faye interjected, meeting his gaze and indicating towards the door to the foyer at the end of the ballroom. Red had just walked through it, accompanied by two large men. One of them was black and huge, he towered over Red, every inch of him looked ready for anything.

Everyone stopped what they were talking about and watched as the two men made their way towards them.

'Well, well, well, what do we have here?' Red asked in his mocking cockney accent. 'All the band together, but with one notable exception.'

The silence was deafening as everyone looked towards the newcomers, each of their faces filled with fear. Red was notoriously unpredictable and prone to violence with very little provocation, and now with this colossus at his side, he was even more formidable.

'Can any of you tell me where Mr Hogg can be found today?' he asked amiably, pointing at each, individual band member. 'Myself, and Jules here…' he indicated at the very large black man next to him, '…' we have a little business we need to discuss.'

'That's a question that we've all been asking this morning,' Carl replied a little rushed. 'Do you know…'

He didn't get the chance to finish his question before Brian gave him a small nudge in the back. He snapped his head around and saw him leering at him; his eyes were saying 'don't mess with this guy'!

'Right, well I've said my piece. I need to have a conversation with the little rodent as soon as I can; so, when he comes in, if he comes in…' He grinned a devilish grin, '…the little minx I saw him leave with last night might have tired him out completely, but do tell him that I want him in my office 'tout suite', understood?'

Everyone mumbled their agreement with the single exception of Carl. His face was flushed with anger and his hands were balled into fists at his sides. Red noticed this and he leaned into Carl, leering right into his face, goading him to have a go. Brian watched with deep concern as Carl's fists grew tighter, his knuckles changing from pink to white in the wink of an eye, they were now almost transparent.

Red looked him up and down before sneering and walking away towards the exit.

'As soon as he comes in... unless that little slut has ruined him that is!' He was laughing as he pushed the exit door before disappearing through. This left the tall black man alone in the ballroom with the rest of the band. He just stood there looking at them; his expression emotionless as if he were weighing them up for body bags or coffins. He smiled a small, horrific smile before walking off himself.

Carl broke away from the rest of the group and stormed off towards the curtains at the back of the stage.

Brian rushed after him. 'Carl, you can't let him get to you like that, there's probably a perfectly innocent reason for George's absence. You can't let Red see you get angry, especially at him.'

'I can handle myself, Brian.'

'I'm sure you can, but you don't know what Red's capable of, and, Jesus, did you see the size of the guy next to him?'

Carl nodded absently, flexing his fingers on both his hands as he did. The smile on his face was a million miles away from light-hearted. 'There's no innocent reason,' he seethed through gritted teeth. 'I just know it. I've only known the guy a few weeks, but I can already see that he's a user, a manipulator. I could tell from the first moment that he doesn't like me.'

'Listen, George is a lot of things, but I think he's a genuine guy. He's just disappointed that he never got the shot at the lead male vocals.' Brain heard his own words echoing in his head and found it hard to convince himself that they were true. If he couldn't convince himself, he had no chance of convincing Carl.

'Well, if that's true and he *is* a genuine fella, what would someone like Red want to see him in his office for? 'Regarding a little business', he said. Have *you* ever been in Red's office regarding business?' Carl asked, the anger still flushing through him.

Brian was lost for words. He'd never been in Red's office regarding business, or anything else for that matter. He shrugged. 'It may well all be innocent. You don't know.'

'Well, all I know is that he left here with my sister last night, and now, the next morning he's late and I haven't heard anything from her.' He slumped his shoulders and turned back towards Brian, there was pain in his features, deep pain. He shook his head. 'You don't know the whole story! She's…vulnerable, easily led.'

Oh shit, Brian thought, thinking back to George and Faye's relationship. 'Listen, I'm sure it'll all work itself out. Now come on, let's practice eh. It'll take your mind off it for a while.'

Carl nodded and made his way back onto the main stage.

~~~~

Faye was sat on George's bass drum; watching, with interest, the exchange between Brian and Carl. Her head was reeling today, and she looked awful. Her skin was pallid and dry. Her pink eyes had a glassy look about them, either from not enough sleep or from crying; or maybe both. She hadn't bothered to put any make-up on this morning and looked like she hadn't even combed her hair.

'Hey, you,' Tam said in his thick Scottish brogue. 'Faye! Are you OK there, sister?'

She snapped out of her musing, somewhat surprised by the sound of Tam calling her name. She smiled a sad little smile at him, acknowledging the fact that this was the most Tam had ever spoken to her in all the years she had known him. She shook her head and pouted. 'I'm fine, I think I'm just getting a bit of flu or something.' She was lying; she knew exactly what was wrong with her. She felt like she had been run over by a steam train and that this feeling would continue until she got herself another fix, but she was trying her very best to convince herself that 'getting the flu' was the truth.

The rouse didn't work on Tam. He offered her a knowing smile. He wasn't completely innocent in the ways of chasing the dragon. He nodded his head before turning away, lighting another cigarette.

Eddie was watching Faye like a hawk. He had studied her for a long time, mostly from afar, with the longing that a man can have for a woman. He'd noticed her health had been deteriorating over the last few months, maybe even the last year, ever since she had begun associating more with George. He knew there was something wrong with her and he didn't like it, not one bit. 'Faye, why don't you take the day off?' he asked her, loud enough so everyone could hear. 'We all know that you know the parts; it's Carl that we have to practice with. It'll do him good to learn both parts anyway. You get yourself home and I'll check in on you later.'

Faye's shoulders visibly slumped in relief and she stood up, gingerly, from the bass drum. 'Are you sure?' she asked in a strained voice.

Eddie winked. 'Go on, before I change my mind. Besides, George is an hour and a half late already, today might end up being a whitewash if he doesn't turn up.' Eddie said to the room.

Everyone looked as if he had said exactly what they had all had been thinking.

She walked up to Eddie and gave him a big hug. The older man hugged her back, enjoying every single moment of it. 'Listen, thanks,' she whispered. 'I *am* feeling a bit rough. A few hours' sleep and I'll be right as rain.'

Reluctantly, Eddie let her go. As she walked off towards the exit, she stopped. 'Will you do me a favour though? If George does turn up, can you tell him I need to see him? Tell him it's urgent.' She smiled and exited the ballroom.

Eddie smiled back at her, nodding, telling her that he would pass the message on, while all the time, deep inside of him, his old man's heart was silently breaking.

20.

GEORGE STROLLED INTO the artist's entrance to The Rialto a lot later than was normal, even for him. As he limped inside, Red was there to greet him. A thin, sadistic smile had crept over his face as he enjoyed watching the drummer struggle up the few stairs to the foyer.

'Georgie, my boy! Step into my office if you would, I've got a little something for you.'

George tipped his head and raised his eyebrows in recognition. He changed direction and made his way over to the office by the cloakroom. As he entered, Red closed the door behind him and stood with his back to it. He was looking intently at him.

George noticed rather quickly that they were not alone in the room. Stood behind the desk, in the corner, was a mountain of a man. His skin was so black it looked almost purple. His alert eyes stood out, bright white in contrast to his dark skin, but it was his height and his build that were the most intimidating part of this man's demeanour. He was so tall that it looked like he was struggling to stand upright in the small office.

Red continued, without introducing the newcomer. 'Now then, I'm putting quite a bit of faith into you, George.' He said this almost genially, which, in-itself was more threatening than if he had put a knife to his throat. He offered George the seat at the desk while he made his way around and took the seat opposite. Without saying another word, he opened a bottom drawer in his desk and removed a large paper bag. He pushed it over to George without taking his eyes of him.

George could feel his heart thumping in his chest as he took the offering and peered inside.

There was a large brown bottle, like a medicine bottle, and several large white tablets.

'The tablets are to be sold by the half, that way you get more money for them. Apparently, they work best if you crush them up, mix them with a little caster sugar, if you can get it, and sniff the powder.' Red spoke, matter-of-factly. 'I wouldn't know any of this of course, not touching the muck myself, but it might be something for you to consider telling your... customers.'

George took the bag and stood up. As he did, Red grabbed his arm; his grip was hard enough for it to hurt. 'You now owe me twenty-five pounds, which is the ten from the previous debt, another ten for all this shit here, plus another five for my troubles...OK?' The question was rhetorical, but he felt like he needed to answer, as Red had raised his eyebrows to him, in a menacing way, indicating that he was not joking. George nodded, took the bag, and got himself ready to leave.

'Before you go, I think maybe this is an appropriate time to introduce my little friend here.' The irony of using the word 'little' was not lost on him. The man towered over Red, and even if George had been sat on Red's shoulders, neither of them would measure up to him.

'This, my friend, is Jules.'

George looked up at him and gulped. He had heard of Jules; the man had a formidable reputation in Liverpool.

He had jumped ship at the docks, where he had been working his passage, and never returned. He quickly gained a reputation as a Dock Road Enforcer, dealing out savage beatings on behalf of pimps and drug dealers - basically, anyone who would pay him. There had been a few disappearances and more than a few murders around the city where the name Jules had been whispered. It was generally agreed upon that he was not a person you would want to mess with.

Red was fidgeting with the key hanging around his neck again as he stared at George. 'Jules is working for me now, kind of a face of the organisation kind of thing. You know, if anyone tries to mess around behind my back, or thinks that they don't have to pay up what they owe.' He stared hard at George. 'You know what I mean. Anyway, he'll be around to pay you a visit on Thursday. Do yourself a favour, make sure you're home.'

George dropped his eyes and nodded. 'Yeah, I'll be in,' he mumbled, making his way towards the door.

'Remember, Thursday. Jules likes being messed around even less than I do.'

George finally made it out of the office, paper bag in hand. He breathed a huge sigh of relief as the office door closed behind him. He lifted his head and exhaled slowly, as if trying to relieve himself of the stress of the situation he had just found himself in. He stuffed the paper bag into the pocket of his coat; he didn't want the others to know what he had, *especially that puff Brian, frigging nosey queen*, he thought.

As if on cue, Faye walked out of the hall and into the foyer. Her sudden appearance grabbed his attention and he became more interested as he noticed that she looked awful. It was just how he wanted her to look; it meant a nice payday for him.

'Faye! Jesus, what's the matter with you?' He asked this with a deep sarcasm, but Faye didn't pick up on it.

'You know what's the matter with me, George,' she spat at him, trying her best to keep her voice low. 'I need more stuff,' she whispered.

'Have you got any money?' George whispered his reply, looking around the lobby for any eavesdroppers.

'You know quite well that I've got the money. I only need a little pick-me-up. I've told everyone that I need to go home and…, get some sleep.' She edged up close to him and began to play with the buttons on his coat, fingering them and looking up at him with the big eyes she knew, or thought, he liked.

He pushed her away as if she was something abhorrent on the sole of his shoe, he didn't want her touching him. 'My God, Faye, look at you. Your face is pale and blotchy,' he pinched his nostrils. 'And you stink. He flashed a humourless and chilling smile at her. 'It does look like you're coming down with something. It's lucky for you that I've got a remedy for that something right here in my pocket. Ten shillings for half a tablet *or* a shot of the opium and you can have them now.' He looked at her, grinning maniacally.

'Ten shillings? That's almost double the normal cost.'

He looked at her again, the glare in his eyes was intense; all his previous humour had died and was currently languishing with his with his 'nice guy' persona, in the morgue of his personality. George was all business now. 'That's because it's harder to get these days. It's a simple case of supply and demand. But, you know, it's up to you, if you don't want it then I know someone else, someone who's more than willing to pay twelve for what I've got here. She's a whole lot nicer to me too, if you know what I mean.' He raised his eyebrows.

She understood his meaning, completely.

'You're a bastard, George Hogg,' she sobbed, shaking her head. The desperation of her circumstances was ingrained into her features.

He shook his head and made to walk away. 'You've called me that before!' he laughed. Before he could get anywhere, she grabbed him by the arm, easily spinning him around to face her again. Her eyes were wide, and her red tinged nostrils were flaring with each panicked breath.

'OK, OK, ten shillings, but I need it right now,' she pleaded, her eyes closed. Tears were racing down her cheeks and she had to wipe them away, twice, as she reached inside her purse to get her money.

George Hogg, like the Cheshire Cat, smiled broadly. He loved being in control and felt himself very lucky that Faye was always willingly subservient. 'This is new stuff apparently,' he said cheerfully, snapping a large pill in half. 'Apparently, you're supposed to crush the pill into a fine powder and mix it with some caster sugar if you have any, if not don't bother. Then you sniff it all up, like snuff.'

She looked at him as if he'd gone mad. 'Are you trying to pull a fast one on me here, George? I don't just swallow it like the other stuff?'

'No, this is the new - what do they call it - 'designer' drug. I think people refer to it as snow. All the movie stars are doing it these days. It cures most of what ails you, apparently. It gives them the energy they need to make it through a tough day's filming and still have enough left in the tank to party that night.'

She took the half a tablet and gave him a ten-shilling note. 'There's not much more of that left,' she said morosely passing over the currency. 'I might have to start paying you in-kind again. What do you say to that eh?' She looked at him and grinned.

As he looked into her red eyes, he could see mucus running from her pink-edged nostrils, mixing with her tears on the cracked skin of her lipstick-less lips. To George, it was the ugliest, most pathetic smile he had ever seen in his life.

'We'll have to see about that eh?' he said pushing past her and walking off towards the main ballroom. 'Desperate women aren't really my thing!' he shouted as the door closed behind him.

Grasping the pill in her hand, she hooked the strap of her handbag over her shoulder, sniffed in a deep breath, and made her way out of The Rialto.

The brightness of the day hurt her eyes as she made her way down Parliament Street, heading towards the river and the trams. A thought passed through her mind; an easy way of her making some money, enough for a couple of hits at least. As she made her way towards the docks, she drew plenty of looks from admiring dock workers and more than a few sailors.

She had always enjoyed the attention of the male of the species. *So, what if I can get paid for it?* she thought.

A shiver passed through her whole body, and she clutched her handbag closer to her, safe in the knowledge that she had what she needed inside.

A large docker wearing a dirty overall and sporting a filthy face, idled drunkenly over to her. 'All right darlin', are you workin?' he asked, his voice course and gruff.

The stink of sweat and alcohol coming from him almost made her balk. The thought of him rutting and stinking on top of her, fumbling and trying to kiss her, all for one miserly pound, turned her stomach.

She turned around and hurried off in the opposite direction.

'I'll take that as a no then, slag!' he shouted across the street.

In the distance she could see the tram approaching, and she whispered a silent prayer.

21.

'GEORGE, WHERE THE Hell have you been?' Carl shouted, as he stormed across the ballroom towards him the very moment he entered. Brian and Eddie closely followed him. Tam stayed sat on the edge of the stage smoking a cigarette and swinging his legs, as though nothing was even happening, and Big Joe was too busy looking for a glass to pour his poison into.

'You were seen last night, leaving the club with Marnie. Where is she and where have you been?' Carl was out of breath and shouting in George's face, while gripping the lapels of his jacket with vice like fingers.

Although miffed by the attack on his jacket, George looked at him bemused, as if he were a petulant child having a tantrum. He took hold of Carl's hands and removed them from his person. 'Whoa there, soldier! I've just this second walked in. A simple hello would have sufficed.'

Carl's face was twisted; he looked desperate and scared. This turn of events interested George. *A person doesn't get that wound up regarding his sister! There's more here,* he thought.

'Don't mess around with me, George,' Carl spat, letting go of the lapels and taking a step back from the smaller man.

George took the advantage to step away from Carl himself and began to make his way over towards the stage. 'Well, firstly, you're right. I did leave with Marnie.'

This enraged Carl even more. 'I knew it!' he snapped.

'Hold on, hold on. I took her home and I went in for a cup of tea.'

Carl grabbed George by his shoulder and spun him around again. 'You best tell me you never.'

George faced his accuser. His eyes pierced Carl's like a hawk eyeing prey. He smiled, but it was an icy one. 'I did, but that was all it was, tea. That, and some good old-fashioned company. We talked a bit, it *was* late when I left, very late actually, and it's quite a long walk from Bootle to Walton, especially when you've got a dodgy leg like mine.'

Carl let him go again and turned away. His face was bright red and he looked angry, he also looked like he was about to cry. Brian was there in a flash; he wrapped his arm around Carl's shoulders and began to rub his hand up and down his back in a vain attempt to calm him down.

George noticed it but put it to the back of his mind, just for now. *I'll deal with that one later*, he thought.

'Look, Carl. Marnie…she's way out of my league. Why would a damned attractive girl like her go for a cripple like me? Eh?' George asked this in a self-depreciating way, he had used this exact same tactic in the past to disarm many potential aggressors.

Carl shook his head and pushed Brian away with a lot more aggression than was necessary. The tall man backed off, a little disappointed, and a lot embarrassed, at being shunned. As he stepped back, he looked like he'd been slapped.

'So where is she, George? I went around to her room this morning and there was no answer. The landlady said she'd had male company until late and hasn't seen her since.'

'Look, we drank tea and we chatted…then I left.' He raised his hand to ward Carl off before walking away again. 'That's all I know, so back off, Carl. If you have sibling issues, then it's nothing to do with me.'

Carl went to have another go at George then, the rage that had been building finally exploding towards the object of his hate. 'Why, you…' he snarled.

Brian lunged after him and managed to grab him by the back of his collar. 'Carl, don't. He's not worth it!'

A noise from behind distracted them as the door to the ballroom opened and Marnie stood in the doorway. She had a sheepish look on her face and was hugging herself as if it was cold in the room.

Carl's face changed in an instant. It was as if someone had turned on a light inside his head. 'Marnie!' he shouted, turning to look at the woman in the doorway. He switched direction from George and ran towards her, throwing his arms around her in an intense hug. 'Where've you been?' he demanded, holding her tighter.

Marnie was struggling with the hug; she barely had breath left in her body to speak, so she pushed her brother away from her as if he were an overenthusiastic dog. 'I just slept in, that's all,' she gasped. 'I came here to see what you wanted. Mrs Jenkins said you turned up this morning at the house.'

Carl loosened his hold on his sister and held her at arm's length, taking in her appearance as if for the first time. Her hair looked as if it hadn't been combed and she wasn't wearing any make-up. 'It was only to make sure you were OK, you left while I was talking to someone and I got worried, that's all.'

'Well, you needn't have. George took me all the way home, safe and sound.'

George had made it to the stage and was sitting at his drum kit. He smiled at her and then waved to Carl with his drumsticks in his hand.

Carl shook his head, not knowing if he was relieved that she was OK, or angry for going home with George in the first place.

'Then he left, and I fell asleep. I woke up this morning and came straight down here to see you.'

'The way I see it…' came a gruff, Scottish-accented voice from the stage; it was Tam. '…Carl, I'd say you owe George an apology. Don't you?'

Carl looked at Tam before turning back to Marnie, and then finally at George. The fight dropped out of him, although he still looked somewhat like a stubborn schoolboy. He knew that Tam was right, he did owe George an apology.

'George, look, I'm sorry for overreacting. Seriously, no hard feelings, eh?' He made his way to the stage area where George sat, wearing a smug, self-satisfied grim. Carl held out his hand and he took it, eagerly, the two men shook enthusiastically.

'No hard feelings,' George replied, still smiling.

'George.' Marnie spoke up from the doorway. 'Can I speak to you a moment? Over here in private?' she asked.

There was a mischievous glint in his eye, as he stood from his drums. 'Yeah, just give me two minutes to set up and then I'm all yours. Again!' He added the last part just loud enough for everyone in the hall to hear, especially Carl.

He deliberately took a little longer setting up his drum kit than usual, leaving Marnie standing in the wings, waiting for him. Everyone else were busying themselves setting up for the practice session they were here for.

The drama had passed and there was no point dwelling on it now it was over.

'What on Earth has got into George? I know he's always been a bit of an arse, but he's off the level these days.' Eddie was whispering to Brian as they stood at the side of the stage watching everyone getting ready.

Brian shook his head. 'I really don't know. He's never happy when someone else joins the band, but it's never been like this.'

Eddie leaned in. 'I'm going to keep a close eye on him. I don't trust him with Faye, and I know that Carl hates it if he even looks at his sister.'

'I know what you mean. I'll do it too; we can't have him ruining all this before it's even really begun.' Brian put his trombone onto its stand and looked over at the new singer, who was playing with a microphone stand, attempting to attach the mic. 'I think Carl's going to work out, don't you?' he asked, changing the subject.

Eddie slapped him on the back, shook his head slowly and walked over to his equipment. He picked up a large, semi-acoustic guitar, and began to tune it in.

Eventually, George finished twiddling with his kit and made his way over to where Marnie was waiting patiently, her arms wrapped around herself, nervously biting her fingernails.

'Sorry about that, love. What can I do for you?' he asked as he limped towards her.

'George, I haven't slept as good as I did last night in months. I'm not stupid, I know you slipped me a Mickey Finn. I'm right aren't I?'

George flicked his eyes to the other side of the hall for a second and then flicked them right back at her.

There was a mischievous look on his face. 'I might have!' He put his arm around her and led her towards the door; he could feel the eyes of the rest of the band boring into the back of his neck as he did. He enjoyed that feeling.

She covered her mouth, hiding the giggle that she couldn't quite keep in, as she allowed him to walk her.

He bobbed his head from side to side, as he attempted to justify what he had done. 'I saw how tired and upset you were, and as I always carry some pain killers around with me because of my condition… I'm sorry, but I thought you could do with a good night's sleep, so I slipped a couple into your tea.'

George braced himself for a backlash, but it was not forthcoming. Instead, she leaned back in and whispered in his ear. 'Can you get me some more?'

Inside he rejoiced; on the outside, he kept his face stoic. 'Marnie, this isn't what you need right now.'

'It might not be what I need, George, but it is what I want. Get me some more.' The last part was not a request.

He looked back towards the band; none of them were taking any notice of them, except for Carl who kept shooting furtive glances their way. 'Listen, I can, but not here. If I hand anything over to you now your gorilla of a brother will be down on me in no time.'

'You leave him to me; I'll sort him out. You're not playing tonight are you?'

George shook his head; they didn't play Monday nights.

'Good, come around to mine at about seven thirty, and bring the pills with you.'

As she turned away, George grabbed her wrist, not tightly but enough to make her stop. Carl noticed this in the background, and he looked up, alerted by what was happening by the door, but he didn't make a move.

'Marnie,' George whispered. 'I hate to do this but… the pills, they're not free you know, they cost quite a bit.'

'I know, I'm not stupid. I've lived a little bit you know. I'm good for it. Seven thirty then?'

George nodded and looked away. 'Yeah, seven thirty.'

'Good, see you then.' She leaned in and gave him a kiss on his cheek.

He watched as she walked out of the room, a wicked grin spread across his face. *Everything is going to plan,* he thought happily as he made his way back to the ballroom for the band practice.

22.

BAND PRACTICE WAS awful! Not one of them hit their stride, and everyone's timings were atrocious. Try as he might Brian couldn't blow a note right, an irony that was not lost on George. He noted how much he had changed since the introduction of Carl into the band. He was like a giddy schoolboy.

Eddie was trying too hard to overcompensate his guitar for Brian's failures. It resulted in an intense frustration and George could see his anger seeping onto his face from time to time. He kept shaking his head and biting at his bottom lip every time he hit a bum note.

Carl was missing his cues left, right and centre, but that was nothing new.

George was loving it. He was adding to the frustration by purposely speeding up and then slowing down his rhythms. Tam had gotten onto his little game and, to his favour, played along with it.

George felt an affiliation with Tam sometimes. It was a very rare thing indeed to find someone else who truly wanted to watch the world burn, like he did.

Eventually they decided that enough was enough and that the rehearsal should be called off as a bad job. Brian polished his trombone and put it away before making his way over to George, shaking and scratching his head. George tried his best to ignore him by stripping his drum kit down, slowly, and methodically.

'What the hell's going on? I don't think I've ever heard us so bad,' he whispered, flicking a furtive glance over towards the rest of the band.

George shook his head and looked up; he was loving what was happing, but he put on a convincing show of concern. 'I don't think Carl's going to work out, you know. I mean if he gets as emotional as that over his sister not answering the door, imagine what he'll be like during a show if it all kicks off like it did the other week?' He made a point of putting down the parts of the kit he was handling and staring at Brian. 'It'd be embarrassing.'

'What would we do without him? We're playing on Thursday and it's Monday night already. There's no way we could get anyone to fill in, especially if Faye's still sick.' George shook his head and shrugged his shoulders.

'I've got a feeling that Faye will be fine, she's a tough broad, and a professional.'

Brian's face changed; the concern he was feeling for the band now passed over to focus on George. 'George,' he asked, pausing for a moment. 'Are you all right? I mean... really all right?'

He shook his head, dismissing the question, continuing to busy himself putting his kit away. 'Yeah, I'm fine. Why are you asking?'

'Well, you've been a bit off, just lately.' Brian was being cautious, he wasn't sure if he was overstepping the mark, as he knew that George could be flaky sometimes.

George stood up and wiped his hands on a handkerchief. He sighed, pulling a thoughtful face. 'Yeah, really! I'm good. I've just got a lot on my mind now.' He indicated towards the rest of the dispersing group. 'It's just all this that's going on here, and...well, Tex isn't the easiest person to live with.'

Brian nodded. 'I can imagine. You're doing an excellent job with him though; I just wish I could do a bit more myself.'

George stopped what he was doing and stared at his friend, an idea was sprouting in his mind. 'Brian, I... Oh, nothing,' he started, knowing that it would pique his nosey friend's interest.

'What is it, George? Go on...'

'Well,' he took in a deep breath and exhaled it, slowly though his nostrils, as if he was having trouble vocalising what he was thinking. In reality, he knew exactly what he was about to say. 'I was thinking, what with you asking and all, I do have a little bit of a money crisis happening at the moment.' His eyes scanned Brian as the lie dripped from his mouth, looking for any signs that he was falling for it.

He was.

'You know, Tex's medicine isn't cheap. I know that we can get it from the doctors, but sometimes he needs more than the doctors are willing to give him. You want to hear him in the night sometimes. Whatever happened to him during the war...' he shook his head, adding another level of conviction to the lie, '... it must come back and haunt him in his dreams.'

Brian's brow was ruffled, as he swallowed every lie George fed him. 'Jesus, that sounds bad.'

George could tell that he was trying to be noncommittal regarding money, but he could also tell that he didn't want to seem unsympathetic to the cause. 'Yeah, it is. I've been trying to score a few extra quid here and there, but I've got myself into a little bit of a... situation.'

'Oh yeah?' George could see that Brian was desperately trying to relieve himself of this conversation now. He was trying to walk away, back in the direction of the rest of the band, back to normality; but George wasn't about to let him off that easily. He reached out and gripped Brian's arm. 'Yeah, I've laid a few bets with Red.' He shrugged his shoulders and laughed a little, it sounded nervous. 'But what do I know about horse racing? They were honest bets, just bad ones. Now, you see, I've ended up owing Red a little more than a few quid; you know what he's like, daily interest rates and stuff. This job just doesn't cover it.' He tightened his grip on Brian's arm, tight enough to leave white welts in his skin. 'And now, with Tex no longer earning, but him still needed that medicine; it all adds up. Do you know what I mean, Brian?'

Brian watched as the rest of the band walk out of the ballroom. He longed, with all his heart, to join them, to be free of this club, this life, this loathsome man before him, but he was trapped. He could see where this was going, and it saddened him. He thought George was a friend, a confidant, but over the last few days and weeks, he'd seen that it was a folly. One great big joke.

He knew what was coming next; and he wasn't wrong!

George's eyes changed. Gone was the levity, the humour, all of it replaced by a threatening glare. 'I need money, Brian, and I need it fast.'

Trying his hardest to produce a sympathetic face, Brian attempted to wriggle his arm free from George's vice like grip. 'I'd love to help, I really would. I love Tex just as much as everyone else, and I'd hate to see him suffer, but I just don't have the funds mate.'

George let go of his arm and shook his head; there was the ghost of a smile on his lips, a ghost with no humanity whatsoever. 'That really is a shame, Brian, it really is.' He put his hand on his shoulder in an almost friendly manner.

Brian nodded as he absently rubbed his wrist. He was relieved to get out of that encounter but, at the same time, felt a little embarrassed that there wasn't more he could do to help his friend. He was also embarrassed by what he had been thinking just a few seconds ago. 'I know mate, I know it is. You know that if I had it, I'd help you out in a flash, don't you?'

George nodded, 'Yeah, I know.'

Brian patted the hand that was on his shoulder and began to walk away feeling a lot more than relief that he'd managed to get out of that situation, relatively unscathed. George had done one thing for him; he'd help him make up his mind about something he'd been toying with for a while now. Today, he would be going into Rushworth's Music House in Islington and putting an advert up touting his skills as a musician around the many other swing bands in the city. He'd had enough of the Downswing Seven, he'd had enough of George, but most of all, he'd had enough of hiding.

'Although...' George spoke up from behind him.

Brian stopped in his tracks and shuddered at the single word. He'd thought he'd escaped, but something told him that his very own Sword of Damocles had just twanged another thread. He watched the other members of the band leave, the door closing behind them. A metaphor that spoke to him regarding his situation, and theirs.

George continued; he was pulling another faux sympathetic face. 'I'd just hate it if anyone was to find out about your little secret!'

There is was, the threat that Brian, with dawning dread, knew was coming sooner or later. Suddenly, he found himself rooted to the spot. A strange sinking sensation descended over him, and everything around him went dark; everything but the door before him, the door that would take him to freedom. He wanted to turn around, to face George, to stand defiant before him. But he knew that he didn't have the courage, he wasn't wired for confrontation, he wasn't capable of standing up to someone who had the ability to manipulate and bully all he wanted. He'd tried so hard to keep his little secret.

Little secret? he questioned himself.

George wasn't even looking at him. He was busy tinkering with his drum kit, as if he, Brian, wasn't even there. As if he hadn't just uttered the one sentence in the entire world that could destroy him, destroy his reputation, maybe even send him to jail. 'What?' Brian finally asked. He shaking body covered in a thin sheen of ice-cold sweat.

George was still refusing to look at him, but Brian knew what the wicked look on his face would be like, he'd seen it a million times. *The spider who caught the fly,* he thought and shuddered again.

'Your little secret, you know? It'd be a real shame if anyone found out about it, wouldn't it?'

Brian was shaking his head 'I don't know what you're talking about. What do you mean, secret?'

George could read the panic on his friend's face and revelled in it; his sinister smile returned. He wiped his hands on a small rag and then stood up from his stool. His face looked friendly, but that scared Brian even more than his nasty one.

'You know what I'm talking about, Brian. You know, that little bit of queer you have hiding inside of you?' He raised his eyebrows. 'How do you think Carl and Eddie would react if they found out eh? Or Tam for that matter; he doesn't strike me as one of the most tolerant people in the world, does he?'

'I... I...' Brian stuttered, he wanted to defend himself, and his honour, but his throat was now bone dry.

'Oh, you can stutter all you want, but I've seen you going into those public toilets in Stanley Park. I've also seen the way you look at Carl and, probably more importantly, the way you *don't* look at Faye. You're a queer, Brian. A dirty little puff. I know it...' he leaned into his face; their noses were almost touching. Brian could smell peppermint on his breath. '...and you know it too.'

Brian flinched as his whole dirty, sordid, secret life was laid open, unravelled before him.

'It's only a matter of time before everyone knows it,' George continued indicating to where the rest of the band had exited the ballroom.

George then said something that made Brian feel physically sick. Something that brought his life crashing down around him, hard.

'Can you imagine if Red found out?'

One million shards of ice stabbed at him. His whole body felt covered in cold, sharp, needles of hate. The full contents of his stomach shifted as the blood drained from his face and beads of cold sweat formed on his brow. The last statement terrified him. How could he do this to him? This man who he'd considered a friend, a close friend, for the last three years, maybe even longer.

'I don't... I... I just don't...' he stuttered.

'What? You don't want them to know? Even Red?' George pulled his face away and regarded him, a sanctimonious smile sat smugly on his lips.

There was an instant of relief for Brian, because for a moment or two he'd felt like George was going to kiss him; he didn't know how he would have reacted to that situation. His stomach was still shifting, and he felt like he was about to throw up. He stumbled backwards, the sudden dizzy spell knocking his balance. He needed to sit down before he fell.

George continued to tinker with his half-dismantled drum kit, acting as if nothing had happened between them.

'Five quid!'

'What?' Brian replied, not fully understanding the context of the words.

'I want five quid, and I want it on Thursday morning!' He stood up and tipped the screwdriver he was holding towards him. 'If I don't get it, then everyone, including Red and Carl, will find out everything about you.' He smiled and began to wipe one of his cymbals down with a white cloth. 'I don't know if you'd even be allowed to continue in the band, *mate*.' He spat the last word, parodying Brian's habit of calling everyone by that mantle. 'Maybe even *any* band, at least in Liverpool anyway.'

'I... I don't have that kind of money lying around,' he stammered.

George shrugged his shoulders. 'That's not really my problem, is it?'

'I don't know why you're doing this to me, I thought we were friends!'

George looked up from his drums at the taller man quaking before him. His face contorted into a look of disgust; his dark eyes regarded him with pure disdain. 'Friends? Me and some dirty puff who goes into public toilets to do God-only-knows what with other men?' He shook his head. 'No, Brian. We were never friends. I tolerated you at best and now, in my moment of need, I'm milking you. Five pounds by Thursday morning or everyone knows you're a queer.'

'I told you, I don't have that kind of money lying around, George.' He was smiling, attempted to make a little light of the situation.

George stood up and steadied himself on his bad leg. He put down the small tom drum he was holding and exhaled a long slow breath. Like a teacher clarifying something glaringly obvious to a slow pupil, George explained it to Brian. 'Listen, this isn't about you and me, and believe me, it's not personal. I couldn't care less what you do and who you do it with. This was going to happen eventually. It's in my nature. Leopards can't change their spots. I got onto your...' he paused for dramatic effect, looking him up and down with an amused look on his face, '...condition the moment I met you and I knew that one day I'd need to use it. That day is now, Brian. Five pounds on Thursday morning or your secret is out, and funnily enough, so will you be.'

Brian shook his head, faster and faster it went, as if the speed of the shaking would have some bearing on the outcome of this altercation. 'I don't have it!'

'Maybe not,' George smiled. 'But I bet your mother does.'

At the mention of his mother, Brian recoiled. He looked at George as if he had just turned into a dangerous, venomous snake; which in a way, was exactly what had happened.

This was exactly the reaction that George had been expecting. 'Yeah, I thought as much. Bring the five pounds to my house by nine on Thursday morning and your vile little secret will be safe with me.'

'Safe for how long eh?'

'For as long as I want it keeping safe! Don't test me Brian, bring me the money otherwise...well, I'm sure Faye, and maybe Carl, might be OK with it; come to think of it, Carl might even be *more* than OK with it, but it's my bet that none of the others will be. Can you imagine what Red will do when he finds out he's been harbouring puffs in his club? He'll be the laughingstock of the gangster community, and it's my bet he won't take kindly to that.' George winked, put the cloth he had been wiping his drums with down, and limped off in the direction the rest of the band had gone.

'Oh, and do me a huge favour, would you? Pack my kit up and put it back in the boxes please. There's a good little homosexual.'

Brian closed his eyes as the word, the one word that he feared more than any other, hung in the air, like a sword. That word hurt more than queer, or puff, or even nancy-boy. It hurt more because it was the official term for what he was, and if you give something a name, suddenly it becomes real. A small tear, *of shame?* He asked himself, trickled down his cheek as he watched his former friend limp out of the ballroom. He took in a shaky breath and began to pack up the rest of the drum kit.

As he looked at a piece of frame piping he had in his hand for a few moments. Without thinking he launched it across the room, towards the door where George had not long left.

23.

FAYE WAS IN a bad place. She was at home, in bed. Sleep was in another country, a million miles away from where she was right now. Her whole body was itching, and she had been raking at her skin with her long nails leaving vivid pink welts and deep red cuts that were covering her bedsheets with bloody stains. Her legs were restless, and the stomach cramps she was experiencing were double, no triple, the ones she had to endure each month when her period was due.

Her pillow was uncomfortably wet. It was saturated in sweat from her brow and her greasy hair, where she'd been tossing and turning in a bid to fight off the excruciating dreams she was experiencing when snippets of sleep had finally, and mercifully, opened to her.

Every time she closed her eyes, dragons appeared on the back of her eyelids. Big, scaly, dragons and more than once they had had leg braces and George's head attached to them.

24.

AS CARL WALKED home, he was dealing with his own demons. He couldn't get the thoughts of George having 'tea' with Marnie out of his head. 'There's something about that creepy, limping, bastard,' he muttered. 'Whatever she's doing with him has got to stop, and it's going to, right now.'

He decided to take a detour towards Marnie's house. He couldn't let her fall into the depths, not again. America had been bad, and she'd only just about clawed her way out of that pit, *by the skin of her teeth*, he thought. He didn't feel that he had the strength to go through everything they had gone through over there, again. She needed to know of his frustration regarding her relationship with George. She needed to know how angry he was with her, and with himself.

He was so angry and so lost within his thoughts that he didn't realise his hands were clenched and that his fingernails were digging into the flesh of his palms.

Fresh blood was dripping from his fists.

25.

RED WAS SAT at his desk in his office. He was fuming that he had given George until Thursday to pay up and then even given him more produce to sell.

'What the fucking hell was I thinking?' he shouted as he pushed the papers that were littering his desk, along with his telephone, onto the floor.

The phone landed with a shrill ring as it hit the carpet.

'Jules, can you come in here please?' he shouted, and the big man promptly walked into the office, bowing his head to allow his huge frame through the door. 'I want you to go to George Hogg's house on Thursday morning and bring him here, by hook or by crook, for seven thirty, you got that?'

Jules nodded his huge head. 'Thursday morning, boss, seven thirty, got it!' He took a small black book from the inside pocket of his jacket and removed the pencil that was tied to it. Giving the pencil nib a small lick, he proceeded to write the time and date into it. 'I'm on that, boss. When it's in the book, consider it done,' he replied in his deep Jamaican accent, before leaving the office, once again struggling to ease his huge frame out of the door.

'I hope that creepy son of a bitch hasn't got the money,' he whispered as he got up from behind his desk and began to pick the papers and the telephone up.

26.

EDDIE WAS FOLLOWING George. He was doing his best to keep a safe distance. It was not proving to be an easy job, due mainly to the slow progress that George made because of his bad leg. He justified this extreme action to himself, as he just couldn't trust him anymore. He had watched, with horror, Faye's speedy deterioration since she began associating with him, and he needed to know what was happening between them. Ultimately, Eddie needed to confront him about it. He knew that it was something nefarious, and possibly unhealthy.

He followed him as he made his way north of the city, towards Walton, where he lived in. He got onto the crowded number sixty tram at Lodge Lane, Toxteth that headed for the docks. Eddie waited until the very last minute and then jumped on himself, staying on the opposite end from George. Even though he knew what he was doing was important, maybe even a matter of life and death, he couldn't help but marvel at how 'Philip Marlowe' it all was.

He assumed that George had been going home, so he was surprised when his target jumped off the tram at Millers Bridge, a good few miles away from Walton. He watched, helplessly, out of the window as George limped his way over the bridge, heading into the heart of Bootle.

In a slight panic at losing his mark, Eddie got off a little further down the dock road at Marsh Lane station and backtracked, running towards where he had seen George get off. As George wasn't the fastest walker, he hadn't made a lot of progress and Eddie was easily able to pick him up a little further down the road. He was heading towards Derby Park.

He kept a respectable distance as he followed George towards the park, and then beyond.

27.

MARNIE WAS EXPECTING George. She was stood in the downstairs parlour waiting for him at the window. Her landlady, Mrs Jenkins, was fussing around her with a duster and a cloth, taking her time in polishing up the knick-knacks that adorned the room. She was not entirely sure if she trusted the young lady lodger just yet. She knew that she'd had, at least one, gentleman caller recently and that was just not the done thing. Plus, she hadn't liked what she had seen when the gentleman had turned up. But, she knew that she must change with the times, even if they had become ungodly.

'Oh, come on now, Missy,' she scolded Marnie. 'If the young man wants to come, he'll come. No watched kettle ever boiled any quicker you know.'

Marnie smiled at the old woman's wisdom as she twitched at the lace curtain for what felt like the hundredth time, looking out onto the street. 'I know, but this one's a little bit different. He makes me forget my past and just slip into... I don't know, numbness maybe.' She smirked at her own joke.

Mrs Jenkins tutted and shook her head. Even though she didn't know if she trusted Marnie, the small act of waiting by the window for a gentleman caller brought back wistful memories of her youth. 'Oh, I remember when Mr Jenkins made me feel like that, God bless his soul.

Best feeling in the world, it was.' She continued fussing about with a feather duster in her hand, turning away from the younger woman, hiding the small tear of nostalgia that was welling up in her eye. 'Enjoy it while you can. It doesn't last very long, dearie, not very long at all.'

Marnie turned and smiled at the old woman. 'I don't think it's like that. He isn't the…' her shoulders fell and her smile broke, just slightly, '…I don't know. He's not really what you would call boyfriend material. Well, I don't think so anyway. He has a crippled leg. He is a very good musician though.'

Mrs Jenkins laughed. 'If you saw a person inside out, would you like what you saw?' She shook her head. 'I don't think you would. Beauty and looks fade, dearie. It's the person that you get to know, and, if you're lucky, eventually love. You'd do well to remember that!'

Marnie gave her a small, sad smile and resumed her vigil out of the window.

28.

AS GEORGE MADE his way to Marnie's street, running parallel to Derby Park, Eddie was hiding behind a lamppost on the corner. He knew it wasn't the best hiding spec as his robust frame didn't allow for thin hiding spots, but it was the best he could find. There was a telephone box on the corner that he could have hidden behind but there was currently a short queue for it, and he didn't want to appear any stranger than he already did. People tended to remember others acting strange, and he wanted to remain inconspicuous.

He watched as George approached the door of one of the large houses and knocked. A few moments later, he was let in.

Eddie looked at his watch; it was seven forty-five pm.

~~~~

'I didn't think you were ever going to get here,' Marnie beamed as she opened the door and gave him a kiss on the cheek. She ushered him inside, taking a quick, furtive glance, up and down the street as she did; making sure there weren't any nosy neighbours casting disapproving looks at her activities. Other than a large man leaning against a lamppost on the corner, and a few people waiting for the telephone box, the street was empty.

When George got inside, Mrs Jenkins looked him up and down. It was obvious that she didn't entirely like what she saw. 'I think it's time that I make myself scarce,' she announced with a scowl. 'I'll leave you two alone.'

'Oh, don't leave on my account, Miss…'

'Mrs,' she corrected him with a cold smile. 'Mrs Jenkins. I'm pleased to meet you, I'm sure…' she left the sentence hanging for George to fill with his name.

'George,' he concluded for her, offering his hand for her to shake.

'I'm pleased to meet you, George.' She took the offered hand and shook it lightly. Mrs Jenkins tried her very best not to react to the cold, sweat-laced palm she gripped. 'I'll be retiring to my room; if you need me for anything, please don't hesitate to ask.' She looked at George and nodded her dismissal before heading off towards the stairs.

'She seems nice,' George lied as the old woman disappeared out of earshot.

Marnie laughed. 'She is! Maybe a little over-protective but nice all the same. Do you fancy a cup of tea?'

'Well, I took the liberty of bringing something a little stronger than tea.' He pulled out an expensive looking bottle of Scotch whisky from his bag.

She squealed and did a little clap. 'Do you want to drink it down here or should we nip upstairs?' She asked this with a little saucy wink and a raising of her eyebrows.

George smiled like an alligator; a big wide grin that any number of nefarious thoughts could be written into. 'I think maybe we should start down here and then make our way up there later, what do you think?'

Marnie clapped again. 'I think that's a cunning plan,' she said leaving the room, heading for the kitchen. 'You make yourself at home and I'll get some glasses.'

George made sure that Marnie was out of the way before making his way into the front parlour. It was set out for entertaining and not everyday living. There were lots of well-polished ornaments laid out on top of the fireplace, the sideboards and within some of the display cabinets along one of the walls.

To George's greedy eye, they looked like to be worth quite a bit of money. He couldn't resist picking them up in turn and flipping them over to read the stamps on the underneath. He marked the ones that he thought would fetch the most money, mentally before casting his beady eyes over the cabinet containing the trinkets, including the golden pocket watch. His interest piqued on the timepiece, and he leaned in to take a closer look, marvelling at the intricate designs around it and the girth of the chain it hung from. Nodding his head, he turned away, making another mental note.

Marnie re-entered the room carrying two glasses, and more surprisingly, she had changed her clothes for the occasion too. She was now wearing a loose-fitting top and a casual, long flowing skirt. George read 'come and get me' into her attire and he smiled approvingly.

'Marnie, you look fantastic,' he gushed, ever the flatterer, as she bent over, placing the drinks on a small, occasional table.

Her face flushed; the pink in her cheeks naturally complementing her blonde hair and she subconsciously began to straighten her dress with one hand, while nervously playing with her hair behind her ear.

He didn't want to arouse any suspicion regarding his unhealthy interest in the gold watch, or any of the other trinkets, so he held out his arms towards her, giving her his full attention. 'Are you going to pour us those drinks or are we just going to look at each other all night?' he asked, a roguish look on his face.

'What? Oh yes, sorry,' she replied nervously. She poured two glasses of the whisky and handed one of them to him. He accepted it gratefully and sat down on one of the two luxurious chairs, the one that was situated in the bay window.

'So, tell me. Did you come here with expectations?' she asked, with a twinkle in her eye. 'I mean, how often do you bring a twelve-year-old malt into a lady's home?'

He flashed his alligator smile again and shook his head. 'Absolutely…' he paused for comedic effect before continuing, '…not.'

They both laughed.

'I think this is only the…erm…' he theatrically looked up towards the ceiling as if counting the times, '…third time I've ever brought drinks to a lady's home and, to be completely honest, it's not even my bottle. Tex, who I share the house with, has a cupboard filled with some of the finest whiskeys from around the world. He collected them while he was on his travels. This is one of his, but somehow I don't think he's going to miss it.' He smiled as he showed her the label on the bottle that was in some foreign language. The only legible words were Single Malt Scotch Whisky.

She laughed again before rolling the dark, amber liquid around the glass before sniffing it and taking a large swallow. George had to admit he was impressed by her lack of flinching, as the liquid must have hit the back of her throat before blazing its trail into her stomach. A thought occurred to him. *If she can knock them back like that then my little plan might not come off.* He decided that he'd play it by ear. He leaned over and poured them both another large drink, careful not to put as much in his glass as he did in hers. He needed her to be on the verge of drunkenness and then what he had in his pocket should take her just over the edge.

'This is good whisky,' she said with an air of authority on the subject. 'Where did he get this one from? It must have cost him a fortune.'

George shrugged. 'Tex had his sources,' he said with a wink. 'Do you like it?'

She took another long swig; he was relieved when she had a big smile on her face after she removed the glass. He could tell the large measures were taking their toll.

She rolled her eyes and smacked her lips before replying. 'Oh yes, very much so. Bradley used to like a wee dram every now and then; he got me into it. American whiskeys don't have anything on the original scotches you get over here. This is lovely.'

She slurred the middle syllables of her last sentence, only slightly but enough for George to be able to tell that she would only need one more glass to put her exactly where he needed her to be.'

'Why don't you come and sit next to me over here?' she asked, patting the cushion on the couch next to her.

George obliged, picking the bottle up on the way and filling her glass again; this time nearly a whole shot more than what he put into his own.

'I think…' she said pointing at him while only just about managing to keep hold of her glass in her hand, 'that you are trying to get me drunk, and then you are going to try to take advantage of me.'

'Me?' He feigned innocence, rather over-dramatically, making her giggle. 'I would never do that to a lady. Anyway, we're just friends remember.'

'Just friends?' she asked, after another swig. 'Do 'just friends' do this?' She lunged at him, spilling a little of her drink in the meantime.

George was shocked at how forward she was, but he allowed the kiss to happen, welcoming it. He enjoyed it immensely; just because he was a cripple didn't mean he didn't enjoy the advances of a beautiful woman, and Marnie was indeed beautiful. It was the part of the plan that he was most looking forward to, although he did think it might have been a little harder to seduce her. She was an extremely attractive woman and knowing that she was sitting on a small fortune in this house, made her even more attractive.

He needed money, and a lot of it, before Thursday, otherwise it wasn't just his drumming career that would be over. 'So, how much do you pay your landlady a week for a room in a place like this?' He eventually asked, levering her off him, gently.

It allowed them both to come up for breath.

Marnie sat up and fixed her top and hair. She looked at him, her eyes taking a little while to find their focus. This made George smile, inwardly. *Gotcha,* he thought.

'I pay her one pound and ten shillings per week, for all the bills and all my food. I have to do my own washing though, but I don't mind that.'

'One ten cash, each week?' he whistled, impressed. 'That's a good chunk of money.'

'I know,' she said leaning forward and draining her glass of the fiery, amber within it. 'But I'm good for it. Bradley left me a few bob when he died, plus his army pension. I think that's one of the reasons why his family hated me.' She put the glass down on the table and turned towards him; the salacious look in her drunken eyes was back again, she wanted less of the verbal and more of the physical. 'Would you think I was being awfully loose if I invited you upstairs to accompany me into my room?'

George smiled a devil of a smile at her. *Finally,* he thought.

'I would *love* to accompany you to your room. Why don't you go first, and I'll follow with the drinks? We don't want Mrs Mop to get suspicious now do we?'

Marnie squeezed her eyes tight as she tried to suppress her laugh. 'Mrs Mop? Oh, she'd love that. Well, I think that's a plan, mister...' she slurred, getting up onto her feet a little unsteadily. As he grabbed her behind to steady her, she turned around and looked at him, the smile on her face stretched almost from ear to ear. 'Easy tiger...' she whispered. 'None of that until we get upstairs.' She giggled before making her way out of the room.

When she was gone, he removed the small brown bottle that he had in his jacket pocket. He shook it and smiled. 'That should do it,' he said as he put the bottle back into his pocket before following the lady towards her attic room.

The door to the landlady's room opened, just the tiniest bit. He saw it happen, but he didn't see the suspicious glare that came from inside the room.

However, he knew it was there!

29.

EDDIE WAS STILL loitering outside the house. From his vantage point, he'd watched George approach the house and put something, that looked like a bottle of scotch, in his bag. He had also seen him pull out something else from his pocket; he was too far away to tell but it looked like another bottle, a smaller one, maybe a medicine bottle. George had shaken it, checking the contents, before putting it back into his jacket pocket. He had then knocked on the door and been allowed in.

Eddie thought George looked suspicious and, by his actions, assumed that he must have felt paranoid too. He had been constantly looking up and down the street, and into the park. Once or twice, he'd had looked right at him, causing him to freeze, Eddie had held his breath when this happened, just in case he could hear him breathe from over the road.

He was surprised, but not entirely shocked, to find that it had been Marnie, Carl's sister, who had opened the door. He didn't think anything about George could shock him these days, but this theory had been proved wrong when she had given George a little kiss on the cheek before ushering him inside.

It seemed that George had found himself another object of his affections and maybe, just maybe, now he might leave Faye alone. That would allow him the space he needed to steal the moment and go and get her; help her pick up the pieces of her life, paving a path to the relationship that he had craved for a long, long time.

Feeling like life had finally, maybe just dealt him the winning hand he had been waiting an eternity for, he got himself ready to leave. He didn't care anything for George, and he hadn't even met Marnie; so, neither of them meant anything to him. Not enough to stay out here on a cold street and catch his death to maybe catch George out on something he shouldn't be doing.

He wanted to go to Faye now, he longed to fall into her arms and be the hero who could patch her back together. He had a plan, and she was a big part of that plan. They were going to leave Liverpool and head to London, together. The swing scene was bigger and brighter down there. A couple with their talents would get work easily and, who knows, maybe even become stars. He genuinely loved The Rialto, and Liverpool had been his home all his life, but he felt like he needed to get away; he needed to get Faye away, especially from George and his seedy ways.

He lit a cigarette, adjusted his collar against the cold of the evening and readied himself for his long walk back to the tram.

Until he spotted Carl.

Eddie's heart began to hammer in his chest at the thought of some delicious drama happening in the street.

Carl looked livid; storming up the incline towards the house. The same house where George and Marnie were currently comfortable and warm; *and God only knows what else.* The thought tickled him with a wicked delight.

He crossed over the road from his streetlamp and slipped into the bushes of the park, opposite. He followed Carl's progress up the street. He felt like he had just gotten front-row tickets to the best play in town.

This could get very interesting, he thought as he bedded in, resuming his vigil.

He watched with interest as Carl stopped outside the house and looked up at the dark windows above; all the lights inside the house were off. He appeared to have lost the bravado that he had on his approach, looking like he was now having second thoughts about knocking.

The singer turned away from the door and regarded. Once again he stared into the exact location where Eddie was hiding. For the second time that night, he thought the gig was up, and he was going to have to come clean and explain himself, but he surprised him by plonking himself down on the step with his head in his hands. To Eddie he looked like a broken man. He turned to look at the house again, before shaking his head. He stood and walked off, away from the house.

Eddie licked his lips as he watched him leave. He held his breath again as Carl walked past him. The man was too far gone to even notice that there was a, not-so-strange, stranger lurking in the bushes. He waited until Carl was at least a hundred yards down the hill before he gave in to his screaming lungs and the compressed cartilage in his knees. He exhaled deeply as he exited himself from his vantage point in the bushes.

A flicker in his peripheral vision alerted him that a light had gone back on in the front parlour of Marnie's house. For a moment or two he was stuck in a dichotomy. One part of him wanted to go home, but the other, nosy part of him, wanted to see what was going to happen now. The nosy parker, not to mention gossipmonger, within him won the battle and, in a flash, he had jumped back into the bush and settled in to watch for a little longer.

A silhouette made its way to the front doorway. By its shape and exaggerated movement, Eddie made an educated guess that it was George. The door opened and he was proved right.

The drummer poked his head out of the door and turned both ways, up and down the road. To Eddie, it looked like he was making sure the coast was clear, that there was no one around to witness whatever it was he was about to do. He disappeared back into the house, reappearing a few seconds later pulling what looked like a large, heavy, roll of carpet.

This whole scenario seemed odd to Eddie and he leaned forward to get a better view of what was happening.

That was when a hand and an arm lolled out of the end of the roll.

Eddie gasped! He involuntarily stepped back. As he did, he stood on some broken glass, a milk bottle or something hiding in the undergrowth, and it broke under his feet. The tinkle of the glass on the deserted street sounded, to Eddie, like the Downswing Seven in full 'Glen Miller' swing on a Saturday night.

George heard it and stopped what he was doing. He narrowed his eyes and scanned the street; searching the darkness and the park opposite for any witnesses to this obviously immoral deed.

Eddie put his hand over his mouth to stop himself from making a sound, any sound. He stood perfectly still. After what seemed an eternity, he watched George continue to drag the carpet down the hill in the opposite direction. Ironically, in the same direction that Carl walked off in. He was headed towards the two houses that had been demolished by a bomb during the May Blitz a few years earlier. The council hadn't yet been able to get around to clearing most of these sites around the city, and they were mostly still just dangerous piles of rubble. The locals had done their best to make them safe and to stop the children from playing inside them, but there was only so much that they could do. George looked like he knew what he was doing and was up for the tough job ahead of him. He was more than capable of dragging the carpet the hundred or so yards downhill towards the sites.

Eddie watched in horror as the drummer from his band dragged whatever, or whoever was inside the roll towards the derelict sites!

That was more than Eddie could take; he'd seen enough. He broke cover and ran across the park. in the opposite direction of the derelict sites, and far away from George as he could get.

30.

WEDNESDAY CAME AROUND. That usually meant a long day of band practice; long enough to run through any new numbers they had been learning, or talking about, and to shake off the rust of the last two days. It was normal for the ballroom to be bustling with music and activity by ten thirty in the morning, but today the only band member who had made it in, and had set up and ready to play, was Tam.

He sat in the empty hall whilst lighting his fifth cigarette of the hour. The irony of him being the only one here, and already set up, was not lost on him. Normally he was the late one. He was usually the one on the receiving end of a tongue lashing by Eddie and disapproving looks from the old mutton dressed as lamb, Faye. But today he was alone. It suited him nicely, as he didn't really like the others much anyway. He just liked to play, get stoned on the whisky behind the bar for the performers, and then maybe, just maybe, entertain a lady back in his room.

He was thinking about packing up and going either home, or to the pub, when he was snapped from his lull by the disappointing sound of the main doors crashing closed.

He turned to see Carl skulking in.

He looked awful, either he hadn't slept, or he'd had a heavy night on the ale; maybe even both. His eyes were red, and his hair was unkempt. The weight of the whole wide world looked to be resting on his broad shoulders.

George's going to enjoy this one... Tam thought.

He looked Carl up and down. 'You OK?'

Carl ignored him at first. He perched himself on the edge of the stage and sat staring, vacantly, before him.

Normally Tam wouldn't have minded the solitude, but today was a bit different from any normal Wednesday, and he was genuinely interested in the man's transformation from a smooth jazz cat to a strung-out junkie in just one day. 'Man, I don't know if you didn't understand me the first time, but I asked if you're OK,' he spoke again in his thick Glaswegian accent.

It was Carl's turn to snap out of his reverie. He looked at the piano player with genuine surprise, as if he hadn't noticed anyone else in the room.

'Erm, yeah, yeah. Sorry man, I'm good. I just got a bit on my mind, that's all. Is George in yet?'

Tam shook his head. 'Nope. Just me, and now you,' he replied lighting another cigarette, his sixth.

Carl began to busy himself with some of the equipment on the stage in a disinterested way, and Tam couldn't help but grin.

Next in was Faye, she looked like she always did, which is to say classy, but ultimately, cheap. Her makeup was flawless, and her dress was stunning. Even for her faults, Tam could appreciate a good woman when he saw one, and the way her dress clung to her curvaceous figure got Tam's seal of approval.

People usually did Tam the disservice of dismissing him on first glance. He was the kind of guy who kept to himself and blended in with the scenery. This gave him a unique perspective on life; it allowed him to see things that others, far too wrapped up in their own little lives, would normally miss. Today, he saw something in Faye that piqued his interest, even though it was only a slight pique. There was something about Faye's eyes that millions of others would have missed, but not him.

There was a void in her eyes, and she was attempting to fill that void with all the wrong things.

He knew it because he'd had that look himself as a younger man. The void had taken hold of him and began to control him, getting him into several bad situations, and it was the main reason he'd had to leave Glasgow.

She was filling her void with desperation!

It seems Miss Faye's in need of a little something, he thought, shaking his head. *A little something that I used to need!*

'Hi, Tam!' she sang her greeting, trying a little too hard to sound jolly. 'Am I the only one in?'

Tam raised his hand in hello but never offered her an answer.

She didn't want one anyway.

He watched her hurry backstage, presumably to get herself together for the practice.

Next in was Eddie, closely followed by Brian. *Well, the gang is all here, or nearly anyway,* he thought to himself. *Apart from Joe, there's only one player missing.*

'Has anyone seen George?' Carl asked, still looking frantic as he came back through the curtain from backstage.

'Why?' Eddie snapped in reply. Tam thought he had answered just a little too quickly.

'I was just wondering, you know, if he'd seen Marnie. I haven't heard from her since the day before yesterday.' His face was a picture of desperation.

Frowning, Brian put a friendly hand on his shoulder. Carl seemed to appreciate the gesture.

Eddie was shaking his head, vehemently. *Perhaps too vehemently*, Tam thought.

'Nope, I haven't seen him, not at all…'

Tam eyed Eddie. His rather sudden and emphatic outburst had caught his attention. He was enjoying the farcical scene that was playing out before him.

'Can I have a quick word with you, please Faye? Backstage!' Eddie asked as he made his way towards the curtain, just as Faye was making her way back.

'Erm…yeah, OK!' she replied as Eddie grabbed her and half dragged her backstage. Everyone, including the frantic looking Carl, watched them disappear behind the curtain.

'What are you doing?' Faye asked as she was manhandled towards the toilets.

'I've got to talk to you. I need to ask you a question and I want it answered with the truth. You might think it's a bit odd, but I need to ask it anyway!'

'Go on then.'

Eddie swallowed, pausing before he continued. 'What, exactly, is your relationship with George?'

'What?' she asked, visibly shocked by the question.

'What's your relationship with George? Jesus, Faye, it's a simple enough question. Just bloody well answer it will you.'

Faye's face dropped at the fury she could see building up in Eddie. It scared her; she'd never seen him like this before. 'I - I don't know, on and off… I think. We used to have something going, but now I'm not sure. I don't think he's that interested anymore, and I know that I'm not!' She was laughing, it was a humourless, ugly little sound as she turned away from him, absently rubbing her wrist. 'Come to think of it, I don't think he ever was if the truth be known.'

As she looked at Eddie she could feel the fear that must have been visible in her eyes. This whole situation was scaring her now, and, for some reason she felt compelled to reach out and touch his face. She was moved by his tenderness as he closed his eyes, savouring her small embrace. 'Why are you asking this, Eddie?' A feeble smile tweaked on her lips. 'You're not going to tell me that you're in love with me, are you?' As she asked this question, a small laugh escaped her, one with more than an edge of bitterness in it.

Eddie was not smiling.

'Faye, I've got to tell you something, and it's serious. I'm scared as Hell, and I mean really scared.'

Faye read his expression and all the humour, forced or not, fell from her own face. 'What is it, Eddie? What are you trying to tell me?'

'I saw him, Faye, I saw George last night.'

She shook her head, not understanding what he was trying to tell her. 'So?'

'I saw him at Marnie's house.' He dropped his head, the shame of what he did, and why he did it, crept into his stomach like a mist rolling over a choppy lake; slow, continuous, relentless. He swallowed hard but it caught in his throat and he nearly gagged. He took in a deep breath and exhaled, getting himself back under control, before he had the courage to continue. 'I followed him there, I wanted to confront him about what...' he paused and looked away from her.

Her heart was beating faster than it had done in a while, she felt more alive right now than she had in weeks. *Maybe even years,* she thought. 'About what, Eddie?'

Deep down she already knew the answer.

'That's not important right now. But you need to know that I watched as he dragged an old carpet out of her house.'

Faye wrinkled her brow and shrugged, willing him to carry on. The context of this conversation was becoming lost on her.

'The carpet had a dead body in it, Faye. I watched him drag it out! He was looking up and down the street to see if there was anyone witnessing what he was doing. I was hiding in the park; he couldn't see me, or anyone else. As he dragged the carpet out, a woman's arm fell out of it. Oh, he put it back in quickly enough, before dragging it into one of those bombed out houses in Bootle.'

Faye just looked at him. She was struggling to take in everything he was telling her. 'Are you sure it was him?'

This question angered him more than anything else.

'Yes, I wasn't that far away, only across the road. He's not hard to identify with that limp. I don't know why I followed him, I really don't, and now I wish I hadn't. It was because I was angry with him, mostly for what he's doing to you...' he paused for a moment or two, trying to gauge her reaction to his last statement. Once he saw that there wasn't any real reaction, or at least not the kind he wanted, he continued. 'But I saw him with my own eyes. I think he's done Marnie in!'

Noises from back inside the ballroom alerted them to the fact that someone else had just entered the hall.

Carl was shouting and someone else was laughing.

They looked at each other, both of them thinking the exact same thought.

'George!' Faye whispered.

She walked towards the curtain and peered through. George was there, limping towards the stage. Carl was hot on his heels, shouting, George was shouting back.

~~~~

'You've got a real problem mate,' George was laughing. 'You need to let go a little. Your sister's a grown woman, she can see who she wants. Remember, man, Hitler failed, this is still a free world.'

'Don't you DARE talk to me like that,' Carl raged. 'I'll tell you something about Hitler you dirty draft dodger.'

George stopped and turned on his heels, a neat trick for someone like him. 'Oh yes, pick on the cripple time is it, eh?' he shouted back, standing toe to toe with Carl. The younger man stood a good few inches taller, but that didn't seem to bother him one bit.

Brian jumped in between them, like the world's worst boxing referee. 'Look fellas, stop this, eh. It's ridiculous. We're here to practice! Let's take our aggressions out on the music, what do you say?'

Carl looked at Brian and then back to George; his body physically relaxed, only a little as his shoulders sagged, then the fight rushed out of him like a deflating balloon.

George's dark eyes regarded him as he sneered and shook his head. The fight was still very much within him. 'Oh, that's right, listen to your boyfriend there!' he spat.

Carl smiled serenely before turning away. He then balled his hands into a tight fist and swung his punch. It was well aimed, and it landed directly on George's chin, knocking the smaller man to the ground with the one hit.

Faye, still behind the curtain, gasped.

Everyone else, including a red-faced Brian, watched as the drama unfolded before them; all of them shocked by what they had witnessed. Well, almost all of them! Tam was the exception; he watched it with a detracted disinterest.

George was on the floor cradling his chin in one hand, while wiping the blood from his swelling and split lip with his other. His eyes flicked from the crimson on his hand back to Carl who was looming over him like a championship fighter, his fists still clenched.

George grinned as he struggled up from the floor. 'I don't understand,' he said, bemusement mingling with real malice in his voice. 'I just left your sister in bed about an hour and a half ago. She asked me to give you her love.'

Carl lunged at him again, but this time George was savvy to the attack and stepped out of the way, he was quicker on his feet than anyone would have given him credit for. Brian and Eddie grabbed Carl and held his arms behind his back, stopping him from attacking George again.

George shook his head, laughing at the situation. He wiped more blood from his chin and showed his bloodied hand to Carl. This was obviously a way of non-verbally saying, 'you'd hit a cripple?' He then turned and limped his way out of the ballroom.

His laugh could still be heard after the doors crashed closed behind him.

Carl tried to shrug off his guard, to go after George, but Brian and Eddie strengthened their grip on him. 'Just leave it...' Brian scolded him, '...it's what he wants you to do. That's how the bastard works!'

31.

'GEORGE, STEP INTO my office, would you? It's not a request!'

Red was standing in the doorway to his office behind the cloakroom. Ron, the bouncer, was standing behind holding his hands before him as if he were in church. George noted that the big man was not looking his best. He had never been what you would call sharp, but today his eyes looked rheumy and his skin looked paler than normal, *I may have a little something to cure you, big fella,* he thought with a wry smile.

Red was gripping the key around his neck, so he knew that he meant business.

George was still holding his chin as he turned to look towards Red. He didn't need this, not right now. 'Hey, Red, what can I do for you?' he asked, trying his best to sound cheery.

Red ignored the question and turned back into his office.

George sighed deeply before following him in.

'I want my money, George, and I want it today!' Red characteristically got right down to business.

'But… you said you wanted it by tomorrow. I've got a few things coming together today and I'll have it for you tomorrow, after the gig,' he protested.

Red sat and observed the snivelling man before him. He was still fiddling with the key around his neck, as he normally did while thinking through his options. He pouted his lips and shook his head. 'It looks like you have everything under control,' he said gesturing towards the blood on George's collar and his swelling lip.

George touched his lip and looked at the blood on his fingers.

'It's simple Georgie, I just don't trust you enough. I want it tonight, all of it, the full twenty-five quid. Me, Jules and Ron will be collecting it personally from your house at eight o'clock, sharp. For the sake of your own health, and Tex's for that matter, I'd be in if I were you. Are we understanding each other?'

George could not believe what he was hearing; but he had understood every word all right. Everything that he had set up was about to fall about around his ears.

'That's all, Georgie. You can toddle off now and beat your skins, or whatever else it is that you guys do.' Red dismissed him with a wave of his hand.

George didn't move, he just sat there looking at the gangster before him. He had always made it a priority to not show Red any fear, but he couldn't help himself now.

The look of shock was all over his face. 'Red, how the hell am I supposed to get my hands on twenty-five pounds by tonight?'

The gangster blinked his eyes as if he couldn't believe the man before him was still there. He shrugged and shook his head. 'That's not my concern now, is it?' he replied. 'So, I suggest that you go and do whatever it is you need to do to secure me my money or there'll be some, erm, shall we say, nasty consequences? I'm sure you know how Jules likes his work and how good at it he is. Now you, get yourself out of my office and get me my money.' He stood up slowly but in an utterly threatening manner. George didn't need to be asked again, he got up and grasped the door handle.

'Don't forget, Georgie. Eight o'clock.'

George continued to walk out of the office without looking back. He hated being called Georgie!

32.

AS THE DOOR closed behind him, a blind panic set in. He knew that Red didn't make idle threats, he wanted his money and there was no way he was going to be able to get around it. Jules had built his reputation on the fact that he always followed through on his orders. George was going to have to accelerate his plans. He would have to get Brian around to his tonight now to extort the money from him, then he would have to get Faye to come around after that. No sexual favours from her anymore, it was just going to have to be cold, hard cash.

His eyes lit up a little as he thought about everything that he had seen in Marnie's house. *I'll need to get rid of some of that stuff today too*, he thought.

He did a quick calculation in his head and he concluded that he might be able to get about six pounds and ten shillings for some of the lesser ornaments in a quick sale but that left him short by a long way.

He made his way back into the main hall where everyone was still sulking and setting up their instruments. There a heavy atmosphere, and no one was really talking. All eyes were on him as he re-entered, no one had expected to see him back.

Carl stood and eyed him suspiciously.

He knew that all eyes were on him, but he ignored them, making his way over to Brian. He grabbed him by the arm, tight enough to

163

make the taller man wince, and dragged him towards the back of the stage. 'I need to talk to you, right now,' he said this loud enough for everyone to hear. He wanted the rest of the band to see them talking together.

'What do you think you're doing?' Brian asked as he was unceremoniously dragged to one side.

'Do you remember our little talk the other day?' George's voice was low, urgent. It unnerved Brian somewhat and he shot George a dirty, disgusted look, that told him he remembered the conversation very well.

'Well, I'm going to have to speed things up a bit. You see I'm in rather a tight spot and in dire need of that money we talked about. Five pounds, wasn't it?'

He gripped Brian's arm a little tighter, his eyes glaring in their intensity.

Brian's initial anger was abating, it was being replaced with fear. 'I don't have that kind of money,' he hissed. 'I told you. I'm just a bloody trombonist in a swing band. Five pounds is more than two week's pay.'

George tightened his grip again, enjoying the way the taller man squirmed as he did. As he moved his face closer, Brian could smell cologne mingled with sweat emanating from his former friend, and current blackmailer. 'You mightn't have it, but it's my bet that your saintly mother has. Do you think it would be too much to ask in return for the keeping of her favourite son's secret?' George gritted his teeth and curled his lip as he closed the, already intimate, distance between them. 'Because, I swear to God, Brian, if I don't get that money, and I don't get it tonight, then everyone will know your *sordid* little secret. And I do mean everyone.'

George's brow was beaded in sweat; it was as if the room temperature had suddenly risen ten or so degrees. Both men just stood there, staring at each other.

Eventually, Brian was the first to relinquish the challenge. He lowered his eyes and turned away.

George didn't smile, although deep down inside he was rejoicing. 'Be at my house tonight at six thirty,' he threatened. 'Don't dare be late, I mean it. How do you think your mother would cope with the police kicking her door down to drag her fruit of a son to Walton Prison?'

Brian lowered his head. He couldn't believe that it was only a few days ago that he considered this vile, evil man, a friend. 'What happened to you, George?' he hissed. 'Why the hell are you so…so bitter?'

George let go of him and walked away. 'Six thirty, Brian! Don't be late.' With that, he walked away, without even the courtesy of looking back at him.

Eddie was watching this conversation from afar; it was obvious that something was wrong, but when George had walked away shouting something at Brian, something that he didn't quite catch, his interest was well and truly piqued. He caught Faye's eye and, raising his eyebrows, indicated in George's direction. Faye frowned and shrugged. He ushered her over conspiratorially. 'I think we should follow him. If he's killed Marnie then I think he might be planning to do something to Brian.'

Faye looked over to where Brian was still standing, gazing into nowhere, contemplate the intense intricacies of the curtain weave at the back of the stage. When she turned back to Eddie, her face was pale.

'Either that, or Brian's in on it somehow!' she replied, turning her wide-eyed face back towards the trombone player. 'Either way, I think you're right, we have to find out what he's up to.'

They both watched as George limped towards the main exit.

'Listen everyone, it looks like we're all a little emotional so why don't we call it a day, and all go home. I don't think there's much practising getting done here today anyway. What do we say? If we all get back here tonight for the usual time, nine, for the gig, I think we know the stuff well enough to pull it off,' Eddie addressed the room.

They all looked at him as if he had just stated the most obvious thing in the world; but still a feeling of relief washed over the room.

Tam shrugged, lit another cigarette and sat back.

Carl turned on his heels and stormed out of the room, without even so much as a by your leave. Brian followed closely behind, not saying a word to anyone. Faye watched them go before sidling up to Eddie.

'How do you do you think we should do this?' she whispered.

Eddie licked his lips; he was relishing the feeling of Faye so close and so personal with him, but there was still something that he needed to ask her - something he needed to know before he could trust her in this little investigation they were about to undertake. 'Faye, I don't know how to ask you this, so I'll just come right out and say it. Are you in need of a fix right now?'

She looked like she'd been slapped, hard! Her face was a mixture of anger, desperation, but mostly shame. She looked up at him, her eyes widening with the shock of the unexpected question, before falling away. There was a long, pregnant pause. She hoped Eddie would be the first to break the silence, but he was just staring at her, waiting on an answer. She swallowed hard before nodding. She wanted to speak but the words caught in her throat and it was a small while before she could regain her composure. She sighed, raised her face and looked her old, but seemingly new, friend in his eyes. Suddenly she was a child who was about to admit to eating all the cake from the cupboard. 'Eddie,' she paused. 'I need a fix all of the time!'

At that moment, Eddie wanted to take her into his arms and hold her, hug her tight and never let her go. He wanted to take all the pain away from her and make everything better, but he knew that now wasn't the right time. Something happening between them, he could feel it, but something bigger was happening around them, that required their immediate attention.

'OK! Come on, we're going to see George and then I'm going to get you away from all this shit.' It was his turn to get the words caught in his mouth, but he was also determined to finish what he started. 'Faye, I love you and… and I think I always have. I wanted to tell you that now, before we go and confront George once and for all.' He grabbed her by the arm pulling her towards the exit.

'What did you say?' she asked, her voice little more than a whisper.

Eddie stopped and looked at her, a small, excited smile crept across his face. 'I think you heard me. I said, I love you, and when all this is over, I'm going to ask you another question and I'm not going to take no for an answer. We're going to confront George and then me and you are leaving this place, Liverpool, The Rialto, for good. Are you OK with that?'

Faye couldn't do, or say, anything, so she just looked at him. To her, it felt like it was the very first time that she had ever seen him. Before today he had always just kind of been there, lurking in the background, not really registering. Her heart fluttered for a moment and she raised her hand to her chest, she could feel her heart's rapid beat as she fought for breath. Looking at Eddie, she realised that it *was* the first time in her life she's seen him.

She liked what she saw.

'OK!' Her voice was breathless.

Eddie looked at her as if she'd suddenly begun talking in Japanese.

'I said OK. We can leave together. There's nothing keeping me here anyway. We can get jobs in any city. What I'm saying Eddie, is that I want to leave with you.'

When he smiled then, his face looked ten years younger. He grabbed her by the hand and ushered her out of the ballroom.

Tam was sat at his piano. He stubbed out the butt of his cigarette in the empty cup of tea he had on top of his instrument, before lighting another. As he watched everyone leave the ballroom, he shook his head, bemused at all the comings and goings, before turning back towards his piano to begin playing his most favourite piece. Mozart's Requiem.

33.

GEORGE HAILED A taxi. It was an extravagance that he could ill afford, but he knew, today, it was warranted. He had a lot to do before Red turned up, demanding money that he still didn't have.

He loved entertaining, and tonight he had a feeling that there would be quite a few comings and goings at 'Chez Tex'. 'County Road, Walton please driver,' he informed the back of the man's head, before settling back into the comfortable seats for the drive through the city he loved.

He nodded off as he passed the Liver Buildings, with the majestic birds adorning it, and the other magnificent buildings that graced the Liverpool waterfront. As he did, there was a small, contented smile on his face.

34

'WHERE ARE YOU going?' Brian demanded as he made it outside, hot on the heels of a fleeing Carl.

'I've got to go and find Marnie.' There was a distant look on his face, and it worried Brian, no end. There was something wrong here and he knew that George was at the bottom of it. 'I've just got a really bad feeling about them, about George and Marnie.' He shook his head as if to shake the demons that were residing inside, out into the open. 'I've got to warn her off him. This isn't the first time she's gotten herself into a, shall we say, unhealthy relationship.'

Without further ado, he sped off leaving Brian stood in the middle of the road, watching as he ran in the direction of the tram station.

'You still didn't tell me where you're going?' he shouted again.

Carl glanced back towards him, his face registering annoyance at the questioning. 'Marnie's. Now leave me alone, Brian, I've got to do this.'

With a heavy heart, Brian watched Carl go. He'd wanted to let him know how he felt about him. He'd made the decision to leave Liverpool for good. He knew it would break his heart, and break his mother's heart, but he was going to stick to the decision. He knew deep down it was the right one.

He also knew that he was going to miss Carl.

For the first time in his life, he thought he had met someone who he could open up to, someone who wouldn't judge him and would maybe even want to be with him. Brian knew what he was, and he had more than a feeling that Carl was the same way. It made him sad that it was all going to be ruined; his nice, cosy, little life. There was no way that he could stay here now, and allow his, former, friend George blackmailed him.

He was going to give him what he wanted, what he demanded, and then he was off. He had bought his train ticket to Wales, to live with his Aunt Teresa. He knew he could get work as a musician there; there were more brass bands out that way that he could shake a stick at, and he would be as far away from George, and Liverpool, as he could get.

Besides, he thought with a small smile, *I've always liked the Welsh accent.*

With the sad smile still lingering, he turned to take one final look at the grandiose building that was The Rialto. He'd had some fantastic times here. There were even some fond memories of him and George; but that was all they were now, memories.

This was the end.

Turning his back on the building, he adjusted his collar against the ill wind that was whipping off the river and slowly made his way towards the tram station.

35.

'WHAT DO YOU mean you can't make it in tonight?' Red was stood at his desk, holding the telephone receiver in one tight fist. He was holding it so tight that his knuckles were pure white. 'Ron, I need you in and I need you NOW!' His face was turning the same colour as his name and he looked like he could easily eat someone right now. 'I don't care if your fucking legs have fallen off, you're my main man in tonight and I have some very important business to attend to. I need you to drive me to… Hello? Hello? HELLO!!! Don't you fucking DARE hang up on me Ron… Ron??? RIGHT… I'M ON MY FUCKING WAY!' he shouted down the receiver, fully aware that Ron couldn't hear him.

He slammed the receiver down with a snarl then turned and yanked his coat off the peg it was hanging on. It snagged a little and resisted. Red, furious now, yanked harder, ripping the little material hook off from the inside.

He intended to drive to Ron's house and drag him out of bed, flu or no flu, but first he knew that he had to calm himself down. He'd do himself no favours driving the three or four miles with this red mist hanging over him. He put his coat down on his desk and sat back down in his chair. He took in a series of long, deep breaths, and closed his eyes, allowing himself to relax.

'Fucking George!' he hissed between clenched teeth. 'It's him who's got me all wound up like this.' He looked at the clock beside his telephone; it was four o'clock. There were another five hours to go before he needed to be at George's house. 'It'll have to be Jules then. God help George if he doesn't have the money.'

He reached his hand into the inside pocket of his coat and pulled out a small scrap of paper, on the paper was a telephone number.

He dialled the number and allowed it to ring.

It was answered in four rings by a deep, exotic accent. 'Hallo!'

'Jules, it's Red. Listen, I need you tonight. Can you get to the club for seven o'clock?'

There was silence on the other end for a small while before the voice came back. 'I'm sorry, boss, but that's not possible.'

'What? What do you mean not possible? What the fuck am I paying you for?' He clenched the receiver ever tighter. Today was not going as planned.

'You pay me for my services, boss, but you also know that I service others too. I have a job on tonight that requires my particular skill set, and I am a man of my word.'

'I'll pay you more than what the other job's paying.'

'Boss, I already have more money than I can spend. I am a man of my word and must do this job tonight. I could meet you at the club at ten thirty, no earlier I'm afraid.'

Red slammed the receiver down on the phone a little too hard, knocking it along the desk. He stood up with a jerk, knocking his seat behind him over. He grabbed his coat from the desk and stormed out of the office.

36.

AS GEORGE MADE it home, the house was unusually quiet. On a normal night, Tex would be pottering about, playing his swing time records on the gramophone and making a mess.

But not tonight.

Tonight, it was as silent as the grave in the house.

'Tex? Tex, are you about mate?' he shouted into the empty room. There was no reply.

George walked through the house looking from room to room but there was still no sign of the older man anywhere. He knew that sometimes he would take himself off down the pub, and he would sometimes go after him, as he was prone to getting himself into all sorts of mischief, but tonight George welcomed the silence. He had a lot of things he needed to figure out and the empty house fit his needs perfectly.

Still nursing his swollen lip from Carl's punch, he went into the kitchen, poured himself one of Tex's single malt scotches, and sat at the small table collecting his thoughts. As he took a sip of the amber liquid, he gasped a little as it bit into his cut lip.

He needed the cash from Faye and Brian badly, and he needed to offload the knick-knacks that he'd harvested from Marnie's house last night. He also knew that it was too late in the day now, and he wouldn't be able to get anything for them until tomorrow night at the very earliest.

The money from Faye and Brian plus the little that he knew Tex had stashed in the house, would have to be enough to satisfy Red, but there was something about him today that unnerved George, something in his eyes.

He was snapped out of his thoughts by an urgent rapping on his back door. Smiling to himself, he eased up from the table and limped his way over. 'First caller of the night,' he said as he opened the door finding Faye standing outside in the cold, in all her glory. He kept her out there for a few seconds, enjoying the moment. She was a very attractive woman, when she put her face on, but George had seen the ugliness behind the veneer, when she was so desperate for a fix that she would do, quite literally, anything to get it.

Tonight, she had that look.

Eventually, he grinned and then moved aside to allow her in. 'Faye, this is not an altogether unexpected surprise,' he said, the sarcasm curdling his words. 'Come on in. you'll catch your death out there.'

He grinned as all she could offer him was a sheepish look; he thought she might have glared at him if her eyes hadn't been dripping with desperation, dulling them of any other emotion, besides need.

She stepped inside the house, the house that she had been in countless times before.

He noted that she did her level best to avoid any contact with him. Still grinning, he closed the door behind her, trapping her inside. He limped back towards the table where his half-empty glass of scotch was languishing. 'Can I offer you a drink, or would you like something stronger?'

His laugh was sickening and condescending. He was loving his moment of power.

As she stepped in, she shook her head at his invitation, choosing to remain standing in the doorway. She was holding one of her arms with her other hand, looking like she was trying to warm herself and even though she was shaking like a scared dog, there was also a kind of brave defiance in her. George could see it and strangely enough, he admired her for it. Even though he needed to conduct this business and move on, he wanted to revel in the moment, the moment before he broke her, and all her resistance, once and for all.

'No, George, I don't. I don't want anything from you, ever again.' She spat the words out of her mouth, spittle punctuating her venom.

He looked at her; for a second or two he reeled, hearing the defiance in her. His smile returned, but there was precious little humour in it. 'Oh, I'm sure you'll change your mind on that one, Faye! Just think about when those cramps start to kick in. You'll be begging me for your fix.'

Faye twitched as a shiver ripped right through her. She could feel his gaze on her skin, and it made her feel dirty, filthy. The things she had done with this man; *to* this man! That thought alone made her shudder again. She could feel his enjoyment, the knowledge that he had the upper hand on her, like he'd always had. But then she thought about her and Eddie leaving Liverpool, George, and her stupid addiction, behind her for good. She lifted her head up high and looked at him; hoping she looked bolder than she felt.

George's face went dark, breaking into a thin, ugly leer. 'Actually Faye, you're looking a little rough right now. Are you sure I can't interest you in a little… something?' He pulled a small brown medicine bottle from his pocket and shook it at her.

Her eyes darted towards the bottle, she eyed it greedily. She knew that what was in there would make all these feelings inside her go away, she knew that it would make her feel good about herself again, for a small while at least, but that was all she wanted, all she needed. She could take the days one at a time, wean herself off the drug slowly, off George, and then, when she was clean again, she and Eddie could finally shake the dirt of this old life off their shoes and hit the lights of London.

George could read everything that she was feeling in her face.

She shook her head, as if the act of shaking it could make all those horrible, negative feelings fall out of her brain so she could squash them underneath the sole of her shoe. She cleared her throat and pulled out her purse.

With a voice that wasn't quite hers, she defied him again. 'No, George, never again. Not from you, you evil little man.'

He wasn't prepared for her determination and he recoiled again. The hits seemed to be coming hard and fast tonight.

Slowly, she reached into her purse.

George eyes her, nervously.

Her eyes caught his. The steely determination within them was catching him out every time. Without even thinking about it, he took a step back, his hand searching for something, anything that he could defend himself with it this *mad bitch* decided to attack.

'There's your money, seven pounds of it, what bleeding good it'll do you.' She gained strength from George's shocked face and taking in a deep, shaky breath, she continued. 'Me and Eddie are leaving, George. He knows what you did to Marnie, and what you've been doing to me, and we're leaving. He... he told me that he loves me.'

37.

'MARNIE... MARNIE! PLEASE open the door.' Carl was standing on the doorstep of the house in Bootle. Even though the night was cold, a sweat had built up on his brow and steam was rising from his unkempt hair.

'Marnie... *Please!*' he shouted again.

He banged on the door with his clenched fists, rattling the wood in its frame again and again, until his white knuckles turned pink and begun to bleed.

'*Marnie!*' he shouted again. There was panic, and desperation, in his voice and it cracked, almost a full octave, mid-shout making his sorrowful wail sound almost comedic.

'Mrs Jenkins! Mrs Jenkins... are you in there?' He continued banging on the door, making far too much of a racket for anyone inside the house to ignore. It was too much noise even for the people not inside to ignore.

A light came on in the neighbour's house, and an elderly man poked his head through the voile curtains, looking to see what the racket was about.

Carl noticed him straight away and switched his attention to him. 'Sir, excuse me, sir, can you help me please?' Carl forced his way through the hedge that separated the two front paths.

Watching the madman approach his house, the elderly neighbour retreated back inside, alarm registering on his face as he did.

Carl began rapping on his window. 'Sir, I need your help. It's my sister... she lives next door. I haven't seen her in a while and I'm really worried about her. *Sir!*' He shouted the last word, his voice faltering halfway through again, sounding less comedic this time and very much more like how he appeared; manic.

He peered into the window where the man had recently been, using both his hands to shade what little light was coming from outside to allow him to see inside clearly. Then he heard the door unlock.

Instantly, he pushed his way through the terracotta plant pots and into the man's garden; within a few seconds he was in the doorway.

'What's all this commotion going on out here? Don't you know what time it is? Decent people are trying to eat you know.' The man was in his late fifties, maybe even early sixties, and he was dressed in a tank top with a small bow tie, he was also wearing carpet slippers and smoking a rather smelly pipe.

'Sir, thank you for opening the door.'

'Well, I could hardly let you...'

'It's my sister, Marnie,' Carl interrupted him. 'She lives next door, she lodges with Mrs Jenkins, you may have seen her, tall, blonde hair.'

'Well I might have, but I don't go about...'

'Have you seen her lately? Have you seen, Mrs Jenkins?'

'Well, erm... no, as a matter of fact. Not today, but then she keeps to herself somewhat.' The man replied, rather relieved to be able to finish a sentence.

'What about yesterday?' He grabbed the man's tank top and pulled him towards him, his steaming breath gushing into the surprised man's flinching face.

The poor man was not expecting the physicality of this confrontation and his face drained of colour as the much younger, taller man leered at him, his teeth were grinding, and his eyes were wild. A woman popped her head around the door, her hair was in curlers and she was wearing a bright orange housecoat. She looked almost as frightened as her husband.

'Dennis... Dennis, what's happening?'

'It's all OK, Alice. Just you go on back inside and I'll take care of this.'

Carl turned to look at the woman while still holding her husband's tank top. 'Did you see them yesterday?' he demanded. 'Either of them. Did you see them?' The last question was directed at the wife.

Dennis's face turned a distasteful shade of purple as he attempted to push Carl away from him.

Carl's anger depleted then, and he let go of the man's garment and fell away from him, backwards onto the path. He flopped himself down onto the doorstep, where he sat with his face in his hands and began to sob.

As Dennis fixed his tank top, he eyed Carl with outright distaste and relief of being unhanded in front of his wife. 'I'll thank you to leave my path, young man, and never return. I'm good mates with the local bobby around here, and he'll listen to me. So why don't you go and crawl back into whatever bottle you crawled out of, eh?'

He then looked a little closer at Carl, his eyes narrowing in suspicion. 'Aren't you the man who was around here a few nights ago? The one making all that racket then too?' He shook his head and tutted. 'I'll be having words with Mrs Jenkins about taking on disruptive lodgers in the future.' He took another puff from his pipe and blew it out in Carl's direction, before turning his back and going back inside.

He shot Carl one last, disgusted look, before slamming the door closed. The knocker rattled against the wood with the force of the blow.

Carl slowly got up and looked longingly over towards Marnie's house. The dark windows depressed him somewhat and shook his head. He didn't want to admit to himself what he thought they meant.

Like a broken man, he walked out of the path, over the road and entered the dark park opposite.

38.

'SO, HE LOVES you, eh? Does he know about me and you?' George was sitting at the small table in the kitchen; the glass of scotch in his hand was almost empty, as he tipped the tumbler to his mouth and drained it.

Faye was still standing, defiantly, in the doorway. Her eyes were dark and determined but there was still a deep fragility to her. 'Yes, I've told him everything. The whole sordid affair.'

George raised his eyebrows. 'The *whole* sordid affair?'

As her face flushed, he gained a level of satisfaction. That single, small, involuntary reaction spoke volumes about what she had, and more importantly, hadn't told Eddie.

He levelled her with a sadistic glare, one that cut right through all of her defences. She felt goose-bumps rise on her arms. She knew this time they were nothing to do with her needs, these were about fear.

'Did you tell him about the sort of things you've been willing to do for me, do to me, just to get your grubby little, drug addicted, mitts on some of this?' he hissed, banging the little brown bottle on the wooden tabletop.

She jumped at the noise, her hand grabbing at her arm in a weak attempt to stave off the fright. Her eyes flicked towards the bottle.

George could see the longing in that look. 'Have you told him about how low you've been willing to stoop, and the money that you've spent? Does he even know where you are right now, eh?'

The questions were coming hard and fast in his excitement; thick, white spittle was forming on his lips as he spat them at her. Her head was hung so low now that he already knew the answer to every question.

He put the bottle down and leaned on the table, fixing his intense gaze on her.

She was still averting her eyes, unwilling to look at him.

'I'm guessing by your silence that you haven't yet told him everything.' He sat back into his chair again. He picked up his empty glass and looked at it. 'That works well for me. Now, Faye, I think you know, by now, that you've always disgusted me. I want you to leave the money that you owe me and then I want you out of my house. Never to return. Have you got that?' He stood up and made his way towards the bottle of scotch that was on the counter by the cooker. He turned his back to her as he began to pour himself another drink.

~~~~

Everything that he had said had been a slap in her face. Multiple slaps in the face. Slaps, she had dealt with her entire life and had learned to roll with, but one thing that had always irked her, sometimes even to the point of violence, was being ignored. So, George's, unintentional, final act of contempt, simply turning his back on her, coupled with the cravings and the cramps that were currently coursing through her decimated body, sent her into a rage. Her sanity was slipping, and her hatred for this vile little man was swelling inside her; growing like a physical entity, rising, attempting to break free of its prison. It started as a small ball in the pit of her stomach and blossomed, like a phoenix from a flame, throughout the whole of her body. Her eyes grew wide, and her pale face turned a deep crimson. The fingers on her hands turned inwards, transforming them into vicious weapons, as venom coursed through her veins. Slowly she raised her head fixing her dark eyes on *him*. George, still with his back to her, ignoring her, busy pouring himself a fresh drink from the bottle.

The roar she could hear seemed to come from somewhere else; from another room maybe, somewhere deep inside the house. Absently, she wondered what could produce such a terrifying sound.

She was honestly astonished to realise that the noise was coming from her; from somewhere deep inside of her!

Before she knew what she was doing, before she could even attempt to regain any modicum of self-control, she lunged at George, claws out, poised for attack. With one bound, she was on top of her target, her fingers were ripping into the exposed flesh around his neck, gaining any purchase they could, aiming to inflict maximum damage.

George reacted quickly, a lot quicker than Faye, or anyone else for that matter, would have ever given him credit for.

As if coming from somewhere else, maybe the same somewhere else that she'd heard the roar coming from a second or so earlier, a loud crunch echoed all around her. It was a strange noise, as if a giant had bitten into a large and extremely fresh apple.

The sound momentarily deafened her. Suddenly the entire world sounded like it was coming in through a large seashell, like the big one she had found on New Brighton beach when she was a child.

Her father had told her to place this shell over her ear and she would be able to hear the sea. She thought this was a rather silly thing to do, as they were already at the seaside and if she'd wanted to hear the sea, she didn't need the shell to help her do it.

Another crunching sound filled her head, but this one came with a shudder that wracked through her entire body, bringing with it a good deal of pain. The tips of her fingers began to tingle as a strange sensation surged through her nerve endings, electrifying every limb in her body. Her vision went funny, everything was shaky and then just a little bit dimmer. She began to see the world as if it was through a long, scary, dark tunnel. At the end of the tunnel, she could see a light, but there was something in the light, something barring her from getting to the sweet relief, and out of the vile dimness of this tunnel.

It was some a monster; a hideous abomination.

The thing was wearing a mask of some sort; a mask that was supposed to make it look human but was ill-fitting and only served to make it scarier, and somehow, even less than human.

She watched as it lifted something over its head; sweat was glistening off the tip of its fake human nose. She was fascinated as the thing stretched the mouth of the mask into a grin, before it brought, whatever it had over its head, down one more time in a wide arch, with devastating strength.

The loud, apple-like crunch came one more time. The physical sensation was less painful than the last one and she felt herself go numb. The crunching was reverberating through her head and she could feel herself sail away on its echo. She didn't want to go but she was stuck in its current.

Suddenly, the tunnel closed, and everything went black.

Faye was finally free of all her addictions.

39.

GEORGE LOOMED OVER the crumpled body of Faye as she lay on the floor of the kitchen. Her blank, sightless eyes were staring, accusingly, up at him. He could feel the accusation burning into his skin like a child using the hot sun to burning ants underneath a magnifying glass. His own blank gaze fell over the empty whisky bottle that was still in his hands and he regarded it as though he had never seen it before.

Faye's hair was stuck to the sides of it in thick, sticky clots. Blood was dripping from it onto the kitchen floor and pooling around her body, as she lay, unmoving, on the cold tiles.

With a shaking hand, he attempted to put the bottle back onto the counter, missing it a few times, before steadying his aim. He staggered backwards, reaching out for the table to stop him from falling over and joining his former friend on the floor. His leg had suddenly started to ache, painfully, and he had to concentrate, all his efforts, not give into it and allow it buckle.

The sting of the deep gouge marks in the back of his neck throbbed in perfect timing and rhythm with his leg, the pain amplified as he thought about it. He rubbed his hand over the sting to see if he was bleeding. When he brought his hand back, it was covered in blood.

This gave him a moment of panic before he realised that this was Faye's blood, not his own.

He flopped down, heavily, on one of the seats at the table and sighed a long, breathy sigh. He looked at Faye's body on the floor. The wound in her head was deep, and there was thick, fresh, blood pumping from it. It was running along the channels between the tiles like a new and hideous grouting. A large, expanding puddle of blood was forming around her head like a perverse, red halo in a religious painting.

This wasn't the first time he'd had blood on his hands; it wasn't the first time that his rage had gotten the better of him. The sight of the poor young girl lying dead on his floor brought back dark memories; memories that he had tried so hard to forget, to repress, but of course, life-changing events like this have a habit of bringing everything back, in deep clarity.

He checked his whisky glass and, finding it empty, he reached out for the heavy, blood-soaked bottle beside him on the counter. He looked at it, at the bloody hair sticking to it, blonde tinged with red, and had second thoughts. As he stood, his leg screaming at him as he did, he felt like he floated over to the cupboard where he knew Tex kept his whisky reserves. He removed a second bottle, this one was full, and he fumbled at the cap with his shaking hands before finally pulling the cork out of the neck. The long swallow he took burnt his cut lip and his throat but he didn't care, it was what he needed, and he relished, welcomed, the burning sensation, the warm, stabilising feeling it gave him when it hit his belly.

He closed his eyes and thought about something that he hadn't thought about for a long, long time.

40.

IT WAS MAY seventh, 1941, and George was getting himself ready for a long, cold, wet, night. As his leg had stopped him from seeing active duty, he had been pressured into becoming an ARP warden - a job he loathed - and felt was beneath him. The ARP (air raid protection) recruited the men who were either too old, or unable to go to war, making sure the populace of Britain was safe in the event of an air raid. It involved him traipsing around the streets of Bootle, with his bad leg aching, making sure that the stupid populace had heeded the curfews set by the stupid government, to protect them from their stupid enemies. His job was to ensure that all illuminations were off, and all blackout curtains were drawn.

It was a job he loathed.

Heaven forbid that Hitler's air force should notice a parlour light on; that way they'd know exactly where to blitz the Liverpool docks.

'Bloody stupid idea this,' he grumbled as he tightened the strap underneath his black tin helmet. He slid on his long black overcoat and checked his gas mask. He was good to go.

He left the room that he was renting at eight thirty and began his patrol. His mood was already dark. His leg was hurting badly and the band that he had been playing with had recently broken up. Mainly because the female lead had said that her father wouldn't let her play anymore, what with the threat of the bombs and stuff. George had offered to sing but the rest of the band, made up of older musicians, too old to fight, had looked at him and scoffed.

It always came down to the fact that he was a cripple.

Eventually, after much procrastination, he left the house and made his way towards Merton Road in the centre of Bootle Village. He was feeling dour and more than ready to take his mood out on anyone who had missed the curfew. People always took the fact that he had a bad leg to mean that he couldn't fight if he needed to. He could, he knew exactly how to look after himself; he had been doing it for years.

The night was cold and quiet. This made him even more miserable than he already was. His only excitement up to then was when he had thought he had heard some kids messing around down by the Kings Park off Stanley Road, but either they had heard him coming and scarpered, or it was just his imagination. This disappointed him as he thought that he could have had a bit of fun with them.

The park was deserted.

As were all the streets.

He looked at his watch and it read just after nine fifteen. He hadn't even been out for an hour and he was already bored, miserable and angry.

There had been air-raid warnings for the last few days, but mostly they were just one-off aeroplanes doing reconnaissance. Everyone had been jittery since London had almost been flattened back in September, before the Jerry's had turned their attentions to Liverpool. There had been another warning tonight, the familiar siren had sounded at eight o'clock and all the families had scarpered into their shelters for the night.

Everyone, it seemed, except him.

George limped his way around Bootle; the searchlights over the Mersey were visible as he was no more than a mile away from the river.

189

'One more pass of Derby Park and then I'm done. I'm not staying out here all night.' His voice echoed back at him as the whole of Bootle was deserted. Even the pubs in the village were quiet, and that was seldom heard of, even at the small hours of the morning.

As he made his way through the park, he thought he could hear giggling coming from somewhere in the darkness. With his heartbeat speeding up somewhat at the thought of a little adventure, he flicked on his torch and went to investigate.

The park was in pitch darkness and it was eerie. The wind blowing through the trees unnerved him more than he wanted to admit, but he pressed on. 'After all, it's my duty to the King and country,' he scoffed.

'Is anyone there?' he shouted into the darkness. The instant the shout left his lips, the giggling stopped.

'I said, is there anyone there? I'm with the ARP, you need to get out of this park and get yourselves into a shelter. There's good intelligence that there'll be a raid at some point tonight.'

There was no reply, but he could now hear whispering carrying on the wind. He knew there was a bandstand in the centre of the park, and it should be just a little further on. The whispers continued; as he got closer, he could tell they were female and, by the sounds of them, they were young.

'Listen, you need to get yourselves out of here and get to a shelter, if not I'll have to call the police and then you'll be in real trouble.'

The whispers stopped again. *Got their attention now,* he thought.

Buoyed on by the knowledge that he wasn't busting into some shady gangland capers where his life could be in danger, he sped up his limp towards the bandstand.

He shone his torch around the structure looking for the kids who were messing about.

And found them.

Two girls, both maybe sixteen years old, he guessed, were lying on a blanket against one of the walls of the stand. They were both covering their faces to stem their giggles as his torch light dazzled their eyes. As the beam swung between them, he saw a large, almost empty bottle of gin lying on the floor. He flicked the beam back up to their faces and noticed, for the first time, that they were both drunk.

Maybe a little more than drunk.

'Come on you two, you need to get up from there and get home. It's not safe out here in the blackout,' he snapped testily at them. This was all he needed tonight, in the foul mood that he was in. 'Where do your parents think you are?'

'Won't we be OK now that a big strong ARP warden is here to keep us safe?' one of the girls laughed.

George swung the torch around at her and shone it full in her face. Her dark hair was tied back with a colourful bow. She had a dark complexion. Even through the bleaching of the torch light, George could tell it was the kind of complexion that spoke of Spanish ancestry. The fact that she was a very attractive young lady was not lost on him.

The other girl was not unattractive, not by a long shot. She had strawberry blonde hair and her skin was a lot paler. On her own she would have been considered a beauty but next to her drunken friend, she paled into insignificance.

'Come on you two, I'm going to have to get you home, or at least somewhere safe until you sober up.' He made a move towards them and grabbed hold of the darker girl's arm.

'Oh, look, Mary. This one can't keep his hands to himself,' she giggled, half-slurring her words. George blushed but as it was night-time no one noticed.

Because of his leg, he'd always been shy with the ladies. He knew it had always just been a fear of rejection, but he had always hated the power that they had over him.

Not tonight though. Right now, he was in control.

He felt the old familiar rage building up inside him. It surprised him a little due to the pure ferocity of it. It almost felt like he was watching somebody else as he lashed out his arm and slapped the darker girl right across the face.

'Shut your filthy mouth,' he spat.

The girl's laugh fell off her face and fear blossomed in her eyes in complete tandem with the red welt which was rising on her skin from where his hand connected with her.

'What the hell do you think you are doing?' the other girl shouted. There was shock and fear in her high-pitched voice, as she watched her friend fall back onto the wooden floor of the bandstand. George turned to look at her. His eyes flashed with a malevolence that she had never seen before.

'You can shut your dirty little mouth too, you slut!' he hissed through his gritted teeth.

The word 'slut' surprised her, and she was stunned into silence.

'Do you want your fathers to know what you two dirty little whores were doing out here during the blackout? Do you?' he continued.

Both girls sobered up rather sharply as they looked at the man in the black tin hat. The paler of the two turned to look at her friend lying on the floorboards, holding her face and crying. A panic overtook her, and she picked up her shoes, that were lying next to her, and ran off into the darkness of the park; leaving her friend alone and at the mercy of the nasty ARP man.

George smiled as he watched her disappear, before turning his smile onto the whimpering, drunken beauty, lying below him.

'Nice friends you keep,' he quipped. 'So, it looks like it's just you and me now, doesn't it?' He was whispering as he got to his knees next to her, smiling a sinister smile. 'It's OK to scream little girl, no one's going to hear you now; everyone will be nestled, warm and comfortable, in their air raid shelters, exactly where you should be.'

The girl was attempting to back away from him. She was slowly moving herself towards the wooden wall behind her, trying to use it as a lever to get up of the cold floor. 'Wh…what, what do you want with me?' She pleaded.

He leaned into her and breathed slowly out of his nose. The girl looked petrified; her mouth was quivering with either fear or the cold, probably both. George hoped that it was the former. He reached his hand out and fixed a lock of her thick, dark hair behind her ear. She squirmed emitting an involuntary whimper at his cold touch.

This enraged and excited him in equal measures and he forced his body right up next to hers, so their faces were almost nose-to-nose.

The smell of the cheap alcohol on her breath and her petrified eyes staring at him elicited a natural, physical response; one that he was rather expecting.

She closed her eyes and George went to work.

It was over in a few, violent minutes. When he was finished, he sat back and looked at the terrified girl below him. In his frenzy, he had given her a bloody nose and black eye and there was a deep cut on her lower lip that was already beginning to swell.

But the worst of it were the tears.

Her tears streamed down her cheeks as she sobbed, silently in the dark, chilly night.

He rolled away, fixing his trousers. He turned to look at her, but she had already turned away, averting her face from his gaze. Her small, frail body was shuddering with every sob. This was the only indication that she was crying.

She made no noise.

He breathed in a long breath of the clear, fresh night air and ran his hands through his hair. 'You had that coming you know,' he sneered. It was all he could think of saying. 'You and your nice friend.

You shouldn't have been out here, alone, and drinking. Let it be a lesson to you.'

The girl slowly turned her head to face him. Her pretty face was ruined by her swelling eye and the tears; he no longer wished to look at her.

'So, go on. Get off home. And don't you even think of telling anyone about this because they won't believe you. They'll think you're a low-life slag who goes with anyone for the sake of a drink. Is that what you want your dad to think of you? Or your poor mum?'

The girl looked at him. Her swollen features were alive in the darkness. Hate poured from every outlet of her once-pretty face. 'No one will believe that,' she spat. 'No one's going to believe that I'd go with an ugly, little cripple like you. You make me sick; you freak.'

George's face was blank, emotionless. It was the perfect poker face for the maelstrom that was building up inside him. His breathing was becoming rapid. The darkness was camouflaging his rage.

The girl was attempting to get up, fixing the top of her dress, where he'd ripped it, and grabbing at her shoes. 'I'm going to tell my dad about this. He didn't go to war because he was too old, not because he was a coward like you. When he hears about this…' she turned to look at him and laughed, as close to a laugh as her injuries would allow, right in his face, '…you're a dead man.'

She turned her back on him to pick up her coat and George saw his opportunity. There was a brick lying on the floor near his foot, a brick that had been left there by God only knew who, but before he could even consider the history of it, the heavy thing was in his hand.

'He has brothers too, my uncles, they're going to hunt you down. You're not going to be hard to find when I tell them a bloody troll, with a gammy leg attacked me. When they find you, they'll rip your…'

She never had the chance to finish her sentence, as the brick swung, with full force, and hit her across the back of her head. She fell, face first onto the cold, damp, wooden floorboards.

Dazed and battered, she was helpless to defend herself as rough hands grabbed her and flipped her over onto her back.

He was on top of her once again, only this time she didn't feel his excited manhood digging into her and he wasn't slapping and punching her. He *was* using his hands on her however, only this time he had them wrapped around her throat. Tighter and tighter they gripped, until her vision clarified, and she could see his ugly, grimacing face leering into her. Spit was drooling from the maw of his mouth and his forehead and cheeks were flaring bright red, as he laboured, harder, to squeeze all the breath, and therefore all the life, out of her. Her inbuilt survival instincts kicked in once her brain registered what was happening. They commanded her arms and legs to fight off whatever it was that was attempting to kill her.

Never in a million years would he have been ready for the barrage of bucking and clawing a dying young girl could produce. He had only read stories about women being strangled. They always depicted the act as a serene, silent death. Now, although it was silent, it was certainly anything but serene. The girl clawed at his eyes, thankfully missing them both but gouging a fair amount of skin from his cheeks as she did. She bucked and tossed her body in a violent attempt to shake him off. Ultimately, he was too strong and heavy for her, and her resistance began to wane. Her eyes began to bulge from their sockets and her bloated, purple tongue lolled, like a fat slug, from her mouth. Eventually, the pummelling on his arms weakened, before stopping altogether.

He kept his hands gripped around her neck for a few more seconds; making sure that she was dead before he could let go. There was no way he was going to allow a snotty-nosed little brat to tell tales on him and ruin his life.

When he was sure she was gone, he released his vice-like grip and fell onto his back on the floor, exhausted.

Who would have thought strangling someone could be so tiring? he thought.

It was at that moment when the bombs from the Luftwaffe hit their intended targets.

In his frenzy of trying to kill the girl, he hadn't even heard the noisy engines of the oncoming aeroplanes from overhead. It wasn't until the deafening explosion, the wave of heat, and the wall of rubble battering against the bandstand that he suddenly found himself in the middle of a fully-fledged air strike and, by the feel of it, a pretty precise one too.

Smoke wafted over the bandstand as he lifted his head out of the debris that was covering him. All he could hear was a high-pitched whine that seemed to be coming from the middle of his brain. He peered over the side of the bandstand towards the intense orange glare through the dense cloud smothering the night. Even though he was more than a little disorientated, he could estimate that the glow was coming from the row of houses on Worcester Road, the street running parallel to the park.

It looked like there had been a direct hit.

He sat fell back into the bandstand and waited for the debris cloud to pass. Eventually, it did, and he could see again, mostly due to the intense orange glow from the fires that were all around. He looked at the body of the dead girl next to him.

He couldn't leave her there; people would notice that she had been murdered and not a victim of the bombing.

Then an idea hit him, a really good one!

He dragged her body off the bandstand and carried her the few hundred yards across the street, towards the blast zone. He had always been physically strong, due mainly to the way he had had to carry himself through life, so carrying her was not really a bother. Working under the cover of the thinning dust cloud and away from the prying eyes of the people he could hear emerging from their shelters all around the street, he dropped her body onto the floor. He looked about for something heavy, something that would fit his purpose, and it wasn't long before he spotted the perfect tool. A large chunk of debris, obviously from one of the stricken houses, had landed nearby. It was a few bricks still held together with the cement and grout that had been used in the construction. He dragged it over to the dead girl, before lifting it over his head and dropping it onto her face with some force. The thud and crunch of it landing was sickening, but at least he was spared the screams of her dying.

The slab destroyed her face thus eliminating all the bruises and cuts that he had inflicted on her.

He looked down at his handy-work and a satisfied grin spread across his features.

She was now an unfortunate victim of the blitz!

He then stood up and began to shout at the top of his voice.

'Help! Help! There's been a direct hit.'

People began to emerge from their shelters, curious and somewhat desperate to view the carnage and destruction that had happened around them, wanting to mark themselves safe, and lucky to survive the bombs. As they clambered out of their ugly brick and corrugated iron constructions, into the hell of fire and thick smoke, the first thing they all saw was their local ARP warden, limping around, attempting to beat away the intense flames and enter the devastated houses.

'We need to get in here, there might be people still alive inside,' he was shouting towards the new, and confused looking, arrivals. A scream ripped out into the already chaotic night. George turned to see where it was coming from.

A smile broke in his mind, but there was no telling indication on his, purposefully crafted, horrified face. Someone had noticed the body of the young girl. He looked around and witnessed the discovery, feigning simulated horror. 'Does anyone know who she is?' he shouted over the chaos as he investigated the ruined body of his victim.

No one could answer. It was good enough for him. All he needed to do now was to find her friend and make sure that no one listened to her version of tonight's events.

41.

BACK IN THE present, he realised that he never did find the girl's friend. He assumed, or rather hoped, that she had become a victim of the blitz herself. It was something that he would never know.

He looked over the kitchen towards the dining table. The cash that Faye had brought, notes, and coins, totalling seven pounds, were still there. With everything that had happened, he was worried that he might have only imagined her handing over the money. A surge of relief washed over him as he grabbed it from the table, counting it greedily, and stuffing it into his pocket.

A noise from somewhere inside the house caught his attention. His eyes flicked towards the cooling corpse of Faye lying on the floor, her thickening blood still pooling around her head. She hadn't moved. *Of course, she hasn't, she's dead*, he thought, but the noise came again.

There was someone else inside the house.

Oh, please don't let it be Tex, he thought, he didn't want to have to hurt his old pal.

He poured another drink from the new bottle before putting it down, back on the counter. He drank it in one, wincing at the burn in his stomach and the damned sting in his swollen lip, before wiping his mouth with his sleeve. All he managed to do was smear blood, his own and Faye's, across his face.

He looked at the lifeless body lying on the floor; at the stagnant pool of black blood that had pumped slowly from the deep, dark wound in her head. Aesthetically it looked strange, the dark blood of the gash was in stark contrast to her light blonde hair. He shook his head at this odd thought and took in a deep breath.

The noise came again, prompting him to look back at the kitchen door.

He jumped, nearly dropping his half full glass.

Eddie was standing in the doorway. He looked like the subject of a tragic painting that should be hanging in the hallways of the Louvre in Paris. He was motionless, his eyes staring down towards Faye's broken body, cooling on the tiles, and the still pool of congealing blood that had formed around her smashed head.

Slowly his eyes shifted from the tragedy on the floor to George sitting at the kitchen table grasping a whisky glass in his hand. He took in the open bottle next to him and the mostly empty bottle that was covered in blood and hair next to that. His eyes roamed from the bottles back to George's face. There was blood smeared all over the stubble on his chin, making it look like he had an ugly, red colourant in his hair.

'She…she… came at me, from out of nowhere,' George stuttered as he gripped the glass in his hand with white knuckles. 'It was self-defence, you saw it didn't you, Eddie? She…she told me that you two were in love and I…I gave you guys my blessing, then she went for me. Look.' He turned his head to show off the deep scratches that she had made on the back of his neck. 'She did this to me.'

Eddie's eyes passed from Faye's broken body, to George's bloody neck and then back to Faye again. Although his face looked impassive, neutral, the grief and disbelief at the scene before him was visible in his eyes. Just below the surface, simmering away like a pan filled with near boiling water, was a healthy dose of anger, maybe even rage. He shook his head slowly, a line of drool hung from the lower lip of his wide, slack-jawed mouth.

He swallowed as his hate filled eyes rested back on George. 'I don't care what she did to you.' Eddie's slow whisper was barely audible, but to George, it boomed throughout the room. It was all he could hear. 'What did you do to her? What have you done to my Faye?' A tear began to trickle down Eddie's face. Absently, he wiped it away as his gaze shifted again to the corpse of the love of his life.

George didn't take his eyes off his unexpected guest. He took another, long, swig of his drink, although due to his shaking hands he very nearly missed his mouth.

Eddie began to sob; his bottom lip trembling as more tears joined the first one, racing down his grief-stricken features. His eyes were deep scarlet and the tears were causing tracks down his face. He reached out and grasped at the doorway, it looked like he did this to stop him from falling backwards.

'We were getting away from here. From you and your spider's web of lies and deceit; from whatever shallow, perverted hold you had over her. You turn everything beautiful into shit, George, that's your talent. That's what you do best. Forget the drumming, or the singing for that matter; you're a bastard, George, a bastard with a Midas touch, only... only in reverse.'

George shook his head; he was in denial about what had just happened. He was almost as shocked as Eddie. 'Please, Eddie,' he pleaded. 'It wasn't like that. She's got problems. Faye has needs, strange requirements. All I was doing was helping her out.'

'You were only helping yourself out. The only help you could give would be from one of those medicine bottles, wasn't it? And look at the price it came with. You took something beautiful, something delicate, and dragged it down to your own grubby, filthy level.' His tears were flowing now.

George could see something in his eyes, something sad, and dangerous. The man was realising that his life was now empty, empty and futile, and that he was succumbing to the darkness of it. He wasn't afraid anymore. He had nothing else to lose.

Eddie shrugged. 'You've ruined my life, George, so I'm about to ruin yours.'

He stepped into the kitchen; George was up from his seat like a shot. He was still holding the whisky glass.

'I saw what you did to Marnie and now what you've done to Faye. You won't do it to anyone else, George Hogg. On that I swear.'

'What did you say?'

Eddie blinked and tore his gaze away from his beloved Faye back towards the monster in human clothing that was George.

'I said, I won't let you get away with it,' he reiterated.

'No, before that. You said something about Marnie.'

Confusion was clouding Eddie's features. He could hear George talking, but he was too far gone, grieving for his lost love, to comprehend what he was asking him.

'What are you talking about?'

'You said something about what I'd done to Marnie!'

'I saw you moving her corpse out of her house; it was wrapped up in a carpet. You dragged it into one of those bombed out sites in her street.'

George couldn't believe what he was hearing. *Has he been spying on me?* He wondered how much he knew. He took a gamble and turned his back on the man standing just inside the kitchen. It was under the pretext of pouring himself another drink from the bottle next to him. Slowly, and ever so silently, he opened the drawer in the kitchen counter, making sure that Eddie couldn't see what he was doing. He wrapped his fingers around the handle of the large carving knife before removing it and closing the drawer again.

'It's… unfortunate that you saw that, Eddie,' he said in a threatening monotone, still with his back to him. 'What do you propose to do with this information?'

Eddie wasn't looking at him, he was still staring at, and weeping over, the dead body of his beloved lying on the floor. He looked to be stuck in a dichotomy of whether cradle her, or to just run.

The crimson pool around her head had stopped expanding and was now developing a film over the top of it. it was this that was stopping him from embracing her. 'In light of what's happened here, I'm going to go straight to the police. You're a madman George, crazy! You've killed two people.' He drew in a long, stuttering, and shaky breath before continuing. 'Two, beautiful, people! Their whole lives were stretched out before them, but your greed and your… your selfishness, has taken that away from them. You need help.' He paused then and sat down on the chair behind him, his head in his hands. 'Oh, my Faye!' he wept.

George's face was emotionless. He'd become every inch the psychopath that Eddie thought he was.

'You know I can't let you go to the police, don't you?' he said, continuing in the same monotonous voice. Draining his glass, his grip tightened on the knife that was still out of sight of the weeping man.

'You can't stop me, George, this can't go unpunished,' he stuttered in between sobs and sniffs.

George closed his eyes and nodded. He took a deep breath and held it in for a moment or two, enjoying how Tex's expensive whisky was dulling his sensations. As he exhaled, he let out a long, resigned sigh. 'Now, you see, Eddie, that's where you're wrong… about a great many things.'

George whipped his body around to face his fellow band member. Eddie had gotten off the chair and was now kneeling on the floor. Apparently, he had decided that he should pay his respects to the woman he loved after all. He was bent over, attempting to cradle the body in his arms. He was holding her awkwardly, as if he didn't want to get any of her blood on him. He looked up at George and saw the long, sharp knife in his hands. He gently laid Faye's head back down onto the floor and attempted to stand.

He never made it. 'Look, Geor…' he began, but that was as far as he got.

George covered the space between them in a fraction of a second, once again showing the speed and agility over a short distance, that no one would ever have given him credit for.

The knife struck home, first time. He felt it sink through the weak resistance of Eddie's skin. He pushed it harder to match the tougher resistance as it passed through the lining of his stomach muscles, to the point of no return.

George was amazed at how easy it was to stab somebody. Not that he had thought about it much in the past, but he had always assumed that it would have been a lot harder to do.

He let go of the blood-slicked handle, leaving the blade embedded deep within Eddie's stomach. He put his arm around the surprised and stricken man's head, as if he were about to embrace a lover. Holding Eddie's head, he gently lowered the man to the floor. His eyes were staring, deep into Eddie's.

They were almost apologetic.

Eddie's own eyes stared back at him. As George's were apologising, Eddie's were accusing.

The older man tried to struggle; he clawed at his stomach, grasping at the slippery shaft of the knife handle, trying to grip it, to yank it from where it was protruding. Gently, George pulled him in closer, preventing Eddie's hands from gaining any purchase on the weapon.

'Shhh,' he whispered to his dying friend as he rocked him, slowly, back, and forth. 'Shhh, now. You'll be with your Faye soon enough.'

Eddie's struggles slowed; all the fight flowed out of his body, evacuating it alongside the copious amount of blood that was pooling on the floor around them. The stream of thick liquid that had been cascading from his wound slowed as a gurgle of blood bubbled from his mouth.

He was trying to say something.

The viscus liquid dripped down his chin, ruining the white collar of the shirt he was wearing.

'Come on now, Eddie. There's nothing more that needs to be said. You just need to relax and embrace what's happening.'

George was rocking and whispering to Eddie in soothing tones, as if he were a baby going to sleep rather than a former friend and colleague, dying at his hand.

Eddie kept reaching for the hilt of the knife in his stomach and George kept removing them.

He rolled his eyes, knowing that if the blade were to be removed from Eddie's stomach, the cleaning up duty would be doubly horrendous. He looked around him at the mess that Faye had made; that was already going to be a huge chore. He hated cleaning up, it always hurt his leg with all the squatting and scrubbing. He didn't think that he'd have the wherewithal for all the extra that Eddie would require. Not after the night that he seemed to be having.

Still with Eddie in his arms, he reached up towards a towel that was hanging out of the drawer above his head and wrapped it around the blade. He tugged on the wooden handle attempting to pull it out of Eddie's stomach, but it wouldn't budge. He was totally unprepared for the resistance that he was experiencing.

The blade refused to come out. Each time he pulled it, it caused Eddie to struggle a little more, and with each struggle came more of the disgusting, red bubbles popping out of his mouth.

Eventually, Eddie's struggles waned. The gurgles of blood from his mouth lessened, until, after what felt like an eternity, they stopped altogether.

Eddie died in George's arms on the cold tiles of his kitchen floor next to the already cooling corpse of his newly found, and newly reciprocated, love.

His wide, lifeless, yet accusing, eyes stared up at George, unwavering in their message. Dead eyes told no lies, *what a great line for a song,* George thought absently as he stared into the paling, waxy face beneath him.

'I know what you've done, George,' they said as they spoke to him in the language of the dead.

42.

BRIAN WAS LOST. Not physically lost, he knew where he was geographically; he had lived here for the whole of his twenty-eight years, so he really should know where he was. He was lost in his mind! That vital organ was somewhere else entirely, somewhere he always knew he would end up; he just didn't know when.

He had lived with his 'condition' for as long as he could remember; for maybe twenty of his twenty-eight years. He remembered being teased by the other kids at St. Monica's school, mainly because he wasn't very good at playing football. The ironic thing about that was he was an excellent football player when he wanted to be, he just didn't have any interest in the game. He had always loved music. This love had been nurtured by Canon McGuff, the priest who ran the school. He had provided extra lessons for Brian, but the lessons had been attended only by other girls, and here he had found himself rather comfortable.

He had convinced himself at an early age that he was the reason his father had run off and joined the Merchant Navy all those years before, abandoning him and his mother to their own fates.

As he grew older, he'd noticed that there was something different about him; something that had separated him from the other boys, but paradoxically, made him long to be nearer the other boys too.

He had tried his best to hide it all his life. While others in his class were out running feral in the streets of Bootle, collecting shrapnel, discovering girls, drinking, he'd spent many a teenage night at home, just him and his mother, listening to and playing music or reading, sometimes both at the same time. His personal favourite had been by Oscar Wilde. He also loved the more romantic classics, and he secretly longed for a rugged Heathcliff to rush into his house, in Bootle, and sweep him off his feet.

He suspected that his mother did too.

The fear of reprisals from the other boys and, as he became a man, the fear of the law, had made him keep his feelings hidden deep inside. He could no more help the way he was than he could help the musician inside him from coming forth.

It was a part of him, and he hated it.

George had been the first, real friend he'd been able to make since he was a boy. The first time they played together in the band they had clicked. He had noticed the talent this flawed human being had from the first moment and he had always assumed that George either knew about his condition and was not bothered by it or was blissfully unaware of it.

He had always hoped the former.

Platonic friends of course.

He held no illusions that George was *his way inclined* and, to be honest, George would not have been his type. This was nothing to do with his physical defect or his appearance, but more to do with his mental state. Brian had always known that George operated on another level. He had thought, at least up until now, that there was a tight bond between the two of them. Like they were misfits, outcasts, teaming up against the big, cruel world around them.

It was a romanticised daydream and he knew it; somewhere deep down inside of him, he had always known it. Recent activity had shown George for who, and what, he really was and had proved Brian wrong once again. George, despite their four-year friendship, was no different from any of the others. He was a queer basher like all the rest.

Now here he was, his pockets filled with cash that he had been putting aside for a rainy day, along with some that his poor old mother could ill afford to lose, heading towards Walton, on his way to pay a ransom that George was demanding of him. Then, along with his trusty old suitcase, he was going to board the overnight train to Betws-y-Coed. He'd stay with his aunt for a while before attempting to branch out on his own. He would do his best to forget all about Liverpool and the troublesome times he had been forced to endure here. He had always loved the city, it would always be his home, but with the likes of George Hogg, running freely, roughshod, over his life, he couldn't stay.

Just this one last errand and he would be free.

He was under no illusion that Wales would be any better than Liverpool. Betws-y-Coed was nothing more than a provincial mining town, but it would be a fresh start; a chance to be who he was, with no suspicious eyes watching him, judging him. Plus, he liked the idea of all those rugged choir singers. In his heart, he was still hopeful of finding someone as sympathetic to his condition as he would be to theirs.

He stood in the chilly night outside George's door. He'd been here countless time before; all of them nicer occasions than what he was here for tonight. Many a night after a late gig, George had invited some of them back to this house for late drinking sessions with him and Tex. Of course, that was back when Tex had been able to function properly. *Better times all round*, he thought with a wry smile.

He paused before knocking on the door, unsure if he really wanted to do this or if he wanted to turn and run. The money in his pocket would go a long way towards him starting that life in Wales, the life he was so desperate for. Then he thought about George and he thought about his mother. He knew where she lived. Was he so rotten that he would take his issues out on her after Brian left? He knew the answer to that one. So, hesitantly, he knocked on the door and waited.

There was no answer.

He held his ear to the wood. There was movement behind the door, tell-tale signs that someone was in. So, he knocked again.

'Hang on, be there in a minute,' George's breathless voice came floating out from behind the door. He sounded like he was either in pain or was struggling with something. Brian hoped that it was the former.

He shook his head. *What am I doing? I'm here like a good little boy, to give this low life… bully, who I thought was my friend, all my money so that he won't tell everyone my secret. And he's asking me to wait a minute before he even answers the door! Brian,* he scolded himself, *no wonder you're where you are today, you just let people walk all over you.*

He turned away from the door, looked out onto the row of terraced houses opposite, then into the fields behind them, towards freedom. *Come on Brian*, he thought. *Walk away. Take that money back to your mum's house and then jump on that train. You can do this; you can shake the dust of this city off your shoes. Who cares if anyone knows you're a fag? You're never going to see them again anyway! They'll never know where you are, so the law won't be able find you.*

He gritted his teeth and readied his escape. He took two steps towards the liberty and independence he craved; towards taking his life back and walking away. In his heart, he was taking one huge, giant leap of faith.

As he reached the gate at the end of the short path, he heard the deadbolt of the door behind him slide from the inside, just before the door swung open. A strong hand gripped him by the shoulder and roughly pulled him inside the house.

It wasn't a rugged Heathcliff sweeping him off his feet!

43.

BRIAN FOUND HIMSELF on his behind, on the floor in George's hallway. He had lost his balance when he was unceremoniously dragged inside. Confused, he turned around to confront his assailant. What he saw shocked him to his core and scared him more than he had ever been scared in his entire life.

Given the life he'd had, this was not inconsiderable.

George was standing in the doorway, looming over him. The clothing he was wearing was his normal fair: a white shirt with a yellow tie, a pair of everyday black trousers being held up by a pair of black braces over the shirt.

Tonight however, his normally impeccable appearance was much dishevelled, and his shirt was covered in a large crimson stain. It was deep, and Brian thought that there would be no way that the stain would wash out no matter how much lye he used. The trousers, by the looks of them, were covered in the same mess, although it was difficult to tell due to the darkness of the dye. It looked to Brian like he'd had a mishap with a bottle of red wine or the blood from a steak. That was until he looked closer and saw that the crimson stains extended up his arms, over his hands, and even into his hair.

His, normally flawless, slicked back hair was sticking up at almost every angle imaginable, and there was a wild look about his eyes and mouth. The stubble on his chin was also covered in the same red stain.

It was then that Brian realised that the stains and the mess were far too thick, and far too sticky, to be wine. His simple brain couldn't fathom what it could have been instead. It wasn't until he looked back up at the man's face that his wild eyes and disturbed hair brought it all into context. That, plus all the red stains that were up and down the walls behind him.

Brian realised that he couldn't be in Tex and George's house after all. No, he'd been pulled into some living nightmare, a hellhole, maybe even hell itself. He knew that it was blood spattered over the walls and there was far too much of it for it to be George's.

His heart sank as the peril of his situation dawned on him.

'George, what the...'

'Shush, Brian,' he hissed interrupting him. His wild eyes were flicking around the narrow hallway as he did, registering all the splashes of red against the beige paint on the bare walls. 'I've got a bit of a problem here and I need you to help me sort it out.'

Brian was horrified. As his gaze moved around the room, he took in the floor and the walls. There was more blood than he had first thought, a lot more. It was everywhere that he could see.

George was covered from head to toe in it, as were the walls, and the carpet beyond the hallway was ruined with it. He closed his eyes. *Why didn't I make that decision to walk away sooner? Even a few seconds earlier would have done it. I'd never have been hauled into this... hell!*

George then produced a large, wooden handled carving knife from behind his back and looked at Brian. There was a new level of craziness beaming from his eyes. Pointing the knife towards Brian, who was still sat on the floor, he leaned in and rotated it slowly before his face. Brian could see the stains on the metal of the blade and the gore that had amassed where the stained wooden handle met the cold steel.

He felt a weakness in his bladder, and he fought a courageous fight to keep it from opening up altogether.

'Now,' George whispered, 'I need you to help me with my little problem,' he whispered, gesturing into the house with the knife. 'And then you're going to hand over that five quid I asked you for. Then, you're going to disappear from Liverpool, Brian. You'll never come back and you'll never talk of this night again to anyone. If you do, I'll release your secret to the world. I'll say that you did all these horrific acts here tonight. People will believe that queers like you will do anything to keep their secrets safe. They'll believe that you did all sorts of vile, evil acts on the dead bodies. I'll tell them that you were making sacrifices to some kind of homosexual God or something. I'll make all kinds of rubbish up. People are rather gullible when it comes to a good, gruesome story. Finally, when you're languishing in Walton Prison, with all the other Nancy-boys, I'll take a little trip out to Bootle to see your mum. Oh, she'll be very happy to see me, one of her son's only friends in the whole wide world; one of the only people who knows that her dearest Brian isn't capable of anything like what they are saying he is.' He leaned in even closer, almost touching noses. Brian could see the blood and sweat beaded on his face and stubble. 'Then, my queer little friend, I'll kill her too. Slowly and painfully.'

Brian's was petrified. He knew that George wasn't lying. His logical brain kept returning to one word that it had picked up from the diatribe of the madman looming above him.

It was a plural word.

'Acts?' he asked, scared out of his wits.

George nodded and pulled away from him. He indicated with the knife for him to stand up. 'Follow me into the kitchen.'

It was not a request.

As George walked towards the kitchen, Brian looked at the front door; it was mere yards away. He would be faster than George, he was a cripple for God's sake! He could dart out the door and be away. But

213

something told him that the door would be locked, and he knew that, even if he did make it, he would still be trapped. Trapped at the mercy of this raving lunatic who he used to call a friend.

Slowly, he got up off the floor, trying his best not to touch any of the stains on the walls and the floors of this house of horrors. Not daring to take his eyes off the large steel blade that George was dangling behind his back. He followed his captor through the house into the kitchen. As they passed through the living room, he noticed a bloody track over the carpet, as if a dead animal had been dragged through the room. Brian knew that George was no hunter and big game animals were hard to locate in the wilds of Walton.

He entire body was shaking!

When they reached the kitchen, there was nothing in the world that could have prepared him for what was there waiting for him to discover.

The bodies of Faye and Eddie were lying on the floor. The tracks of blood that he had followed through the living room, led him to this grisly discovery.

The sight of two of his closest friends lying motionless and pale on the cold, tiled floor shocked him and chilled him. George had done half a job of trying to cover them up with white bed sheets, but their wounds must have still been wet and the sheets had soaked up quite a bit of the blood that had flowed from them, turning them into two-tone death shrouds.

Two pairs of lifeless eyes stared accusingly at him where the sheets had fallen away from their faces. 'Why didn't you stop him?' they asked. 'Why didn't you help us?'

Brian wanted to close his own eyes, but the horror of the situation had rendered him unable to turn away. They remained wide open! His head was reeling at the impossibility of the situation, and he felt like he was about to faint. His face turned towards George, just in time for him to administer a slap; a hard one.

Feeling like he had been dowsed with freezing water, the force of the blow caused him to fall back into one of the cupboard doors. The shock and the sting sent the blood filtering back into his face, snapping him out of his terrible thoughts, and back into the terrible reality.

He didn't know which one was worse.

'What? What?' he stuttered. He was trying to finish his sentence, but his voice didn't want to join in the game, it seeped out of his mouth in a strange, high-pitched whine.

'It was an accident,' George replied regarding his handiwork lying on the floor while he absently wiped the knife on a tea towel that looked like it had already been used.

'Both of them?' Brian gasped while shaking his head. 'You've got to go to the police, George, you have to. You've... you've killed them.' The last words made him balk and he could feel the saliva building up in his mouth, the precursor to vomit.

'Brian, I swear, if you faint on me or vomit, I'll kill you right now,' he flashed the knife towards him for emphasis. 'I'll stick you so hard with this knife you won't even know you're dead.'

He didn't need the threat; he already knew what George was capable of. His small, innocent brain was trying desperately to get a handle on everything that was happening around him. Every time he thought about it, he just couldn't comprehend the fact that two of his best friends were dead at the hands of another of his best friends. 'George, how do you think this ends? How do you think you're going to get away with this? These people are going to be missed; people are going to ask questions. Shit, George, we have a gig tonight! What are we going to do about that?'

George put the large knife down on the counter and bent over the body of Eddie. He examined it for a short while as if calculating his weight, before looking back up at Brian. 'Oh, you don't need to worry about the gig tonight, Brian. The majority of the band can't make it you see. Preoccupied. All you need to worry about right now is helping me get these bodies out of the kitchen and into the bath at the end there.' He indicated a small bathroom at the end of the kitchen, inside it stood a tin bath.

Brian was shaking his head in disbelief. 'And then what?'

'And then… I'll think of something,' he snapped in retort.

Brian took another step backwards.

George flashed him a smile. 'Don't worry, Brian, it'll be something that I'll do whilst you're on a train to who knows where, and no one even cares. Now help me with this or I swear to God I'll stick you with that.' He pointed at the knife on the worktop. Brian didn't need to look at it to know it was there. He decided that it would be best to just help George and at least get out of this situation with his life still intact.

'How do we do this then?' he asked as he looked down at his dead friends. Another gag rose from his stomach and there was a second or two where he thought the vomit was going to flow.

'How the hell do I know?' George snapped. 'I've only ever done this once before and there wasn't so much blood that time.' He looked closely at Brian's face. 'Do I have to tell you again about vomiting?'

Brian glanced over at his former friend and realised that he had never even known the man. Not one little bit. George Hogg was a complete and utter stranger to him.

'You've done this before? When?'

George wasn't looking at him, he was bent over the body of Eddie and grabbing him by the arms, trying to get the best angle for pulling the dead weight along the tiles. 'It was ages ago, during the war. Now come on, help me with this, will you?'

Brian steeled himself. He rubbed his sweaty hands on his trousers before bending to grab Faye's hands. He faltered. The thought of touching her cold, lifeless digits was abhorrent, but he knew that he was going to have to. He had to appease George. He closed his eyes and gripped Faye's dead hands. They were freezing cold already, and stiff. The nausea he felt at the feel of the dead skin crept though his body once again. *I'm going to vomit at some point,* he thought grimly, *it's inevitable, and then he's going to kill me with that knife. I'm going to die with vomit down my shirt.* He held his breath before tightening his grip on Faye's hands. He wasn't OK with the creepy feeling of unresponsive limbs. It was a strange phenomenon for him to be gripping a person's hand and not have them grip back.

Despite this, they managed to drag both the bodies out of the kitchen and into the small bathroom. It was harder work than either of them had imagined and they had both built up a sweat when it was done; damp and covered in blood.

As they heaved the stiffening body of Eddie into the bath, George was panting. It had been a long and arduous day, and this had been the cherry on the cake. He wiped his mouth with the back of his hand, leaving another, fresher, bloody swathe in its wake. He looked at Brian. His face looked a lot older than his twenty-eight years. 'Do you want a drink?'

All Brian could do was stare at him. He was looked at him as if it was the first time he had ever seen the man in his life, like he was a stranger on a train who he knew nothing about. He realised that George was ugly. Not necessarily physically ugly, it was nothing to do with his appearance, it was a deeper, more spiritual type of ugly.

He shook his head; he couldn't believe what this stranger was asking him. 'A drink? You're offering me a drink? After what you've just made me do, you offer me a drink?'

George was taken aback. He had never seen Brian angry before, had never heard him shout; it seemed funny somehow.

'I hope you burn in Hell for this. I came here tonight to pay you your dirty blackmail money, to pay off my debt, and to let you know that I'm leaving.' He reached a bloodied hand into the front pocket of his trousers and pulled out a train ticket. He threw it on the table in front of George, who looked at it. 'All I wanted to do was leave, to get away from here, away from you, but now you've embroiled me in this seedy affair.'

The tears that had been threatening while moving his friends' corpses finally fulfilled their threat.

'They were your FRIENDS, George! Does that not mean anything to you?'

George looked at him and then switched his gaze towards the bath. It was a cold stare.

'What about me, George? Your oldest friend. You sold me out for what? Five quid? You're sad and you're deranged. You deserve to rot in this…' he paused, indicating the mess that was the kitchen, '…this hell of your own creation. But you won't drag me down with you…' he was still crying. Real tears were streaming down his face. 'You won't implicate me in this degradation. I won't allow it.'

With his head held low, he walked off in the direction of the front door, through the kitchen, careful not to slip on the bloody tiles beneath him.

'Brian.' George called after him, his voice sounded filled with feeling, almost tender.

He stopped and turned back into the kitchen. There was a hopeful look on his face. *Maybe he's changed his mind. Maybe he will go to the police after all*, he thought.

'What?'

The two men regarded each other; a wordless, silent moment passed between them.

'You didn't leave the money,' he said coldly, stuffing his bloodied hands into his pockets.

This simple statement sent a shiver ripping through him; he couldn't believe what he was hearing. He shook his head, slowly regarding the monster before him. 'You are a piece of work,' he hissed, his face looking more disgusted in the man than the deeds he had performed.

With a curled lip, he pulled out a roll of bank notes.

He threw the roll on the table; the blood on his hands rubbed off, onto the money. 'There you go, George,' he said looking at the red stains on the banknotes. 'That's a rather fitting endorsement - it's your blood money. I hope you will be very happy together.'

George looked at the notes and the pile of change on the counter and then back to Brian.

He was making his way out of the kitchen, out of Liverpool, but mostly out of this parasite's life, for good.

'Brian,' George's voice made him stop again. 'There's just one more thing I need you to do, mate.'

Brian felt his heart sink deep into his stomach. He could see the front door; his exit, his salvation was so close. This monster calling him 'mate' had made him feel physically sick. He stopped and looked up to the ceiling, half distressed and half angry. 'What now? Don't you think you've had enough from me for one day?'

'It's only a little thing. But, I'm going to need you to go out through the back door. You're covered in blood mate. I can't have any of the neighbours seeing you leave looking like that.'

Brian turned to face him; his eyes were dark with disbelief. 'Are you serious?'

'Deadly.'

The word had its own double meaning. Coming from this man right now, in this situation, Brian could feel the level of threat, but as George was smiling as he said it, he could also see the dark, sick humour in the small pun. 'It's the very last thing that you can do for me and you'll never see me again. You'll be free of me, and free to live the rest of your life in whatever way you want. I've seen the way Carl looks at you. I think you and him might even have a future together.'

At the mention of Carl's name, Brian's eyes looked wistful for a split second, before life crashed right back around him, with a bloody slap. He began to shake his head. 'I'm not having this conversation with you. In an hour, I'll be on my way out of this city and I'll never be coming back. I've seen the dark side of this business, and it looks exactly like you.'

George exhaled slowly. 'Listen, please, I know I don't deserve it, but just do this one thing for me, go out the back way and through the yard. No one will see you, and it'll give me time to think this whole thing through.'

Eyeing George with mistrust, Brian slipped his coat back on, covering most of the bloodstains on his shirt and trousers. He brushed passed his ex-friend standing in the doorway and went through into the kitchen and stormed towards the back door at the end of the bathroom.

As he entered the small room, he couldn't help but glance into the tub where the gruesome sight of the lifeless bodies of two of his closest friends in the entire world greeted him. Their dead eyes staring into whatever abyss came after this world, and their once lively faces, now expressionless and cold. Suppressing the urge to shout and rave and cry, and still holding in that vomit - he knew it would come sooner or later - he crossed himself as he passed. He eventually closed his eyes as the awful image before him became too much for him to bear.

He tried his best to blank the scene out of his mind, he thought that if he could forget about it, he could live his nice new life in Wales, in blissful ignorance, believing that this terrible situation never happened. He could tell himself that Faye and Eddie had made it out of the clutches of The Rialto, out of the shadow of George and everything he stood for; he could pretend that they were living happy, contented lives somewhere else, maybe in the club scene of London.

Lost in his own daydream with a small, sad smile etched on his lips, he reached for the latch of the back door. He was moments away from a new life himself, one that he deserved.

He never heard George sneak up behind him. In truth, he never even felt the tip of the blade as the kitchen knife slipped, almost effortlessly, into his back. All that he felt was an odd feeling of deflation, like a balloon being let down slowly.

The world was now moving in slow motion. He forced his lethargic body to turn.

George was standing behind him.

This simple act of moving was a whole lot more complicated than it should have been. His body screamed, not in pain so much but in disobedience, it was like it didn't want to move, or it couldn't.

As George was the smaller man, he was looking up at Brian. His face looked sorrowful somehow, as if he was sorry for something that he'd done - something that he didn't want to do but, ultimately, felt like he HAD to.

Brian smiled at him. He didn't know why he was smiling, but he felt sad and different somehow. He wrapped his arms around George as if to hug him, to embrace him, to let him know that everything would be all right. He wanted to tell George not to look so glum, things would be better in the morning; things were always better in the morning.

Brian's world then began to take on a different look. There was a hue to the room that he was sure hadn't been there before. He couldn't tell if it was lighter or darker exactly, he just knew that it was…different. He fancied that he could hear the whistle of a steam train somewhere in the distance. This might not have been too far of a fancy as the train lines were less than a mile from where they were currently situated.

Suddenly, a ferociously pain ripped through the middle of his back; it felt like he was being torn apart from within. It brought the world back into sharp focus.

George wasn't smiling at him like he had thought; instead there was a vicious snarl on his face. His bloodied upper lip was curling like

Tex's used to when he was singing a ballad. His eyes weren't sad; they were filled with malice and hate, they were bright and alert, and dangerous.

The whistle of the steam train was back, only this time it wasn't in the distance. This time it sounded up close and personal, and nothing like a whistle at all.

It sounded more like a scream.

A scream that was coming from him.

As the sharp pain began to subside, he felt his legs buckle underneath him and he fell forwards towards George. The pain came back again, then again and again, each wave more ferocious than the last.

Brian's eyes began to dim, and he could no longer see George's face in any clarity. His features, and the details of the room around him, began to darken; there was no mistaking it this time.

He felt George's hands on his chest, supporting him, stopping him from falling.

He looked down and saw that they weren't supporting him at all, they were pushing him; not viciously, just lightly. Something behind him caused Brian to lose his balance.

Another excruciating pain in his back screamed as he felt something long and thin slide out of him. Brian flailed his arms as he attempted to stem his fall but there was no purchase behind him, and his useless legs finally gave way.

This time George let him fall.

He landed on something that was both hard and soft, and wet and sticky. Due to the agony in his back, he was glad that he hadn't landed on the floor, *I might never have got up again,* he thought with a lucidity that he would never have again. He moved his arms with a degree of difficulty and felt around him.

It took a small while to register where he was. His eyesight had dimmed considerably, and his body was feeling cold and numb. After a few moments of disorientation, he succumbed to a brand-new experience, terror!

Slowly, he turned his head. He didn't want to see what he was lying on, but he felt like he had to, he needed to know for the sake of his own sanity. His eyes were wide; the pupils fully dilated, allowing as much light into his receptors as was possible. Although the room had been adequately illuminated a short while ago, everything was now dark and grainy, like a poor-quality photograph, or a news real on the cinema.

The very last thing he saw before full darkness enveloped him, before finally taking him away from Liverpool, and this sad life, forever, was the wide, vacant, dead eyes of his two closest friends.

Faye and Eddie.

He tried his best to scream but there was no sound to be made. The abundance of air that he had used to full extent to make sweet music and fantastic riffs from his trombone, and a saxophone too if he put his mind to it, was gone forever.

Brian's life force seeped from his dying body into a cold tin bath, accompanied by the cadavers of two of his dearest friends.

44.

GEORGE'S FACE STRAINED and his back cracked as he shifted Brian's body around in the bath, creating enough space to accommodate the three bodies.

'How the hell did tonight escalate so quickly?' He wiped at his head while blowing an exhausted raspberry, leaving a fresher crimson swipe over his forehead than the one that was already there. He looked down at himself and marvelled at his shirt, which was now completely void of the white that it had been this morning when he put it on. It was one huge, dark, drying stain.

A bloody cocktail if ever there was one.

Once he was satisfied with the position of the three corpses, he looked at the clock that was hanging on the kitchen wall. It was nearly seven o'clock, which meant that Red would be here in less than an hour for his money. He made his way into the kitchen and grabbed at the bloodied notes, lying in a roll on the tabletop, and counted them.

There was five pounds. He added that to the seven that Faye had brought in earlier, making twelve. He knew that Tex had at least another three lying about the house, making fifteen. It was not even nearly enough to pay Red off. He cursed himself for taking the taxi ride earlier, that had cost nearly ten bob. He reached into his pockets and searched around; he knew he had at least another few bob in there; that would leave him just shy of sixteen. It was still a far cry from the twenty-five he owed Red.

That would not go down well at all.

He sat in the chair in the living room; no longer caring about getting any bloodstains on it, his mind was too busy thinking about the nine pounds he needed.

He thought about the money that he would be gleaning from the knick-knacks out of Marnie's house.

He'd been promised thirty pounds in total for the things he could remember while talking to the dealer, and who knew how much else for all the rest of the stuff. *Including that gold watch,* he thought, mentally rubbing his hands together. The problem was that he wouldn't be able to get at any of it until late tonight, at the very earliest, but more likely tomorrow morning. Red would not take another delay in payment, not even a few hours; he'd made that abundantly clear today in his office.

George took a moment to think about his situation. *Shit, was that only today?* he questioned himself, marvelling at how much had happened between then and now.

He looked back into the grisly bathroom, at the three bodies in the bath, when an idea occurred to him.

As he got up from his chair, his back and legs screamed at him to stay put, but he had to ignore them for now, there was far too much to do. *When this is all over, I'll have myself a nice relaxing bath, that will sooth all those aches away,* he thought. He then looked back into the bath and erased that thought. He made a mental note, never to have a bath again.

He made his way into the bathroom, not taking his eyes from the cadavers. Even though he knew they were dead, he still half expected them to jump up at him, trying to gain revenge from beyond the grave for taking them too soon.

A shiver ran through him as he thought about touching them again. He bent over the bath, poising his hands over the bodies, flexing his fingers. He didn't know where to start.

He began with Brian, as he was on the top, his assumption being that by the time he got down to Faye, he would have desensitised himself to the whole experience.

He grabbed his ex-friend and turned him over, reeling in revulsion at how fast his skin had turned cold, clammy and waxy.

It reminded him of cheese.

He made another mental note, never to eat cheese again.

He began to rummage through Brian's trousers, searching for a wallet or any small change he might have in his pockets. There was a few coins and two notes. Dropping them onto the floor, he turned his face away and held his breath as he reached in again to get at the other pocket. He then moved onto Eddie.

Finally, he fished out Faye's purse.

Between all three of them, he managed to find a little over three pounds.

That made just shy of eighteen pounds out of the twenty-five owed. It was a little better, but it still wasn't to give to Red when he turned up.

He sat back in his chair and lit a cigarette; a sardonic smile broke on his face as he puffed at it. 'Maybe I can lure him into the bath,' he spoke, a small giggle escaped him. 'Well, maybe not, not with that big goon Ron waiting in the car outside, and maybe Jules too. The bath's not big enough to fit them all in.'

He finished his cigarette and made his way upstairs to the bedroom, stripping off his spoiled and sticky shirt and trousers on the way.

45.

RED WAS OUTSIDE Ron's house. He was sat in the driver's side of his car and was beeping the horn repeatedly. His face was like thunder. A few of the neighbours twitched their chintz curtains in an attempt to see what all the racket was about. When they saw Red's car and realised who was glaring at them from inside, they hurriedly closed their curtains and found something, anything, else to do. All of them remembering who it was that their neighbour worked for.

He pumped the horn a few more times but still no one came out of the house. Angrier than ever, he got out of the car slamming the door behind him before storming over and hammering on the door.

'RON! Are you in there?' he shouted, the rage building in him with every bang.

There was still no answer.

'Listen, I don't care if you're on your fucking death bed, get this door open now.'

A noise came from the other side, a kind of shuffling. The latch was unlocked on the inside and the wooden door creaked open.

A woman in her mid-seventies half-opened the door and slipped her head around the crack. Her hair was tied up in a scarf and she was wearing a housecoat with slippers, the half-smoked butt of a cigarette was burning out of the corner of her mouth.

'Oh, Mrs Quinn,' Red began, his demeanour changing almost instantly to one of respect. 'I'm so sorry to disturb you, but I need to see Ron. Is he in?'

The older woman looked Red up and down as if judging him. She took another drag on her cigarette and blew it out slowly. 'Yes, he is, he's in his room upstairs.' She gestured inside before shaking her head and turning away, back inside the house. 'I don't think he'll be going anywhere with you tonight though. Go on up if you want.'

'Thanks, Mrs Quinn, I do apologise for my language out there by the way.'

'Oh, don't you worry yourself about it son, my language is fucking atrocious at the best of times...' She laughed to herself as she shuffled back inside, towards the kitchen. 'Do you want a brew, Gerald?'

He watched her enter the kitchen before he shouted back to her. 'No, thank you, Mrs Q. I'll just go and see him for a moment and then I think I'll be off.'

'OK son, whatever suits you best.'

Smiling, Red made his way upstairs towards Ron's bedroom. The smell from inside hit him well before his eyes adjusted to the gloom enough to see the large lump under the covers on the bed. He covered his nose and mouth with a black leather-gloved hand and proceeded inside. 'Jesus, Ron,' he half-whispered, half-balked. 'Is that you?'

He was replied with a grunt.

'What the hell's the matter?' he asked, trying to hold in his gag. The stink was almost physical. It was a mix of sweat, farts and a sweet sickness.

Ron grunted again and turned his sweaty head around on the filthy, grime-stained pillow. He looked at Red with pink, rheumy eyes, only vaguely recognising his boss. The pale moistness of his skin spoke volumes to Red; Ron did have the flu and a bad case of it too by the looks of things. He'd seen the flu up close; it wasn't anything like a heavy cold. He'd seen it beat big, strong men down to almost nothing. He'd even seen it kill.

He backed out of the room with his hand still over his face. He really didn't want to be anywhere near Ron in this condition or to even breathe any of the vile air surrounding him. The last thing a man with his responsibilities needed right now was a bout of the flu.

'Right, you stay there in bed, mate. We don't want you to get any sicker, do we? Take a few days off and get yourself better and I'll see you next week, yeah?'

Ron grunted again and shuffled about beneath the covers. Red could hear a disgusting scratching noise coming from somewhere underneath, he didn't even want to think about what might be happening in there.

He beat a swift retreat and made his way downstairs towards the hallway. Mrs Quinn was sat at a table in the kitchen, smoking another cigarette and drinking a cup of tea. 'Mrs Q, thanks for letting me in. I've got to go now. I'm going to leave Ron alone; bed is the best place for him if you ask me. See you soon.'

'O fucking K' she shouted from the kitchen in reply, raising her cup and cackling to herself as she did.

Red got out of that house as quickly as he could. He shivered as he got into his car before starting it up. 'Looks like I'll have to do this on my own tonight then.'

He checked his pocket and brought out a small black device. He looked at it lovingly in his gloved hand before pressing a silver button on the side. With a strange, spring-like sound, a cold, sharp, metal blade shot out of the side of it, turning it into a weapon. He smiled, put the blade back inside the handle, and started the car up. As he checked his mirrors, he felt a small stirring in his nose. He bit off his glove and put his bare hand against his brow, it felt a little warm.

Then he sneezed.

'Aw shit,' he muttered before pulling off into the road and away towards Walton, sneezing again as he did.

46.

CARL WAS SAT on a bench in Derby Park next to the bandstand. The exact same bandstand where, all those years ago, George had begun his downward spiral into becoming a murderer, and the same one that he himself had performed on a few times as a soldier in the military band.

Tonight, brought back none of the great memories it should have though, because right now, he was convinced that something had happened to his little sister, something sinister. He had more than an inkling that George was at the centre of it.

His thoughts slid back towards all the trouble that they had had in America and how he'd had to step in and sort it out for her; taking the blame, and therefore all the consequences, for that trouble. He knew only too well that if she had fallen under the spell of someone as unsavoury as George Hogg then there was a chance of history repeating itself, and that was the last thing anyone needed.

From his vantage point, he could just make out his sister's house through the bushes and the trees. The day had begun to darken into night and even though lights had begun to appear in the surrounding houses, Marnie's remained completely dark. People had been back and forth, up and down, the busy road all day too but not one person had entered or left her house. It was almost as if it was not there or as if it was the notorious haunted house on the street that people scurried past, without so much as a second glance. *How can everyone else ignore that house when it's the epicentre of my world right now?* he thought. It didn't take much for his brain to become unhinged and that was exactly what was happening right now.

47.

RED HAD TO break a few of the speed limits making his way along the deserted roads towards George's house; as he prided himself on prompt timekeeping. He pulled into the street alongside the house, and left the engine running and the headlights on. He wanted George to know that he was here. His plan was to sit in the car for a short while before he knocked. It added to the allure of his business and his stature. It gave his clients time to adjust to the idea that he was here to talk business and he would tolerate no messing about.

After about five minutes, he got out of the car and made his way to the front door. As he stood, admiring the brass knocker, he shrugged his shoulders, cricked his neck and cleared his throat, all of it helping him slip into the hard-case character that he portrayed so well.

George answered the door after one knock, just like Red knew he would, and just as he liked it. He looked somehow fresh and the smell of Lifebuoy soap coming from him was almost overwhelming. noticed that his hair was wet.

'Red! Right on time as per usual. Come on in will you.' George greeted him with a thoroughly unconvincing smile.

Red didn't say anything, but he tilted his eyes suspiciously. He knew that George didn't want him here and he had an inkling that he wouldn't have the money that he was here to collect. So, deciding that he needed to keep his wits about him, he kept his eyes on his host as he stepped around him and inside the house.

George poked his head out of the door and looked up the street towards Red's waiting car. 'Can I get you anything?' he shouted back inside. To his surprise, he noted that the waiting car was empty; there was no Ron the bouncer sat in the driver's seat or no Jules in the back. It meant that Red was here alone. George's heartbeat sped up in his chest. Maybe, just maybe, the small joke he made to himself earlier might could become a reality. He turned his head to look up the other end of the street, making sure that Red hadn't dotted any other of his bouncers anywhere else. Happily, convinced that his guest had turned up alone, he re-entered the house, closing the door behind him.

'Just my twenty-five pounds, George. That's the one and only thing you can get me tonight.'

'Are you sure, Red? Tex has got a lovely bottle of twelve-year-old single malt open in the kitchen.' He looked at the bottle on the floor next to the bin, Faye's hair and dried gore was still all over it. 'It's bloody good,' he stifled a small laugh at his own joke before entering the front room where his visitor was waiting. 'We could have a glass or two while we conduct our business.'

Red raised his eyebrows and nodded a little. 'Well, why not? There's no reason to not be pleasant while we do this, eh?'

George winked at him. 'Be right back.'

He headed into the kitchen, leaving Red alone in the parlour. As he looked around the room, he noted with a wry smile that it was the room in the house reserved for 'special' visitors. This made him happy, it made him realise that George really did know his station in life.

His host returned a few minutes later with two large glasses of whisky. He handed one over to Red, who accepted it without question, and sat down on the comfortable couch, uninvited. 'So, George, there's a little thing about my twenty-five pounds,' he said giving his drink a long sniff before nodding his head approvingly. He took a small sip, rolling it around his tongue, savouring the taste.

George watched intently as Red swallowed the amber liquid, grimacing slightly as the heat hit his stomach. He smiled. The smile was filled with dark malevolence, irony and a touch of humour.

'Oh yeah, the twenty-five pounds.' He reached into his trouser pockets and pulled out a large roll of notes, along with some small change. 'Look, I know you said you needed it all tonight, but I could only manage to get nineteen together today. I can have the rest of it to you tomorrow. I'm good for it, you know that.'

Red's excitement went up another level, and he revelled in the butterflies that were now fluttering around his stomach. He exhaled menacingly, curling his lip over his teeth. His dark, beady eyes piercing into George's head. He leaned forwards, placing his empty glass on the table, picked the money up from where it had been placed and began to count.

George was licking his lips watching the thin, dangerous man count his money. His eyes kept flicking towards the empty glass next to him.

Red looked at him with real disdain. 'What is this?' he asked in a quiet voice, indicating the money in his hands. George shook his head and shrugged his shoulders.

'What am I going to do with nineteen pounds? It's six pounds less than you owe me; six pounds less than you promised me.'

George was looking at him; he was still licking his lips and flicking his eyes towards the empty glass. 'Can, can I get you another drink?' he stuttered.

'No, you can't get me another drink, George.' Red stood up from the chair; even though he was small, he still struck an imposing figure. 'Is this what you think of me? Is it? Do you think that I'm some sort of cheap spiv who'll take nineteen pounds today when I really wanted twenty-five? Are you calling me a joke, George?'

George backed away, sensing the danger he was in. 'Red, I never…'

'No, you never, did you, George? Not if you thought I'd come all the way here for six pounds less than I wanted.'

'I can get it to you tomorrow!' George was pleading now, and his eyes flicked again towards the empty whisky glass on the table.

The anger was ingrained in Red now. He hated being played and this loathsome little man was attempting to do just that. He began to finger the key on the chain around his neck - it calmed him, and as he knew he needed all the control he could muster when dealing with this man, it could only be a good thing. He shook his head as he advanced. 'No, no you can't, George. That ship has sailed.' He removed his coat and began to roll up his shirtsleeves; all the while not taking his eyes off the shrinking cripple before him. He loved being in control of a situation and it had been some time since he, personally, had administered a beating. He was now looking forward to getting his knuckles dirty. 'I gave you an opportunity, but it looks like you've abused my generosity.'

George backed up even further, out of the parlour and into the kitchen. He knew that he shouldn't show Red any fear but that was another ship that had sailed.

It seemed a lot of ships had sailed today, for a great many people.

'What opportunity, Red? You brought the payment date forward for no reason other than just because you could. I think nineteen pounds is a good return, considering.'

Red feigned light-hearted surprise and flashed an amused grin George's way. 'Oh, do you now? All things considered hey?' His face changed. It was like watching a shadow crawl over the sun; everything gradually got darker. 'You think that it's good trying to rip me off do you? Do you think this is a game?' His mask had completed its slip and the malice emanating from him came on in the wink of an eye. His eyes were wide and wild, and he gritted his teeth. 'Let me tell you what happened to the last person who tried to rip me off, George,' he hissed before producing the flick-knife that he always kept in the back pocket of his trousers, for emergencies, just like this one.

The small black handle was carved and polished, but George fancied that it was well used.

'I used this to cut him before beating him to within an inch of his life.' He flicked the knife and George flinched, as the blade appeared out of nowhere. 'I cut him to ribbons before bashing his fucking teeth in, then I broke his knees and removed one of his thumbs.' Red was still talking in a quiet, calm manner that was terrifying George beyond all his expectations. 'I didn't kill him, no… I wanted him to live, I wanted him to remember the day he thought it would be a good idea to cross Red. I wanted everyone who knew him to know what happens if you cross Red. He's not a pretty sight these days, George, I can tell you. Do you want to know what the funny thing about it is? He only owed me five quid. Can you imagine what I would have done to him for six? I don't need to use you as an example, George! I already have one.'

In a flash, he lunged with the knife held high, ready to swoop it across George's face.

George cowered into the corner of the kitchen cupboards, holding his hand up to protect his face from the cutting that was forthcoming.

At the exact moment that Red started to bring the knife down towards George's face, a funny, numbing sensation began in his nose. It culminated in a mammoth sneeze. He fell forwards into his lunge and stumbled against the counter above where George was cowering. He put his hand, the one holding the knife, onto the wall to steady himself, and raised the other one up to rub his eyes.

In the seconds that Gorge had, before Red could regain his concentration, he ducked and darted out from underneath him. Once free of the madman's clutches, he snatched the wooden handled carving knife from the kitchen unit where he had placed it earlier, in the event that he might need it, and turned, lunging himself as he did. He buried the blade deep into the other man's lower back.

Red raised his head and bellowed in pain and rage. His face was one of utter disbelief. The hand holding the flick knife dropped and he grasped at his back. The small weapon clattered onto the floor.

He turned towards George, who was directly behind him, and looked at him with a sense of disbelief etched all over his face. Red sneezed again. As he did, blood sprayed from his mouth and nose, splashing over George's face, ruining another white shirt.

He was too stunned by his own actions to even notice.

The stricken gangster fell to his knees. His eyes not once leaving George's as he fell. He couldn't believe that he had been outfoxed. He, the notorious Red, had been bested by George Hogg. *He's a fucking cripple,* he thought as he fell forward onto his hands and knees. Blood was pouring from his mouth as he tried to reach for the knife sticking out of the small of his back.

'You… you're a fucking… dead man. You won't get away… with… this!' he spluttered as thick, almost black, blood dripped from his mouth.

George bent down and watched as Red bled out. He leaned his face into the dying gangster's and whispered. 'I think you've got that one wrong, Gerald! It seems like you're the dead man here.' He smiled a playful little smile and theatrically looked all around him. 'And it looks like I've already gotten away with it.' He was laughing as Red's blood-shot eyes turned to regard him. George fancied that he could see the familiar rage in them but also something new, something that looked like fear. 'I don't think you're going to be collecting that twenty-five quid, Red. You see, I don't care that I'm six pounds short because, as it turns out, I don't need it anymore. I'm going to take this nineteen pounds and keep it. Who would have thought that you're the chump now, and that you're about to die here on my floor?' He leaned in even closer and grabbed Red's face, forcing him to turn around and look at him. 'And it was me who killed you,' he spat into the, soon to be deceased, gangster's face.

George let go of him and watched as Red lay dying on the floor of his kitchen.

Each time, it seemed, was a little easier than the last.

He was alarmed and shocked that even though he'd killed four people in just over two hours, he had become almost desensitised to the experience already, and was now concentrating on the practical issue of how he was going to get Red's body into the, already full, bath.

Just as the final breath gurgled out of Red's mouth in a pink froth, another good idea blossomed in George's head. As he had done earlier with Eddie, but with a whole lot more confidence, he fished around in Red's trouser pockets until he found what he wanted.

The keys to the car out front.

48.

CARL WAS AT his wits end. He was attempting to light another cigarette; his fifteenth within the last few hours while sitting on the bench in the park, but the combination of the icy wind and the adrenaline-fuelled shaking of his hands, was causing him a lot more difficult than he'd thought.

He couldn't believe that he was going through all this again. *After everything that had happened in America, she goes and gets herself mixed up in another bad situation. Why is she attracted to the wrong type? Every time, the wrong type!*

He cast another wary eye over the house; he guessed that he had cast the same furtive glance at that house at least a thousand times that evening alone. Finally, the cigarette caught, and he took a deep, satisfying drag on it.

After a couple more, he stood, wrapping his jacket around himself against the chill of the twilight and dropped the cigarette on the floor, crushing it with his shoe. He began to make his way down the road, towards the public telephone box he knew was on the corner.

His destination took him past Marnie's house and he couldn't resist giving it another look over. His eyes scanning for signs, or anything, to indicate that there was life inside those walls.

There was nothing, not even a flicker of curtains or the flash of a light.

He made it to the corner where the telephone box was. There was already quite a queue formed outside it, the people of Bootle waiting patiently for their turn. With a sinking heart, Carl counted six people shuffling about in the cold of the early evening.

He toyed with the idea of walking down to Marsh Lane police station or maybe even actively seeking a policeman on the street along the way. He wondered what he would say to them. If he told them he was worried that his sister was missing or that something had happened to her. They would end up asking him questions, they would want to know *his* name and where *he* lived. Then, when they began to make their own inquiries, they would end up picking up some information about him that could cause some upset, maybe even culminating in his own arrest. No, the policeman route couldn't be done. He'd have to do this on his own.

He decided that it would be best to just wait patiently in the line with all the others.

49.

GEORGE HAD DRIVEN a car several times before tonight's adventure. It had been during the war when he was an ARP warden and Bootle had been seriously short of drivers. The government had decided to give people crash courses on how to handle motorcars. He smiled a little to himself at how apt that description had been - they had been more crash than course.

It had been a while, but he figured that it must be like riding a bike, once you knew how, you didn't forget.

He was right; he hadn't forgotten how to do it and he navigated the gears like he'd been driving for years. It was one of the few scenarios where his clubfoot gave him a distinct advantage as it allowed him to negotiate the double clutch with relative ease.

He manoeuvred the car into the tight alleyway around the back of his house and parked up adjacent to the gate of his yard. He turned off the headlights as he didn't want to attract any attention from his very nosy neighbours. The alleyway was dark, and he struggled when getting out to open the hatch on the large car boot. He had a feel about inside and was satisfied that the space the boot offered would be quite satisfactory for the job at hand.

Using spare bedsheets from the linen cupboard, George proceeded to drag the heavy bodies out of the bath and wrap them in the sheets, one by one. Over the next hour and a half, he managed to single headedly drag the four stiffening bodies from the bath at the end of the kitchen, through the small yard and, somehow, struggle them into the back of Red's car. Red and Faye were the smallest and therefore the easiest, but it was still demanding work and he had to stop several times to get his breath and ponder how a dead body could be so heavy?

With each body in the boot, George could feel another, small, part of his soul die, and another muscle in his back, that he had been previously unaware of, scream in protest of the unexpected manual labour. It was disgusting work. He had been completely unprepared for the natural waste a cadaver would excrete when disturbed and more than once he had had to stop to baulk at the smells coming from each of them. Eventually, when they were all in the car, he covered them with a blanket, closed the rear door and went back inside the house to commence the one job he was dreading the most - cleaning the remaining blood of his friends and colleagues.

The place was like an abattoir.

There was still blood from Faye and Eddie visible on the floor, which had been added to by the moving of Brian's and Red's bodies. He had already cleaned up the lion's share of the spillages, but he wanted to leave absolutely no trace of the struggles that had occurred in the house. The last thing he needed was to explain everything that had happened to Tex. He hated the thought of what he might have to do to him if he came home and found the house like this, disturbing him in his work. *It might be a blessing to the old duffer,* he thought with absolutely no malice towards his old pal and landlord.

He went into the small kitchen and searched about for more cleaning materials. As this was a house occupied by two men, they were few and far between. Eventually, he found some soap crystals, although he hadn't ever seen them before and thought that they might have been there from the previous occupant of the house. He knew that they would do the trick, so he boiled some water, added the soap and went to work.

He found himself whistling a jaunty little tune as he commenced the gruesome job and more than once he had to remind himself what he was doing.

Another hour of constantly scrubbing the floors, the walls and the table and he thought that he was ready for the next part of his plan. He needed to get rid of the bodies, and he knew exactly where they were going to go.

It was somewhere he had used before.

50.

'WHAT THE HELL is going on here tonight?' Seamus, one of the doormen at The Rialto was scratching his head as he regarded the lengthy line of punters waiting to dance and watch the Downswing Seven in action. 'Has anyone seen, or heard from, Red?'

Patricia, who was normally found in the ticket booth at this time, was standing next to him looking equally as dumbfounded. 'Not heard from him all afternoon. He's usually here when the band get in, he's got the keys.'

'So, the band aren't here either? Jesus, what are we going to do? This lot will lynch us if they don't get in there.'

One of the other doormen came huffing and puffing back up past the line of disgruntled looking punters. His face was bright red; he was obviously not used to running too much. He bent over when he reached Seamus and Patricia, attempting to catch his breath. 'I've just been to the payphone,' he panted. 'I rang the number for Red's office... there was no answer.'

'Did you ring Ron's number?'

The doorman was still gasping for air as he nodded.

'Yeah, he's in bed, flu apparently. Although his mum said that Red called around earlier looking for Ron to do a job with him. She never said what it was.'

'This doesn't look good.' Seamus said, looking worriedly down the line. 'No Red, no band. What do we do?'

The girls who worked the bar appeared from around the back, both smoking. 'I know what I'm going to do,' Linda, the younger of the two spoke up. 'I'm off home.' She dropped her cigarette on the floor and squashed it with her shoe.

'Me too,' Patricia responded. 'If he was going to turn up, he'd be here by now. He's never been late before.'

As she started to leave, she looked at the two doormen who were stood looking confused in the doorway. 'I'll leave it up to you then, Seamus. You know, to tell this lot that there'll be no dancing tonight.'

She'd shouted this, just loud enough, so everyone in the queue could hear. Seamus' shoulders slumped. 'Oh, for fuck's sake, Pat! What did you have to do that for?' he mumbled under his breath.

'What did she just say then, lad?'

'Is there not going to be any band on tonight?'

'Jesus Christ, it's my birthday! I've been looking forward to this all week.'

The shouts coming from the punters, some of who had been waiting in line for over an hour, were angry.

Seamus spared one further look over towards where Patricia had walked off, before putting his hands in the air ready to address the crowd; to give them the unwelcome news.

51.

CARL HAD BEEN stood in the queue for nearly twenty minutes. He looked at his watch and could hardly believe that it was almost ten o'clock. He hadn't seen or heard anything from Marnie for over a day now. Although the other people in the queue were generally polite and the atmosphere had been rather convivial, his temper was beginning to fray.

He was spluttering and muttering to himself, much to the annoyance of the others waiting. A few of them, mostly female, had even walked away from the crazed-looking man.

Eventually his patience snapped, he'd had enough of waiting. His phone call was, quite literally, a matter of life and death. He needed to contact the police and he needed to do it as soon as possible. 'This is ridiculous,' he mumbled as he stormed to the front of the queue and wrenched open the heavy red door.

The man inside was cradling the hand piece to his ear. He looked at Carl with shock at the intrusion. 'Ay lad. Do you mind? I'm having a conversation here,' he scolded the intruder.

Carl leaned in, his face maniacal, and wrenched the handset out of the man's hands before slamming it down, back into its cradle, almost hard enough to break it.

'Hey, soft lad, what game do you think you're playing at here?'

Carl glared at him; his eyes were wide, threatening, but most of all, desperate. The man, although almost the same size as Carl, thought twice about shouting at him again, and he began edging his way out of the tight phone box into the dark street. He breathed in as he passed Carl so as not to touch him, in case whatever madness was surging through him was contagious. When he'd made it outside and the heavy door had closed behind him, he turned towards the rest of the queue. 'He's a bleeding nutter, he can't be doing that. A man has a right to make a phone call you know,' he shouted with all his new-found bravado.

Carl heard this and the anger surged inside him again. He swung open the door and stuck his head out towards the unhappy queue. He was wearing the same expression on his face, the one he had used when he had challenged the man. Everyone in the queue cowered away from him. 'EVERYONE JUST LEAVE ME ALONE. I NEED TO CALL THE POLICE!!!' he shouted and slammed the door closed again.

'Yeah, well make sure you report yourself, you lunatic,' the man replied in a half-whisper, just loud enough for the rest of the queue to hear, but not loud enough for the crazy man inside. The crowd began to mumble to each other in disgusted tones as they slowly began to disperse into the night. The drama and theatre of what had just happened overtook their need to make a phone call.

Inside, Carl picked up the receiver and dialled zero. A nasally, officious, female voice on the other end asked him where he wanted to be connected to.

'I need the police. It's an emergency.'

'Please hold the line, sir.'

Carl was now floating in darkness on the end of a telephone line; the few clicks and shuffles, the only telling indication that he hadn't lost the connection. 'Come on…come on!' He gripped the receiver tight within his sweaty grasp.

'This is Marsh Lane police station. Can you state the nature of the emergency please?' an authoritative male voice spoke on the other end.

The voice startled Carl for a second and he paused prior to continuing. 'Erm, yes. I… I want to report a… a…' Carl coughed a little to disguise his hesitation. 'A murder!' he continued, rather boldly, perhaps a little too boldly. It wasn't until the words were out of his mouth that he realised how ridiculous the accusation sounded, but he had started something now, and had to see it through. 'Yes, a murder.'

'Murder you say, sir?' The man on the other end of the phone line sounded intrigued. 'Alright then, these are serious accusations. Can you relay me your current location?' the interested voice asked.

'What?' Carl replied, his frenzied mind not fully understanding the question.

'Can you tell me where you are?' the disembodied voice asked again, slightly impatiently.

Carl took a moment to compose himself. 'Oh, right. Well, I'm in Bootle, in Liverpool.' He looked out of the windows of the red box suddenly unsure of where he was, but quite aware that he had the full attention of the operator on the other end.

'Where about in Bootle, sir? I need your exact location for me to deploy constables accurately.'

'Erm, I'm on the corner of Hawthorn Road, I think. Yes, Hawthorn Road, but I think the murder has taken place in…' his thoughts were buzzing around his head now, making it hard for him to concentrate on what he was doing. Had there even been a murder or was this all in his mind? It was too late to back out of this conversation now.

'Sir, I need an accurate location to deploy personnel. You do know that giving false information to a police officer is a serious offence, don't you?'

It took him a moment to think of the name of the road. He knew it, he'd been with Marnie when she had gone to visit it, but now his mind was blank.

'Oh, Jesus, erm… I think it's taken place on Worcester Road, Bootle,' he answered eventually. 'Yeah, she lives on Worcester Road.'

There was a pause on the other end, it was almost as if the policeman was evaluating if this was a prank call. 'Can you confirm that a murder has taken place, sir? And who SHE could be?'

Carl was silent for a few, long, moments; his brain was hyper-aware of the passing of time, making the mere seconds feel like minutes.

The voice on the other end sounded concerned, maybe even suspicious, Carl couldn't tell. A lot of thoughts and doubts were running through his brain. He could feel bile rising from his stomach and suddenly he felt the need to vomit.

'Hello! Sir? Are you still there? I need to know your name,' the disembodied voice spoke, angrily, on the other end. Accusation came through the receiver like a black cloud attempting to envelop and squash him. He had to ignore the question as his paranoia heightened, and he tightened his grip on the black plastic earpiece because he didn't know how to answer the question. If he told the operator his name, then it would be out there; they would start putting two and two together, and he could ill afford any snooping by the local authorities. He made a split-second decision, one that might just save him. He dropped the phone receiver, allowing it to dangle towards the floor and swing. In a daze, he stepped from the telephone box and out into the night. As soon as the freezing air hit him it turned his stomach. The bile in his stomach, that had been threatening to rise, rose. Projectile vomit spurted from his mouth, narrowly missing the few remaining people waiting to use the phone.

Everyone in the queue stared at him as if he were something that had just descended from the sky; all of them taking a step back from the vomit, no one sure of what to do or even if they should say anything.

'Sir? Sir? I need your name, sir! It's for our records,' the voice on the other end of the phone was still shouting, sounding tinny and far away.

Without any thought or intent, Carl walked off into the direction of Derby Park.

After a few moments of watching the madman skulk away to wherever he was going, a woman braved the telephone box and picked up the dangling receiver.

'Huh! Hello?' she spoke into it.

52.

GEORGE DROVE THE one and a half miles from Walton, where he lived to Bootle with four dead bodies in the back of the car. He had covered them up with a blanket so anyone nosy enough to peer into the car would not be able to easily identify them as corpses.

He drove slowly and precisely, causing no concern to policemen who might otherwise pull him over in the course of their duties. He didn't want to think about what he would have to do to them if they did. He appeared calm and collected at the wheel, but his insides felt like someone was stretching them through a mangle. His stomach was churning, and his heartbeat was so rapid that he could hear it beating through his ears.

The car was also beginning to stink.

He had wound down the window letting in the frosty night air, but it was doing very little to combat the smell of death and early decay coming from the boot.

His lights were on and he remembered to indicate at every turn too; he wanted no suspicions. As far as anyone else on the road was concerned, his was just another car going about its totally innocent journey.

As he turned into Worcester Road, he drove up the slight incline past Marnie's house, and spared it a small glance. He stopped further up the road and parked the car outside the ruins of the three houses that had been hit during the May Blitz, the fateful night that, when he thought about it, was really the precursor for his little, bloody adventure today.

He opened the door and struggled to get out of the car due to his leg not being used to driving. It had gotten stiff, and he had to work it, taking a little time to stretch out the cramps. Once he had control of the blood flow back through the limb and the feeling had started to return, he leaned back into the car.

He looked both ways, up and down the street, and over towards the park on the opposite side, for any potential witnesses. Happy that there were none, he entered one of the piles of rubble that had once been a nice, cosy home.

53.

BACK AT HIS vantage point, on the bench next to the bandstand, Carl was moping around, wallowing in self-pity and misery. The noise of an approaching motorcar turning onto the quiet road made him look up. So few cars drove into this road, that he was drawn to watching as it made its way up the incline. His attention was piqued even more as it passed Marnie's house before parking a little further up, outside one of the bombed-out houses.

What he saw next made his heart beat ten times faster in his chest.

A man opened the driver's side door and struggled to get out. Once he was out, Carl watched as he limped about; stretching his leg as if it was hurting him. Even without the limp, he would have recognised George Hogg instantly.

He thought about rushing him, knocking him to the ground and accusing him of Marnie's murder before beating the living hell out of him. He even stood up, put his cigarette out, and readied himself to accost him, when George did something that made him stop.

He was looking all around him, up and down the street, Carl presumed for witnesses, before he leaned into his car, retrieved something and disappeared into one of the derelict sites. He was gone for just a few moments before returning to the rear door of the car.

His curiosity got the better of him and he hid in a bush, pulling the branches apart to giving himself a better, unobstructed view. He watched as he opened the car's back door and gently pulled a rolled-up swathe of material out of the boot. He was overly careful not to drop the end of the heavy-looking wrap on the road. He then began to drag it, meticulously, inside the demolition site. Once he was inside, he was out of view for a good five minutes, maybe longer. Carl considered making his way over to the car to see if there was anything else in the back, but before he could, George returned and repeated the process. This happened again, and then again. In total, Carl counted four journeys with four swathes of rolled up material, each visit took George around about the same amount of time.

Four times he entered the site with a bundle and four times he came back out empty handed.

Once he was finished, he took another look up and down the street, while wiping his hands on his trousers, before getting back into the car and driving off.

He only drove up a few hundred yards before he spun the car back around to face the way he'd entered. He drove a little further and stopped the car right outside Marnie's house, almost parallel to where Carl was currently hiding.

He watched with interest as George headed up the path towards the house, still looking all around him. Carl followed his gaze up and down the empty road. Both men satisfied that there was no one taking any notice of this nocturnal visitor. George rummaged around in his pocket, presumably for the key, before he let himself into the house, closing the door behind him.

No lights came on inside.

'Got you, you bastard,' Carl whispered underneath his breath. He put his hand inside his jacket pocket and produced a small wrapped bundle of his own, only this bundle was wrapped in an old rag that was slightly greasy with oil. The weight of it in his hands was reassuring; it made him feel calm and in control for the first time since Marnie had got herself involved with the crippled weasel currently inside her house. Carefully, he unwrapped the cloth, exposing the treasure inside. It was an Enfield No.2 Mk1 service pistol. It was his service issue pistol from the war; he had neglected to hand it back in when he was demobbed. The MOD had no way of regulating who had handed what armaments back, and he was sure that he wasn't the only one who had kept his. The weapon was clean, oiled and fully loaded. Six bullets, one in each of the chambers, fully arming the weapon. He had an idea that he would only need one bullet, maybe two, if needs be, but thought it better to be fully loaded when dealing with slippery eels like George Hogg.

He looked up from admiring his package towards Marnie's house, noting that there were still no lights on inside. He thought it prudent to get evidence on this horrible little runt before dealing with him in his own special way. Emulating his enemy, he searched up and down the street making sure that his coast was clear, before he left the sanctuary of the bushes and continued to, what he hoped would be, the conclusion of tonight's mission. He headed towards the bombed-out house that George had just recently vacated.

Using his well-trained stealth and vigilance, he made his way to to the ruins and entered the site. Inside, the footing was difficult for him, an able-bodied man, and he wondered how George had kept on his feet, both with his clubfoot and with the large bundles that he had been dragging through the rubble.

Dark marks on the white dust were noticeable in the limited light. It looked like whatever had been dragged through the rubble had left a trail behind it, as if it had been leaking. He knelt to investigate what the dark trails consisted of and was not overly surprised to find the matter wet and slightly sticky.

Carl had seen enough active duty during the war to recognise blood when he saw it, be it daylight or dark. Absently rubbing the sticky residue from his hands, and with a heavy heart, he stood up regarding the ruins around him. He noticed there were other drag marks through the dusty room, all heading in the same direction.

Marnie...

His heart began to pound, and he could feel his own blood rush around his head, the rhythm banging in his ears.

He followed the trails as they led deeper inside the half-destroyed house. There was a smashed door frame that opened onto a stairwell that leading down into what Carl could only presume was a cellar. He reached into his deep coat pocket and gripped his hand around the sandalwood hilt of the pistol; his other hand explored his other pocket and produced a small metal flashlight.

Feeling fully armed and ready, he shone the light ahead, following the bloody trails down the steps to see what secrets the room below kept.

He was no more than a few steps down when a thick, sickly-sweet smell hit him. It was a smell that he recognised only too well; one that he was familiar with from his time spent in the trenches on the Maginot Line with the Allied Forces. It was the smell of newly decaying flesh.

The smell itself didn't hit him too hard; what did hit him was the thought of what that smell represented, the thought of what he might find down here, that was what sickened him to his stomach.

Marnie... please don't let it be Marnie, he pleaded to whatever God might have been listening at that moment.

The room was pitch black. The light from his little flashlight travelled in straight lines, trying its best to cut through the gloom encasing it but ultimately failing due to the thick concrete dust hanging heavily in the air. Crumbled masonry and broken timber lay strewn all over the floor, making navigating across the room not merely hazardous but positively treacherous. The occasional pieces of ruined furniture, battered and broken in corners or against the walls, were the only break from the monotonous grey, giving small flashes of colour in this terrible room.

His flashlight picked up on something out of the ordinary. There were four bundles; obviously the same ones that George had struggled bringing in earlier, strewn against the far wall, lying haphazardly next to each other.

The dark grainy air, the dim illumination from his torch, and the discovery of the four bundles gave the room an eerie atmosphere. Carl felt like he had entered into the worst kept crypt in history.

A cold shudder ripped through his bones as he made his way over towards the grisly discovery. Doing his utmost not to slip and fracture an ankle, or break a bone, he traversed the obstacle course that was the cellar of the bombed-out house. His only concern was Marnie. He knew, deep down in his broken heart that one of these bundles must contain the remains of his beloved sister. He cursed himself for not being there to help her, for not stopping George sooner, for not pointing out to the others what was happening. He had no idea what or more precisely who, was wrapped up in these other death shrouds, and he didn't really care, all he cared about was his sister.

He stumbled on some loose rubble and fell forward, almost dropping his torch. The beam bounced around the room erratically, illuminating another grisly discovery.

There were not four bundles in the room... there were five!

Four of them were wrapped in white sheets with large, dark, dirty stains on them but the fifth was wrapped in something different. His heart dropped into the pit of his stomach as he thought he recognised the material that the fifth bundle was comprised of.

'Four!' he whispered in the darkness. 'There were only four from the car, I'm sure of it!'

As he struggled towards them, he was becoming more frustrated by the unsteady footing in the room hampering his progress. He reached the first bundle and placed his gun on a pile of rubble next to it before clasping the shaft of the flashlight between his teeth. Shining the beam at the top of the sheet, he began to hastily unwrap the package, dreading but steeling himself against what he was about to find inside.

Once it was open and the contents revealed to him, his hands covered his mouth in shock, and he reeled back, stumbling on a loose plank of timber behind him.

The shock didn't come from finding the dead body - he had been expecting that - it was whose dead body it was that shocked him.

Brian's lifeless eyes stared up, past him, towards the ceiling.

'What the…' he mumbled as he frantically grasped at his friend's throat, desperately searching for a pulse or some warmth on the cadaver's neck. He already knew by how cold the skin was to the touch and the colour of his face, even in the bleaching light of the flashlight, but he had to make sure. It didn't take long for his fears to be confirmed; Brian was stone cold dead.

In a frenzy, he ripped at the next bundle. The vacant and purple face he saw leering out of the blanket was one he would never ever have suspected. 'Red!' he gasped.

His dark beady eyes hadn't lost any of their malevolence in death, and his face still looked threatening.

With his heart racing and his blood boiling in his veins, he undid the next one. The uncomfortable feeling in the pit of his stomach was rising. He felt like there was a wild animal running loose in his stomach, scrambling for freedom from the confines of his belly. The bitter taste of bile rose to the back of his throat and as he burped, a small amount of vomit entered his mouth; he swallowed it down, grimacing at the bitterness of the taste.

When he saw whose face it was, wrapped in the shroud, relief and sorrow, in equal measures, swept over him. Relief because it wasn't Marnie lying there; sorrow for poor Eddie.

With a heavy heart he looked at the last of the original four. The size and shape of it, and some of the more delicate curves, told him everything that he needed to know about this one. It told him that it was a woman.

He took hold of the torch and wiped the saliva that had dribbled from his gaping mouth with the sleeve of his coat. He put the torch on the bricks next to his gun and looked at the bundle.

Inwardly he cursed George and rued the day he'd seen the audition notice for the ill-fated Downswing Seven. He sat down next to the bundle and began to weep. His tears making wet tracks down his dust-lined face.

He put his hand on the package next to him and began to unwrap it. He couldn't bring himself to look at what he was doing. He had loved his sister more than anything in this world and thought he had done enough to make her safe again; but sometimes, just sometimes, lost souls must stay lost, and no amount of help can bring them back into the light.

He whispered a silent prayer for all those who had passed, as he turned to face the cadaver in the bundle. His eyes were closed, and his cheeks were now muddy from the moisture and the dust. He dared to open one eye. At first, he couldn't tell what it was he was looking at. The face was so distorted and badly beaten that it was hard to discern. When he noticed the blonde hair, his heart sank into his chest. It was the same colour as Marnie's...

But it was a different style!

Marnie's hair was shorter, with less of a curl.

He leaned forward resting his head on the bundle that contained the decimated body of Faye and began to cry again. The fresh tears made further, cleaner tracks down his dirty face, as he mourned for the poor delicate soul of someone he hadn't known for very long, but someone he had known, and liked.

A terrible thought occurred to him then. All the bodies of his friends in the bundles looked fresh as if they had been killed tonight, maybe no more than a few hours ago. If that was the case, then the smell of decay must have been coming from the fifth bundle.

He stared over at the roll of fabric and another dreaded realisation hit him. He knew exactly where he'd seen the material that was currently acting as a make-shift shroud for the fifth body. He picked up his torch, the weight of it in his hands felt heavier than it had any right to be, but he lifted it, and shone it on the bundle. In the dark, and underneath the intense scrutiny of the torch light, the fabric looked a little different from the last time he'd seen it. The last time he had seen it, it had been clean and had been hanging over the windows of Marnie's bedroom.

He approached and gently laid his hand on it, lowering his head, reverently, as if in prayer. A cloud of dust, at least a day's worth, rose, revealing the lime green colour of the material underneath.

His heart began to pound again as he thought long and hard about the last time he had seen his sister alive.

It was more than twenty-four hours ago!

He frantically ripped at the death shroud, the one that used to be Marnie's curtains.

'Oh, Christ, no... Please no, not Marnie.' He was sobbing again. 'Please not my Marnie!'

A noise from somewhere behind him disturbed his attempts at removing the curtains. They were made of a heavier fabric than the blankets and were causing him some difficulty. The noise came again; this time he recognised it. It was a shifting of the rubble.

He turned, grabbing his torch as he did, and shone the dimming beam on the silhouette of George Hogg who was standing behind him at the foot of the stairs.

54.

'WHAT ARE YOU doing down here, Carl?' George asked in a calm, careful, and calculated voice.

Carl swung the torch light around the destroyed room, making for a rather hectic scene. 'George!' he spat. 'What have you done? What the Hell have you done down here?' He was struggling to catch his breath between sobs.

George produced a storm lamp and lit it with a twist of a small knob at the bottom. It illuminated the room in a way that the failing torch couldn't. Shadows danced across his face as he stared at Carl, his eyes full and dark. 'I was in a fix and I did what I always do, what I do best… I got myself out of it.'

Carl blinked and swallowed his words as he indicated towards the bundles. He couldn't believe what he was hearing. 'Do you call this getting out of a fix? These are your friends, George, my friends too,' He was spluttering as the dust and his emotions were having detrimental effects on his ability to talk.

George looked from Carl to the bundled bodies, then back again. He shook his head and spoke in a whispered voice. 'No, Carl, they were obstacles.'

Carl couldn't believe what he was hearing. He had known this man for only a few months, and he knew that he could be cold, but he never, in a million years, thought anyone could be *this* cold.

'Don't you be an obstacle too, Carl.' He took a step towards him and pulled the long-handled carving knife he had become so fond of using, from behind him. He lifted it up, showing it off, as if it was a trophy to be marvelled at. The sharp blade glinted in the light of the storm lamp.

'Do you know what? I really think that this knife could go down in history.' He was looking at it as if it was a revered artefact. 'Behold the knife that killed the infamous Red!' He thrust the blade forward, reliving his unsavoury deed. 'It slipped right into his back like a hot knife through butter. I never knew how easy it was to kill someone.' A hideous, and sinister, smile spread across his face as he looked from the blade towards his colleague. 'Well, that's a bit of lie.' He took another step towards Carl, his eyes back on the glinting blade. 'He wasn't the first one!' he laughed. 'Not even the first tonight.'

To Carl, George was now a ghoul, a monster from in one of the horror pictures that he had caught over in America. A small, involuntary smile came to his lips at the thought.

George shook his head. 'What's so funny, Carl? You do know that your chances of getting out of here alive are rather... slim, don't you?'

Carl raised his arm in a straight line. His hand gripped the service revolver, as he pointed towards George's face.

The look of fear he had expected from the man, at the appearance of the gun, never came. This unnerved him. All he did was scoff at him.

'Why? Why did you pick Marnie? There were millions of other girls out there, why did you have to pick the one girl that I loved more than life itself.'

George's shook his head. 'She had what I needed Carl. And there was that something else about her that I could see in her from the very first time we met. Do you know what it was?'

Carl didn't answer, her just adjusted his grip on the gun he was holding.

George smiled before continuing. 'She had a hunger in her, the same hunger that I feel. Believe me, mate...' The last word was spat, '... she was more than a willing participant in it all.'

This enraged Carl and he lunged forward towards the smaller man, still pointing the gun into his face. George still didn't flinch.

'Don't you talk about my sister like that. Don't you *ever* talk about her, at all.' Thick sweat, mixed with concrete and dust, dripped from his lip, and trickled into his mouth, causing it to spray as he shouted. He wiped at his stinging eyes with the sleeve of his coat, smudging the dust that had settled on his face, giving him an odd, almost tribal look.

'Throw that knife over here, slowly, he demanded, thumbing the safety of the pistol, fully arming it. 'I don't want any sudden movements. I know what I'm doing with this thing.' The composure was back into his voice now.

'What do you want, Carl?' George asked as he tossed the knife, slowly and deliberately.

Carl bent to pick it up before setting it down next to the bundles, well out of the other man's reach. 'I want to know why you killed my sister. After everything I'd done for her in the past, a little piece of *shit* like you turns up and wipes her out of existence, like she was nothing.' He was indicating the fifth bundle as he spoke.

George smiled; his hands still raised in the air. 'She told me all about the things you did for her in America, you know.'

'Shut up!'

George noted the small waver in the arm holding the gun; he eyed Carl like a fighter who has his opponent on the ropes. While he didn't relish the fact that he had a gun to his face, he knew that in a moment or two, the man before him would snap, that would be his cue. He knew that he had to be ready for it.

'She told me all about what you did for her. About the cover up that you instigated and how you took the blame for everything, just to keep her safe. About how you smuggled her out of the country and back into Blighty, and how you're now a wanted criminal in America. Public enemy number one she called you.'

More tears were falling from Carl's eyes, stinging them, drawing more dust onto his face. 'I did what I had to do for her. It's like what I have to do right now,' he whispered.

'She told me how you turned up after she sent her letter home, explaining how awful it was over there. How no one would talk to her, how her own husband would beat her and make her... do things.'

George had closed the gap between them now. He was speaking deliberately slowly and concise, like he was teaching a primary school child how to read. It was having the desired, almost hypnotic, effect on Carl. He looked lost in memory.

'Oh yes, she told me about how she murdered her husband over there. She told me in fantastic detail how it felt to sink the knife into him, deep into his fat, alcoholic, stomach and chest, again and again and again.' George's teeth were gritted together as he spilled his tale; in truth, he was enjoying every bit of it. Enjoying how he was making Carl suffer. He could see his gun hand wavering as more tears poured from his red eyes. 'She told me how it felt afterwards; when he was dead, and she was covered in his hot, thick, blood. The surge of power that coursed through her whole body, the power she had over life and death.' George laughed then. 'She told me it felt almost sexual.'

Carl's weapon was wavering; there was a distant look in his eyes, like he was lost in time. In the warm glow of the storm lamp, they looked like the glass eyes of a child's doll, vacant and dark. 'I'm warning you, George, you need to be quiet right now; you don't know what you are playing with here.'

'Now, you see, I do, Carl. You're forgetting I told you that she told me everything. She's quite the woman, your sister. A woman after my own heart, in many ways. She knows what she wants, and she knows exactly how to go about getting it.' He shook his head, all the time keeping eye contact with the unstable man before him, the unstable man with the gun. 'We had lengthy chats about how she had premeditated the murder. She'd wanted him dead for a long time. She'd even dreamed about killing him. A real woman of passions that one! And a talker too, especially after sex! Oh, mate, she loved the sex.'

Carl's face looked explosive. 'Shut up! I swear to God I'll fucking kill you, right here, right now.'

George smiled and continued. 'There was a letter home, and then you turned up. She knew that you'd always been a protective big brother. You'd protected her many times growing up, but she also knew that you could be a little... too protective. Bradley McFell was wealthy, and Marnie was legally entitled to that wealth if something were to happen to him. An accident or maybe something a tad more sinister? It couldn't be Marnie who did it, they'd have hung her from the nearest tree. A Limey killing her husband? So, she sent for her mentally unstable brother, the war hero, knowing that you'd do absolutely anything for her, including taking the rap for Bradley's murder. She called you and you went running, like the good big brother you are.'

Carl's eyes were closed now, saving them from the sting of the sweat that was dripping into them, but he tightened his grip on the gun. 'None of that is your business, George. I'd have done anything for that little girl. I *did* do anything for her. But now you've taken her away and I've lost everything that I hold dear. It's time you paid the price, George.'

George put his hands in the air and smiled an odd smile. 'Before you shoot me, why don't you look in the bundle you're protecting. Go ahead, take a look.' His smile widened. 'But mind the smell, she might be a bit ripe now.'

'You take a step backwards...' Carl ordered still pointing the pistol at George, '...then I'll look. Maybe you'll feel a little remorse at what you've done to my sweet sister, maybe you'll feel something for the first time in your miserable life, right before I take it away from you.'

George dutifully stepped back as Carl turned towards the fifth bundle. Using the hand that was not holding the gun he began a more conducted unravel of the thick curtain that was wrapped around it. He'd gone at it earlier in a frenzy and it got him nowhere. It was hard work; mainly due to the dried blood sticking to the fabric, that coupled with the fact that he was working with only one hand. Tears and sweat dripped from his chin in dust-filled blobs.

He was dreading this bundle more than the others. Oh, he had loved the others as new friends, well, everyone apart from Red - he didn't think there would be a lot of people mourning him - but this package was different. This one contained the body of the girl he had loved and protected since they were children.

As the covers finally came away, Carl did indeed gag. The thick fabric of the curtains had been keeping the lion's share of the stink of decay contained, but as he pulled it away, it released, stinging his nostrils and the back of his throat.

Without thinking, he used the hand that was holding the gun to cover his nose, to protect him from the stench. As he did, George moved towards him. Realising his mistake, Carl turned and raised the weapon again, stopping the smaller man in his tracks.

As George raised his hands again the wicked smile stretched back across his face. He was cocking his head to peer into the bundle himself, like a carpenter proudly reviewing his work.

Carl slowly turned back towards the bundle, his senses getting used to the stench. He gazed upon the body inside.

Marnie's blonde hair was hanging limp from the end of her shroud and was obscuring her face. His heart sank as he looked at it. He ran a shaking hand through her hair and then realised something strange. The hair was the same length and colour as Marnie's but on closer inspection, he saw that it wasn't the natural colour of a woman in her mid-twenties. It was the artificial coloured hair of a woman much older. The hair was dry and brittle, with grey at the roots.

His eyes widened and his mouth fell agape. Drool dangled from his lower lip, like a grape on a vine.

'It's... It's...'

'Not Marnie!' George finished for him.

Carl face George. For a moment he found he couldn't talk, he could barely think, but when he could, there was only one question he had the mind to ask. 'If it's not Marnie...who is it?'

'It's Mrs Jenkins.'

A female voice spoke from behind George, it was a voice that Carl knew well and instantly recognised.

He felt his heart almost miss a beat at the voice. At first, he thought it must have been his mind playing tricks on him, allowing voices from the dead to come back and haunt him. 'Marnie?' he whispered. His distraught face transformed; like a child waking on a snowy Christmas morning, when he saw her stood in the old crumbling doorway of the cellar.

'Yes, Carl, it's me, Marnie. I'm still alive,' she replied.

'It's... It's really you? Oh, thank the Lord you're alive. Where've you been?'

'Never mind where I've been Carl, I need you to do me this one last favour.' Her tone was business-like and demanding, just like it always was when she wanted something from him.

He was shaking his head in joy and disbelief. 'Anything, Marnie, you know that. I'm just glad that you're still alive. I thought that he'd…' he indicated towards George with the gun in his hand. George was watching the proceedings with a smirk on his face.

She shook her head and smiled a gentle smile. 'No, Carl, he didn't.'

'So, what happened to Mrs Jenkins?' he asked, the gun now pointing towards his feet.

He looked at the body wrapped in the curtains and fresh tears welled in his eyes. His elation had had begun to revert to fear and disillusionment. 'You never! Marnie, please tell me you never!' he pleaded. 'Tell me you didn't do it again Marnie. Please tell me you didn't.'

George cleared his throat to make his presence known and to interrupt their reunion. 'It was more of a joint effort. You see, she had what I needed. Her house is worth a small fortune with all those ornaments! Some of them are antique China porcelain. Worth hundreds, if not thousands, of pounds. And that gold pocket-watch! Jesus, that's worth a fortune in itself.'

'We decided we'd go fifty-fifty,' Marnie continued.

George smiled over at his companion.

Carl was not happy that Marnie was smiling back at George, the same devilish look in her eyes that he had seen before; many times, before.

'We have something in common you see. Both of us know the real rush that you get when you kill another person, so we decided that we'd give it another go. I went to your sister's house that night thinking she was an easy target, one I could get hooked on the drugs that I sold for Red, and maybe get a little bit of something else in return, like I did with Faye. Your sister here was onto me trying to drug her, and we ended up talking all night. She told me where Mrs Jenkins kept the deeds to her house. The whole thing was perfect.'

'*Is* perfect!' Marnie corrected him with a smile. George returned the smile. 'And easy,' she finished looking back at her brother.

Carl was confused, he could see genuine affection in her smile; it was something that he'd never seen in her before.

'So, I killed her,' she finished.

George tutted, it was a playful noise and that made everything even more sickening. 'Well, *we* killed her,' he gushed affectionately, turning back towards Carl. 'You should have seen her in motion! Your sister is very graceful, Carl. You would have been proud. She beat the unfortunate woman half to death with a lamp. I think the poor woman's heart had given up before I moved in and 'sealed the deal' so to speak. She never fought back when I was strangling her.'

'We both decided that I should lay low for a while, so I stayed at George's house. Tex can account for my whereabouts the whole time.' Marnie explained.

Carl was listening and shaking his head. His tears were now long gone, replaced by a look of sheer horror. He couldn't quite believe what he was hearing, especially not from his little sister.

George laughed, it was a horrible sound, and sat down on a pile of rubble, stretching his leg. Marnie climbed over to help him. 'So, as you can see here, Carl, it all got a little out of hand.' She bent down and began to rub George's leg, while looking up at her brother with big, puppy-dog eyes. 'Which is where you come in.'

There was something about Marnie bent over George and rubbing his leg that he just couldn't stomach but he needed to know what she needed, what his role in this sadistic pantomime would be. 'Me? Where do I fit into all of this?'

'Yes, you, Carl.' Marnie replied with a smile, the kind of smile that she knew her brother could never resist. 'I...' She turned back around towards George and took his hand in hers, '...sorry, we, need you to take the blame for all these murders. I can't do it, Carl. Can you imagine me in prison?'

'And I can't do it either,' George interjected. 'I wouldn't last five minutes in prison with a stupid clubfoot, now would I?'

'And it's not like you haven't done it before, is it?' she asked playfully. 'You did it in America and got away with it, I'm sure you could do it again? You took all the blame for Bradley's death, remember? And we smuggled ourselves out of the country on that ship. All you need to do now is to do it all over again, one more time. For me.' She was speaking in a little-girl-lost voice.

The corners of Carl's lips turned downwards as his face transformed into a mask of sorrow and regret. His shoulders slumped and his head fell. Fresh tears poured down his face, dripping into the dry dust of the rubble below him. Still holding the gun, he put the heels of his hands to his eyes in an attempt to block out everything that was happening to him right now. Everything that had happened to him in the past, too. He had been a patsy for her far too often and he wasn't going to let it happen again. Not this time, not after all he'd done for her.

'Why do I allow you to do this to me every time?' he sobbed. 'Every time! I've always covered up for you, ever since we were children. I took the blame for everything, when it was always you! And you let me... you watched while I took the strap from Father, when I received the disapproving looks from Mother... you watched, with that same innocent look on your pretty little face.' Carl's face was distorted almost beyond recognition due to the grief pouring out of him.

'That's what big brothers are for, Carl,' Marnie replied, moving her hands away from George's leg.

'You've always been there to protect me. You're my rock, you know that. That's why I need you so much right now.'

'*No*!' he shouted in reply, swinging the gun back around to point it between the pair of them. 'Not this time, Marnie. I'm not going to take the blame for you anymore. You've got your man here to do it now. Let him take the blame for everything you do. I'm done.'

Carl re-cocked the safety on the pistol as he pointed it at the poisonous couple.

'Come on now Carl, let's not be hasty here. Put the gun down eh? You don't want to shoot anyone here, especially not someone as special as your sister. Let's talk about it eh?' George said in a soothing voice as he attempted to stand up.

Carl's face changed again as a calmness descended over him. Lucidity shone from his eyes; George could see it in the dim, dancing light of the storm lamp.

He tightened his lips together and exhaled a long breath from his nose. 'There's nothing more to talk about. I'm not going to be the scapegoat for her anymore.' He repointed the gun at Marnie to exaggerate the word 'her' in his last sentence, while tightening his grip on the gun.

Marnie's face flinched as worry crept over her features like a dark cloud on a summer's afternoon. The strange, far-away look in his eyes scared her. Right now, she believed that he could do this to her. She felt her brother, the same brother she had been able to manipulate all through their lives, might actually be able to kill her! 'Carl... come on, put the gun down now,' Marnie ordered in a commanding voice that was almost a million miles away from how she felt.

Carl's eyes blazed and he shook his head. 'Not this time, Marnie. Not ever again.' He repositioned his grip once again on the revolver, his sweaty finger caressing the trigger.

Marnie closed her eyes and turned away from the barrel, awaiting the final, fatal shot.

George swallowed hard, he thought about stepping in front of the lady, maybe even taking the bullet for her, but thought better of it; after all, he was a coward at heart, and didn't fancy getting shot for anyone, not even the woman he thought he might, finally, love.

~~~~

The hot blast and the smell of the acrid smoke remained in the air after the initial shock and the ringing in her ears of the loud report died down.

~~~~

I'm still alive! she thought opening her eyes. *He missed*!

The shadows made by the storm lamp were at odd angles and for a moment she wondered why. Then she noticed that the lamp had fallen and was lying on its side on the rubble-strewn floor.

Her head was spinning as panic encapsulated her, and she spun around the ruined room, the shadows disorientated her, making her dizzy as she searched the room for George.

She found him huddled in a corner, his back was to the join of the two walls. He looked unhurt but his eyes were wide open. She followed his wide-eyed gaze towards where her brother had been.

She now understood what had happened.

Carl was lay on top of the five bundles in the opposite corner of the room. He was half-hidden in the shadows cast by the fallen lamp. A large, dark splatter of blood, bone, and God only knew what else, adorned the wall behind where he lay.

His service revolver was still in his dead hand, smoke was drifting out of the recently used barrel.

55.

'WHAT'S ALL THE noise going on down here? I'm warning you, if it's you down here Ted McCluskey you're going to be in serious trouble. Pat won't be letting you off this time, laddie. There'll be a serious tanning of someone's hide in store.' The gruff voice was coming from the stairs leading back up to the ground level of the house. 'I'm warning you, Teddie, if it was you making that anonymous phone call reporting a murder, then it won't just be Pat who administers a thick ear!'

Both Marnie and George were surprised to see two policemen poking their heads around the door, both holding flashlights and their truncheons at the ready. Neither looked like they wanted to be in this dirty, and dangerous room.

'I don't think it's Ted this time, sir. I'm pretty sure that sounded like a gunshot. I recognised it from my time abroad,' the second policeman responded.

Marnie took her cue and swung into action. She threw herself onto the dusty floor and began to cry. 'Oh, Officers, thank God you're here,' she feigned. 'I can't believe it; he had a gun. I thought he was going to kill us.'

George took her lead and crouched next to her. He wrapped his arms around her body, as if offering comfort and succour. 'He's a madman. When I heard the shot, I thought he'd shot me, but when I knew I was all right, I feared the worst. I think she's OK though. It looks like he might have shot himself instead. He's over there, constable.'

Both policemen were out of their comfort zones, they hadn't signed on tonight to investigate a possible murder, or suicide. They both entered gingerly into the precarious basement, one of them illuminating their path across the treacherous floor, while the other shone his light everywhere else within the gloom of the musty room.

The beam picked up both Marnie and George, revealing their scared and dirty faces in the sheer light. It traced over them looking for any wounds or blood, before quickly moving on after not finding any. The beam continued, illuminating the floor around them, looking for weapons and the like. Once the policeman was confident there wasn't anything to be found, the beam moved on again towards the wall at the back of the room, the one with the large dark stain. Eventually, it found Carl's body, slumped on the top of the other five bundles.

'Sweet Baby Jesus!' the larger newcomer blasphemed before crossing himself as both torch beams concentrated on Carl's body. Marnie and George heard the other gasp; neither policeman had been expecting anything like this. The younger man cast his beam a little further afield to illuminate the dark spatter on the wall behind their grisly discovery.

The remaining beam moved further towards the bundles that Carl was slumped upon. 'Oh shit,' one of them muttered beneath his breath. 'Michael, have you seen this?'

'Holy Jesus up above, help us!' the larger policeman blasphemed again, and crossed himself once more. 'I think we're going to need some back up here. Trevor, can you go and whistle for someone? I'll look after these two.'

'Yeah, no problem, will you be OK?'

'Yeah, you go, but be quick.'

The older policeman exited through the door he had appeared in, leaving just the one left behind. He turned off his flashlight and the strange shadows cast by the storm lamp reappeared.

'Is he dead, Officer?' George asked in his best 'victim' voice.

The policeman was negotiating his way over the rubble on the floor, attempting to get to Carl and the other bodies. 'It certainly looks like it. Are you both all right? Do you have any injuries?' he asked as he made it to the bodies.

He shone his torch at the bundles and took a quick peep inside. He looked away again, rather sharpish, holding his nose in disgust as he did.

'No, I don't think either of us are hurt, but I'm not sure about our friends over there. I think we might know who it is in them bundles, Officer, I think he might have killed them earlier. I was looking out for Marnie here, when I saw him dragging these bundles down here, I followed him thinking the worst about my Marnie. We know him; he's the singer in our band.' George looked at the bodies making sure that the policeman was watching him. He pulled a fantastic mime of devastation that would have fooled even the harshest theatre critic, before continuing. 'Was our singer, anyway, of what's left of the band. I think that they're the other members. He spotted me watching him and he dragged me down here too. He had… a gun, a service pistol it looks like, and a long knife.'

'He… he's my brother!' Marnie cried, from out of nowhere. 'He's my brother and he tried to kill me.' She began to wail now, taking deep, deep sobs.

George looked at her; inwardly he was impressed. If he hadn't known her, and knew that she was in on this caper, then he would have thought they were real tears that she was crying. He pulled her in close and continued to comfort her.

The poor policeman was well out of his depth. He hadn't ever had to deal with anything like this in all his years of service; both during active service and on civvies street. Drunk soldiers and drunken louts in pubs, yes; not multiple murders, kidnapping and suicide! He didn't have a clue where to start.

'He said if I didn't leave George, he'd kill all our friends, and then kill me.' She put her head in her hands and continued to weep. 'It looks like he meant his threat. He's never been the same since he came back from Europe,' she sobbed.

George cleared his throat; this whole situation was going even better than he had planned. A thought had occurred to him that would get them out of this situation, completely and with exoneration too. 'If you do your checks, Officer, I think you'll find that he's a wanted criminal in America. He killed Marnie's husband, I think, before following her back over here. She's feared him ever since.'

The policeman moved his beam over to Marnie who was still hiding her face in her hands. 'Is this true, ma'am?'

She nodded, and rubbed her eyes, her mascara had mixed with her tears and the dust, making them a lot darker than they really were. 'Yes. He's always been the jealous type. He followed me over to America and killed my husband, then he threatened me. I had to leave and come back. I was hoping that Bradley's family would have caught him or handed him over to the authorities, but it seems they never. You can check all of this out if you want. There's a warrant out for his arrest in Utah.' The shake and sob in her voice was working to full effect, the policeman was swallowing every word.

'Come on then, love, I think you're safe now. Let's get you out of here and back up to the surface. Are you OK getting her up here, sir?' He asked George.

'I'll try, but I'm a little lame in the foot, sir.'

'What?'

'I've got a clubfoot. I'll try my best, but I might need some help.'

'That's OK, son, I'll get her up there, then I'll come back down and give you a touch too.'

The policeman turned his torch back on and shone it towards where Marnie was now getting up. He leaned down and offered the lady his arm to support her up and over the rubble. As he did, he turned around and illuminated their path out towards the stairs.

As soon as the policeman's back was turned, George was clambering over the rubble towards the bundles of dead bodies on the other side of the room. There was something he wanted, and he knew exactly which bundle to get it from. This was not a mission where he would welcome any witnesses. The policeman shone his torch beam over to where he was. 'Are you OK there, sir?' he shouted across the dusty room.

'Yeah, I, erm… I just lost my footing, that's all. I know this is awkward, but I don't think I'll make it back over the rubble, what with my leg and all. I'll hang on till you get back.'

'Yeah, not a problem. Just give me two ticks while I help her up and then I'll come back for you.'

The policeman led Marnie up the steps towards the ground floor of the ruined property. He watched as she scrambled up the last few steps. Then, when she was safe, he turned back downstairs. When he was back at the bottom, he reached over the rubble and stretched his hand out to George.

As the light from the policeman's torch found him in the darkness, George had just managed to stuff something small into his trouser pocket. The policeman didn't even notice; it was just another glint of more twisted metal.

With a grateful smile, George reached out and accepted the policeman's hand and was hauled up to safety.

56.

IT WAS SATURDAY morning and Ron was making his way, grumpily, through a soaking wet and miserable afternoon towards The Rialto. His bout of flu hadn't completely passed yet, and it had taken more than its fair share of energy out of his system. He had ended up taking four days off work. He was still longing for the warm delights of his bed, but as he hadn't heard from Red for a few days, he thought it might be best for him to drag his sorry behind out of his pit and get in to work. He knew his boss wouldn't tolerate him taking any more time off. So, against the better judgement of his mother, he had gotten himself up, into the bath, into his suit, and into work.

As he turned onto The Rialto's street he was on autopilot, lost in his own thoughts. When he reached the front doors he pulled on them, eager to get inside, out of the rain.

In his daydream, he continued walking, his brain failing to register that the doors hadn't opened, and he walked into them. With a scowl, he peered through the grimy window to see why the doors were still locked, but it was far too dark inside for him to be able to see anyone, or anything. He looked at his watch and wondered if he'd slept through more days than he thought. Realising that was stupid thought, he began to hammer on the door. After a few moments of banging and rattling the door frame, a light appeared from inside. He could see that it had come from the door to Red's office.

He straightened up, and dusted off his long, wet overcoat. He didn't want Red to see him still looking rough. He removed his wet hat and slicked his thinning hair back.

The doors began to rattle, as a key was inserted into the lock, and then finally they opened.

He stepped inside; his head was still low as he crumpled his wet hat in his nervous hands. 'Red, I'm so sorr…' He stopped mid-sentence as he regarded the person who had opened the door.

It was not Red.

In all the years that he had worked for him, Red had never, not even once, looked this good.

It was a woman, and a very attractive woman at that. A very attractive and familiar woman.

He couldn't think of anything to say. He had never been very good with the ladies, especially the attractive ones. 'Ahem, excuse me, ma'am, for asking, but who are you?' He put on his most gentleman-like voice.

The woman smiled a disarming smile before holding out her hand. 'You must be Ron. My name's Marnie. I'm your new boss and co-owner of The Rialto.'

The big man stared at her, he had never been, what you would call, sharp, he knew this, it was part of the reason he had got into this line of work in the first place, but this situation was confusing him more than he had ever been confused before.

'You're who now? Where's Red?'

A man's voice spoke from inside the office behind the cloakroom. It was a voice that he knew but not one he could identify right away. 'Red is no longer with The Rialto, Ron. Me and Marnie own the club now, he handed it over to me, lock stock and barrel, so to speak. It was all done and finalised while you were off sick.'

George stepped through the door from the office and into the foyer. He was walking with a black cane with a golden tipped handle and was dressed in a splendidly-fitting, expensive looking, suit with a rather distinctive looking gold watch adorning the pocket and the buttonhole. Around his neck, there was a fine golden chain, and on that chain, there was a single metal key; he was fingering this key as he walked towards Ron.

'I'll be expecting you to continue your role as one of the senior doormen at the club. Is that OK with you? If you have a problem and need to talk to me regarding your support and your loyalty then, please, step into my office and we can continue this inside.'

Ron was still crumpling his hat in his hands and was now shuffling his feet from side to side. He was confused; he knew that he never always got these situations, and he never always understood why Red had wanted him to hit people for him, but he did understand that whoever held that little metal key around their necks was the one who would be paying him each week. He might be a little bit on the thick side, but he knew which way the wind was blowing. 'No, boss, you can rely on me completely; no worries at all.'

George smiled and gestured into the office for someone who was inside to step out.

Ron looked past him, and his eyes widened in fear, and a little in awe, as a tall, wide black man, dressed in a tuxedo, bent his head in order to allow his exit through the doorframe.

'Good, good... You do know Jules here, don't you?'

Ron nodded, not taking his eyes off the huge man.

'Excellent. Well, he'll be the head doorman of the club as of today, and mine and Marnie's number one man. Do you understand that, Ron?'

The large man leered at him as Ron, who was not a small man by any measure of the word, looked up at him. For the first time in his life he felt small.

'Nope, I've got no problem with that at all, boss.'

'Excellent. Now listen, do you know Tam?'

'Yeah, the Scottish guy, the one who never speaks?'

'The very one. Well, I want you to tell him to get a new band together as soon as he can. Tell him the Downswing Seven have disbanded and all the members have gone their separate ways. I don't think he'll ask many questions anyway. I need you to do that as soon as you can, Ron. The Rialto is going to start moving forward with the times, from here on in. You got that?'

'I do, boss, contact Tam. Right away.'

Ron left the room still looking confused but happy that he still had a job.

'What do you need from me, boss?' Jules asked looking down at the smaller man in the nice suit. 'You've got me on retainer now. I'm yours, to do whatever needs doing.'

'I'm sure some of Red's shall we say 'friends' are going to start asking questions about what's going on here, and, more importantly, where he could be. I need you to keep your ear to the ground, Jules. I need you to stay close, and keep me, and Marnie, safe.'

Jules raised his eyebrows and smiled; his white teeth were in stark contrast to the darkness of his skin and the black of his suit. George took a moment to realise that his face didn't quite suit smiling.

'That's going to cost you a fair packet, boss. Are you good for that?'

George smiled and fingered the key that was hanging around his neck. 'Yeah, I'm good for it,' he nodded his reply.

Jules smiled and nodded before walking away.

57.

GEORGE SAT BACK in Red's old chair. A small smile adorning his face. He was going to take a while for him to get used to calling it *his* chair. He put his hands behind his head and, spreading his grin even further, surveyed the office around him.

He snapped out of his private reverie as Marnie breezed into the office, dressed in an expensive silk evening gown. Her hair had been cut into one of the new, expensive, fashions that all the top-class socialites in London were wearing these days. He leered at her, as he drank in the fantastic vision before him.

She was holding a bottle of The Rialto's most exclusive Champagne in one hand, and two glasses in the other. She sauntered over to him and he moved his seat back to allow her easier access. She sat on his knee, placing the glasses on his desk. She handed the bottle to him indicating to him to pull the cork, which he dutifully did. Both marvelled as it popped, giving the explosive liquid inside an escape route. He poured the fizzing alcohol into the glasses, almost to overflowing. She pulled two large cigars out from the low-cut front of her gown and leaned over, picking up the heavy cigarette lighter that was positioned on the edge of the desk. With a salacious glint in her eye, she inserted one of the cigars into her mouth and raised the lighter.

She puffed on the cigar like a seasoned smoker and then blew on the lit end, before popping it into George's mouth.

She lit the other and took that one for herself.

She removed the cigar and puffed a plume of grey smoke into the air around George's face.

He removed the cigar from his mouth and regarded the beauty sat on his lap. He took in a deep, satisfied breath and picked up his Champagne glass.

She reached over for hers and raised it towards his. 'Well, honey,' she purred into his ear. 'It looks like we did it! We finally got what we wanted.'

George looked at the glowing end of his cigar before blowing on it, he then looked over to the other side of the office where a large safe had been concealed into the wall. The door was open and inside were stacks of cash, along with bags of expensive looking jewellery. Eventually he looked back at Marnie and grinned. He didn't think it would be possible for his grin to widen even more, but it was; and it did.

'Do you know what, sweetheart?' he asked, chinking his full glass with hers.

As they came together, a beautiful musical note hung in the air around them, and the light from the ceiling glistened on the small, metal key that was hanging from his neck.

'It looks like we did!'

Marnie, giggling, fell into his arms where they shared a passionate embrace.

Author's Notes: D E McCluskey

I met Tony Bolland back in 1991 when I was eighteen years of age. I had managed to blag myself a job in Rushworth's Music House in Whitechapel, Liverpool. I was young and full of dreams of rock stardom. Tony worked in Curly Music which was adjacent to Rushworth's and right next door to the famous Hessy's Music store. There was a friendly rivalry between the shops, mostly regarding which one The Beatles bought their first guitars from.

A few years later I left the music shop as I decided I should try my luck in university, and there were a few people from that life that I thought I would never see again. If it wasn't for the power of the mighty Facebook, then I don't think I ever would have. Luckily for me, I found Tony, by accident, and requested a friendship. We hadn't spoken in nearly fifteen years and I wondered if he would even remember me.

He did…

You see, Tony kept diaries.

He had almost every event of the heady days in the music shops recorded for posterity in pages and pages of books. We began talking and soon found out that we shared another passion, besides music. That passion was writing.

Tony's forte is non-fiction, historical books about Liverpool, the music scene, the comedy scene, and the histories of iconic shops and locations; mine was for fiction. We got talking and it turned out that he was attempting to write a small screenplay about the history of Hessy's in relation to several of its more colourful customers. He asked me to help, and I jumped at the chance.

The play is still languishing in the 'incomplete list', something for us to do in the future. But in the course its development, Tony began to regale me with tales of his uncle Bill who used to play drums with the swing bands in the forties.

There were some crazy tales. We decided that we could take these tales and make a period novel/screenplay around them.

And that ladies and gentlemen is what you have just read. Some of it is real, some of it not so real... we'll leave it to your own speculation which parts are which.

We hope you enjoy this book, if you do, even half as much as me and Tony enjoyed writing it, then everyone is a winner.

Just a few acknowledgements before I sign off...

Tony Higginson: Without his book knowledge and editing skills, this book would have been a hash of out of time references and dialogue.

My fantastic team of proof-readers: Michaela Bromilow, Clare Kabluczenko, Lisa Piggot, Stella Read, Paula Lynne Heaton and of course, Lauren Davies. Without this team working in the background, editing, proofreading, fixing stupid grammatical errors that I don't even have a clue how to fix, then this book, and all my books would be complete messes... So, thank you guys!!!

Simon Green has done a fantastic job at re-creating The Rialto for the front cover. He picked the fonts and the style, doing all of this after telling me my original idea was rubbish... He was right. He is so talented, but if anyone tells him I said that, then I really will be in the mood for murder!

I must also thank my mum, Ann McCluskey for all her reference help with dates, slang and fashions etc... and for being a fantastic mum. We'd all be lost without you.

And most of all YOU!!! You for reading this, if it wasn't for you fantastic people out there, then there would be no point at all in us doing it.

Love and Peace...

Dave McCluskey
Liverpool
July 2017

Author's Notes: Tony Bolland

Not dissimilar to the mighty words of my co-author and colleague Dave McCluskey whom I met while working in a rival musical instrument shop in Liverpool City Centre in the 1990s. When I say rivalry, we were all good friends and would often visit each other's stores... not to spy (honest!). When I met Dave, I was automatically drawn to his sense of humour and magnetism. We got on so well from the onset. This could well have been due to the mutual enjoyment we got from winding up the junior staff by sending them to each other's shops for non-existent objects to take back to their workplace. Sometimes the poor unfortunates would be stood for hours waiting for fallopian tubes, sky hooks, or even better, the infamous 'long stand'.

Dave and I met years later online and took up again by chance through this social network environment of ours. We began just normally, as you do, asking what we were both up to these days, when we found out that we were both vehement writers and published authors. My books were about non-fiction whereas Dave's where fiction. Before long we'd began a writing partnership producing several ideas, which we often would say 'has legs' along with our own projects. Our frenzied and prolonged brain storming sessions had already created a natural complimentary union, and a short script regarding Hessy's Music Store. This script proved a little cumbersome for us to complete, so we delved into other ideas. It began with me talking about some historical accuracies regarding some of the more unsavoury historical aspects of the Liverpool and Merseyside music scene, and Dave creating an exciting fictional prose around them, it wasn't too long before we had the first draft of the novel you have in your hands right now. We have so much material and ideas, our partners and family have had to become resigned to our creativity.

We are hoping that this will not be the only visit to The Rialto down Memory Lane. There is also another project in place regarding a fictional character's career at a prestigious Liverpool music shop, from the 1960's through to the late 1990's.

My acknowledgements are short and sweet...

I would like to thank my wife, Kathy for having to put up with me, and my cruel mistress... writing. I also need to offer a huge thanks to my daughter, Lisa-Marie, her partner Kevin plus my grandchildren Ethan, Amelie and Penelope who always support me in everything I do.

Tony Bolland
Manchester
2017